The Lucas Stick

Peggie Herron Miller

Panther Creek Press
Spring, Texas

Published by Panther Creek Press
SAN 253-8520
116 Tree Crest, P.O. Box 130233
Panther Creek Station
Spring, Texas 77393

Cover photos by the author
Cover design by Adam Murphy
The Woodlands, Texas

Manufactured in the United States of America
Printed and bound by Data Duplicators, Inc.
Houston, Texas

1 2 3 4 5 6 7 8 9 10

Library of Congress Cataloguing in Publication Data

Miller, Peggie Herron

    Lucas stick, the

    I. Title   II. Fiction, historical   III. Kentucky IV Tobacco farming

ISBN 0-9747839-4-3

The events and characters in this novel are fictitious. Certain
authentic locations and recognizable public figures are referred to,
but all other places, characters, and incidents cited in these pages
are inventions of the author's imagination.

Peggie Herron Miller

The Lucas Stick

In loving memory of my parents,
F. B. and Robbie Shelby Herron

With appreciation to Dr. Guida Jackson, Scott Keltner,
Bette Garland, Jackie Barker.

To Cliff, whose book this is almost as much as it is mine.
With love to our children, Michael Phillip Miller, J.D.; and
Teddy Miller Causey; and to our grandsons, Dustin Causey
and Derek Causey

Chapter 1

"That's Nora Ballard's little bastard," Mae Dee Corlew whispered, giving Georgie Rae Gardner a sharp poke to the ribs.

"Nobody knows who her daddy is. Though, as I've said before, I'd wager it's that Paul Luke Lanier." Mae Dee reached for a jar of iced tea on the floor. "There was talk, you know. Him and that Nora Ballard. Two of a kind, if you ask me."

The women sat in ladder-back chairs near the counter of Corlew's General Store. They were breaking Kentucky wonder bush beans, dropping the pieces into a tin tub between them. A languorous afternoon stretched ahead to be spent, as was their custom, probing the transgressions of local citizens. The women occasionally chortled like two hens over a fresh beetle, and with as much zeal. Interruptions were rare; few ventured into the afternoon heat of late June. Since mid-day the sole customer had been the child standing a few feet away, scrutinizing licorice sticks in a glass jar.

The child appeared to be little more than six years old, but she displayed a confidence that fit like a well-used garment. She wore an ankle-length camisole, tied at the waist with a bit of soiled ribbon. Encircling her left wrist was a wide gold bracelet. Black stockings and high-topped patent leather shoes completed the girl's outfit. Bangs straight as a platoon of soldiers marched across her forehead, disappearing into the cropped yellow hair above her ears.

Georgie Rae Gardner adjusted her bifocals and inspected the child. "Such a shame," she said.

The girl raised her head and eyed the women. Their lips curled about the words like cats eating sardines. She responded in an old familiar way; attack, hit hard, and draw back.

"You're a lying old bitch," she declared, her gaze falling with equal contempt on both women. Turning, the child strode away, not banging the screen door as she left, but closing it gently.

The women's words stung. "Nora Ballard's little bastard."

Malevolent words about her mother. About Paul Luke. They were vile words, *bastard* and *bitch*, forbidden words. Even so, the girl had overheard her own Little Granny once when she was waiting in the wagon. "Let me get this straight, Mae Dee. I certainly know a *bitch* when I see one, but now, exactly who're you calling a bastard?"

The matter quieted some after that, but now it surfaced again, like a cottonmouth in the river, across Cutter's Bridge and a mile further on. Head down, the girl wandered along the side of the building, trailing her hand against its whitewashed boards.

A short distance away, half a dozen farmers dawdled, sitting on nail kegs and straw-bottomed chairs beneath a giant persimmon tree.The Great War had ended almost six years previously, yet battles and killing often were the subject whenever idlers gathered. Without interest one of the men glanced at the girl. He spat and a puddle of tobacco juice formed in the dust.

"Weren't that the battle Mae Dee's boy was kilt in?" he said, gouging his knife into the stick he whittled.

Saree Ballard—who went by her mother's surname—squared her shoulders. Without hesitation she chose one of two dirt roads, which converged and formed a wye creating the space occupied by Corlew's General Store.

The black locust trees surrounding the Lanier mansion dripped with blossoms. Now and then a bee droned across the veranda. A young man knelt beside a wicker settee, his eyes intent on his companion's face.

The woman laughed: Low, throaty, a sound not of innocence. She wore a voile afternoon dress. From her coal black hair cascaded a cluster of locust blooms only slightly fairer than her complexion. She tilted her head, regarding her companion from under half-closed lids.

A few years past thirty, Paul Luke Lanier was tall and well built, possessing a natural elegance. His eyes, of a brown so dark it might have been black, could mesmerize the unwary. The lights that gleamed in their depths flickered like bits of gold in a whirlwind. More than one vulnerable young woman alluded to mischief that went well beyond his glance.

Colleagues who faced Lanier eye to eye in the Kentucky General Assembly observed from a different standpoint. "If he's not on your side, you know he's out there watching," they would say. "Just don't look back."

Lanier's reputation as a state senator stood impeccable. Depending upon which side of a question one stood, the man was either an unrelenting foe or a prudent ally.

Today Paul Luke was on a personal conquest, as his companion, Miss Lockett Lakewood, would soon learn. He bent forward. Lifting her chin with his hand he leaned toward her, his eyes fastened on hers.

Suddenly the man froze. A sound; a motion. Not heard; not seen; but sensed.

"Paul Luke, are you my daddy?"

Saree Ballard was without shoes and stockings. From one side of her dress the satin cord trailed on the porch. Dust mixed with sweat, or tears, lined her face. Her bangs stood like spikes impaled on her forehead.

Paul Luke's glance darted to Miss Lakewood. He faltered for a moment. Then, taking one long stride he swept the child into his arms, and set her down out of Miss Lakewood's hearing.

"Now, Saree, that's an odd question," Paul Luke said, his voice not quite natural. "Why on God's green earth would you come here asking such a thing?"

"Down at Corlew's store they—they said if you're not my daddy, then maybe I don't got a daddy."

"Foolish, meddling old biddies!" he muttered. He pulled Saree against his shoulder.

"Now you and I know," he continued, his composure regained, "that every living creature has a mother. And it has a daddy, too. And some, like you—" He squeezed her. "—are lucky enough to have a granny, to boot. Don't you go paying attention to what gossipy ladies have to say. Promise?"

Saree nodded, but her eyes clouded. "Paul Luke, what's a 'bastard'?"

He winced and glanced down the veranda. The settee was now vacant. Paul Luke shot an anxious glance toward the guest room window.

"I suppose you heard that at the store, too?" He lifted the little girl and carried her into a hallway that led through the house.

"Well, Saree, I'll tell you what a bastard is, and I want you to remember. A bastard is a mean, low-down somebody who tries to hurt other people. They spend their time tending to other folks' gardens while the weeds take over their own."

The two emerged into the afternoon glare. Paul Luke glanced across the lawn where a black mare and buggy waited.

"I'm going to take you home," he said, "before somebody begins to worry. Only one thing, Saree. You must promise never to pay any attention to store talk. Just remember to weed your own garden, and let the other fellow do likewise." He swung her over the side of the carriage.

"Oh, yes, Paul Luke," she said, "and I'll *never* call anybody old bitch, either. Granny said."

With a bewildered look he flicked the black mare's reins.

Appearing unaware of the heat blanket around them Paul Luke listened while the child chattered. A single dimple flashed near the left corner of her mouth. Little puffs of dust rose behind the black mare's heels.

Mae Dee Corlew and Georgie Rae Gardner continued breaking beans in annoyed silence after Saree left. "That little gal needs to be looked after," Georgie Rae observed after a while.

Nodding agreement Mae Dee reached for her tea. A muffled jingle drew their attention to the narrow road.

"Let me go tell that Goose Wiley to hitch up the team," Mae Dee said, glancing toward the persimmon tree for her son-in-law. "If I can find him." She peered through the screen door until the carriage vanished.

Saree jumped to the ground from Paul Luke's buggy. Turning to wave, she headed toward the house where she lived. Remnants of yellow paint clung to the clapboards.The porch, set several feet above the earth, furnished a retreat for Old Puddin,' Saree's custard-colored collie. She glanced at the rope swing dangling from a black walnut tree. Perhaps Little Granny had not missed her.

Behind her, Paul Luke flicked the reins and the black mare moved toward home.

Fields of tobacco pushed against both sides of the road, stopped only by dry little ditches. The rows ran past Boatwright Lake all the way to the Ohio River.

The Lanier land holdings had come through Paul Luke's mother, Naomi Ruth. Her grandmother, far removed, sailed on a ship that delivered a cargo of settlers to a Georgia colony in 1735. Mary Leighza Conlin had not traveled as a woman. Disguised, she existed undetected for two months with a shipload of male offenders; men released from an English prison to become laborers in the new land.

Upon reaching her destination, Mary Leighza worked in a hostel. She eventually married Christopher Prentiss, a soldier in the king's army. His death in an Indian raid left the widow with five children to support on an unreliable stipend from the crown. Ultimately, the young mother realized she could not hold her family together. The two oldest sons were sent to work in a wealthy household.

It was the youngest child, Eve Prentiss, who had been Paul Luke's grandmother generations past. Eve had inherited, from some obscure ancestor, two key weapons in her quest for selfhood—a lyrical voice and an unfaltering ear for music. Prominent families paid her to entertain at their social affairs. In return Eve required access to private tutors hired to educate the sons of rich men. While daughters of the gentility learned embroidering and needlepoint, Eve Prentiss learned to read and to cipher.

Eve often visited her brothers at Oakland, the plantation where they worked.

One March afternoon as she maneuvered across a rock- covered bluff she was startled by whimpering. Her investigation revealed a fox's lair shielding two pups, cold and weak from hunger.

About to continue on her way Eve noticed dried blood on the rocks. A vixen, dead of bleeding from a gunshot wound, lay to one side. Her pups vainly sought sustenance from the stiff corpse of their mother.

Repulsed, yet enraged, Eve seized the pups by the scruff of

their necks. Wrapping them in the tail of her cape she hurried across the field.

"You, there!" she called to a workman emerging from a corncrib. "Take these animals to your master. Tell him they have been orphaned by some hunter. He must see to them. Be quick now!"

The man stared at her in astonishment. "Ma'am—but ma'am—those are fox pups—"

Eve unwrapped the creatures and thrust them toward him. "Yes, indeed. And cold and near starved, too. Someone on this plantation, I suspect, shot their mother and left them to—" Her eyes blazed. "I am Eve Prentiss. My brothers work here. Are you an acquaintance?"

"I certainly am acquainted with the Prentisses," he said. "My name is Newt Tyree."

Eve gasped. The man before her was not a workman as she had supposed, but the owner of Oakland.

"I probably shot that vixen myself, this morning. Last night three of the peafowls I had brought from Great Britain were demolished. I have no pity for these little beasts." He spat, an end to talk.

Eve was not to be intimidated.

"But, Mr.Tyree—sir—that animal was providing for her family in her natural way. Is the law of nature to be condemned? Your pea fowls should have been better tended."

Newt Tyree's eyes widened. Eve held the wriggling animals, waiting for him to take them. He swore under his breath. Aloud he said, "Oh, all right, but you must come along, too. You have a share in this. If you had left them in the field where they belong-"

After that meeting Eve's visits to Oakland became more frequent. She spent many afternoons in Newt's library. Observers wagged their heads. Her conduct ill became a woman, unmarried, and without prospects.

One rainy dusk the following October, Eve stood in the foyer of Oakland watching the somber clouds. Newt came to the door of his study and summoned her. She expected him to offer her a carriage ride home; instead he proposed marriage. Two weeks later Eve became mistress of Oakland, Newt Tyree's Georgia plantation.

One year following, on the day of Newt's death in a hunting

accident, Eve Prentiss Tyree gave birth to a daughter, Eliza. With no husband and with a child now fatherless, Eve decided to sell Oakland. This business completed, she set out in a covered wagon with her infant and two brothers for a new beginning upon the acreage she had inherited from Newt in the dark and bloody land, Kentucky. The year was 1775.

Years later at the age of seventeen, Paul Luke's mother, Naomi Ruth Shelby, an only child born late, had dutifully enrolled in the Tennessee finishing school her mother had attended and where Lucas Lanier was a professor. Had Lucas Lanier been less keen for learning he likely would have been a wealthy merchant. But, to the dismay of his father, a Tennessee banker fallen into distress after the Post-War carpetbaggers descended on the South, Lucas Lanier spent every dime he could scavenge getting knowledge, of which there was no end. Finding the dark-eyed Kentucky lass his intellectual equal, Lucas began sharing with her his great cache of learning. The thought that she was falling in love never occurred to him.

On the day of her graduation Naomi Ruth appeared at his door with a valise and declared that she would not leave. After thinking it over, Lucas Lanier confessed that he had never before contemplated the discipline of love, and that he most earnestly wished her to stay.

After the scandalous marriage of teacher with student, Lucas could never again secure a permanent teaching position. The two wandered about with a chautauqua while Lucas lectured in schools, barbershops, tents or wherever a crowd gathered. Only when Naomi Ruth became pregnant did they put aside their nomadic life. With the Tennessee stranger she'd wed, Naomi Ruth returned to the rolling hills, limestone earth, and Kentucky bluegrass she loved.

With tobacco a major money crop, Lucas determined to absorb every fragment of information he could uncover about the cultivation of Burley tobacco. Ultimately, Lucas Lanier became clothed with an aura of respect accorded to few in Hunt County.

A shift in the black mare's gait ended Paul Luke's reverie. He turned his attention back to the afternoon's events. Saree relied on him, entrusted him with the knowledge of her pain. More unpleasant incidents would arise; this was not the first.

The carriage entered the circular drive lined with locust trees. A team of matched gray mules harnessed to a buckboard stood in Paul Luke's hitching place. A wooden plank reached across the wagon from side to side.

As he approached, the French doors of the Lanier mansion flew open and a thin black woman greeted him.

"Mr.Paul Luke, they's two ladies in the parlor. Say they here to see you about business."

"Thank you, Ruby Gem. Who are the ladies? Anybody we know?"

"Well, sir, one's Missus Corlew from the store. Other one's Missus Gardner. Been waiting about half hour, I reckon. Say it's real important. I poured them up some lemonade." Paul Luke nodded and strode across the foyer, entering the sitting room through its arched door.

"Well, ladies—Miss Mae Dee, Miss Georgie Rae—how pleasant of you to call! Ruby Gem tried to make you comfortable, I presume—in spite of the heat?"

"Oh, Paul Luke, wonderous comfortable!" Georgie Rae gushed. Mae Dee glared at her.

"Yes, thank you, quite. But I'm afraid it's not pure social," Mae Dee said. "Only a matter of grave importance could drag us out in this heat."

Paul Luke settled on a maroon velvet sofa.

"It's that Nora Ballard's little—er—child. Name's Saree— um—yes—Saree."

Georgie Rae interrupted, "Ballard—" Mae Dee elbowed her in the side.

"She's what I call a neglected child," Mae Dee said. "Seven years old, six at the very least, and not a smidgeon of respect. Using blackguard talk. Words not fitten to be spoke at all, let alone in polite company. I'm telling you it's disgraceful. Disgraceful."

Risking another reprimand to the ribs, Georgie Rae spoke. "We thought that you, being a senator up in Frankfort and all, you might know of a—school—or—or a place to send her to—uh, for her own good, you see. Politeness and all."

Paul Luke appeared startled by the venomous attack on the

child. "Is that the truth? Why I thought her mother and Little Granny Ballard were doing a right decent job rearing that child. You want me to help you send her away, to a—a school? Is that it?"

"For—for her own sake," Georgie Rae said.

Mae Dee seemed to sense an uncertainty in Paul Luke. "Now, Paul Luke, I never would of come to you about this, except that—except that—I feel a little close to you. On account of—my poor Cleve—" She sobbed briefly. "You and him was always so devoted—"

A shudder passed over Paul Luke. Her words recalled the death of his boyhood friend, Cleveland Corlew, one wintery night on a French countryside. He turned to Mae Dee.

"Yes, ma'am, Miss Mae Dee. I respect your concern for that little girl, and I agree. Her education must be implemented with all haste."

Paul Luke walked to the window and gazed through lace curtains. After a moment he turned to the women.

"I believe you will be pleased to know, ladies, that we have already begun Saree's education. Why just today, she asked me—you'll pardon the language—what a `bastard' is." He looked Mae Dee in the eye. "And, ma'am, I told her."

Chapter 2

The clatter of Little Granny's breakfast preparations in the kitchen awakened Saree before daylight. She slid into her chair just as Nora Ballard entered the kitchen.

Nora's short hair was brushed into a shimmering halo, but her face remained bare of cosmetics except for a hint of pink across high cheek bones. Although Little Granny sewed her dresses, Nora's appearance rivaled that of fashionable ladies in Lexington or Louisville who spent great amounts of time and money in exclusive shops. Local women headed for Wickliffe, the county seat, or to Corlew's Store where they bought yards of the same fabric but could never achieve Nora's look. In private they called Nora "shameful" and "a vain baggage—you'd think she'd want to hide herself, that child with no daddy and all." But their hearts burned with envy.

In addition to a pair of antique tortoise shell combs, Nora owned only one piece of jewelry, a string of glowing pearls that she was never without.

"I don't think I have time to eat," Nora said, glancing out the window. "Amos always gets here soon as it's light. You know how he hates to wait."

"Amos and his old car," Saree mumbled. "Other people got horses that can go in the dark. Besides, he's always in a hurry."

"Saree, Amos *is* the supervisor and he can't be late," Nora explained as though for the first time. "Besides," she teased, "suppose one of Willie Shoe's hogs got out and Amos accidentally hit it in the dark?"

"They're not Willie Shoe's hogs, they're Paul Luke's," Saree said. "Willie Shoe just tends to them."

"Speaking of Paul Luke," Little Granny said. "Were you riding in his buggy yesterday?"

"Yes'm."

"Went down to the store, didn't you? And me thinking you

14

were playing paper dolls upstairs. You go wandering off like that again, little girl, and you'll be in a kettle of bad fish."

Amos McCann's Ford stopped in front of the house. At the canning factory ten miles down the road, Nora peeled tomatoes or peaches or whatever seasonal produce was available. Although Nora paid Amos McCann a dollar a week for her daily rides, tongues wagged at Corlew's Store, where fact often fared second best against the hint of a raised eyebrow.

Amos was thirty-five years old. Unmarried, he lived with his mother, Nellie McCann, the probable source of Little Granny's information concerning Saree and Paul Luke. Nellie spent her days rocking in a chair while life ambled along on the road in front of her house. Nellie McCann owned one of the few telephones around. She seldom missed a conversation on the party line, whether or not she was involved.

Speculation held that Nellie McCann once lived in a bawdy house roundabout Louisville, and that her son Amos was the result of some liaison during her misspent youth. The two had suddenly appeared one day in Wickliffe. They rode around for days in a hired hack, returning every evening to Moseby's boarding house. For some reason Nellie picked that particular spot down the road from Corlew's. She settled herself and Amos like a bird with one nestling. For months their coming had been the subject of persimmon tree conjecture. However, Nellie appeared to possess enough resources to chill any overt meddling. She reminded Amos, "When money talks, it demands silence." And that was that.

Amos' only distinction, besides owning a motor car, was his red hair and triangular sideburns. He was seldom seen except on his way to and from the canning factory, and in Mt. Pleasant Presbyterian Church on Sundays, where he sat with his mother.

Nellie depended on a cane when she walked, having lost the use of one leg years before in a train accident. That accident, in which Amos' father died, was the actual source of Nellie's wealth. It had been awarded to her in a lengthy litigation against the Georgia Southern Railroad. Church members at Mt. Pleasant noted Amos' devotion to his mother and remarked approvingly, making no secret of the notion that he "would certainly be a good catch for some young lady." It went without saying that the young lady they had in mind was not Nora Ballard.

Amos' attentions toward Nora were not lost on her mother. Amos seemed kind, was church-going. "But, Mother, he's so dull," Nora once said. "And so attached to Miss Nellie, it's—" Nora shuddered. "He'd have to beg her, and she'd never give approval, even if that was the only obstacle."

Little Granny never mentioned the idea again, but she hoed for long hours, chopping until no weeds survived amid her rows of cabbages and squash.

Sometimes Nellie's rheumatism kept her away from Sunday services and Amos would give Nora and Saree a ride home in his car. Sitting still through Reverend Wakerich's sermon was more tolerable when Saree found Nellie absent, and a car ride in the offing.

Streaks of daylight burst into a bright sun-washed morning. Saree sat in her swing touching her bare feet against the earth. A short distance away Little Granny, almost hidden by stick tepees supporting bean vines, hoed tomatoes. No need to worry about weeds taking over *her* garden, Saree mused.

"Suey, pig! Here piggy, pig, piggy!"

A black boy stood in the road. A straw hat, its usefulness outlived in summers long past, clung to the back of his head as though determined to spend one more season in the sun. Overalls rose six inches above his ankles.

"Willie Shoe! Have you done lost your hogs again?" Saree called.

"Just that bar' hog Mr. Paul Luke going to put in the smokehouse this winter. You ain't seen him, have you?"

"No, but I reckon he could of got hit by a car," she said, feeling her devilment rising. "Amos McCann just went by while ago."

"Oh, lordy! I got to find that Mr. Pig!"

Saree left the swing dangling and joined him. "Whyn't we go look down by the swamp?" She pointed toward the river bottoms. "That hog could be most anywheres. Paul Luke's sure going to be mad."

Willie Shoe glanced toward Little Granny absorbed in her garden. "You think you can?"

Saree studied the distant figure. The sun would rise several degrees higher before the old lady became sweaty in her long-sleeved shirt and sought the indoors. The risk of being missed seemed low. Saree nodded, and the two walked along, breaking the silence with "Here, piggy, pig!"

Shortly, they came upon Holloway's pond, almost dry from lack of rain. Water covered with green scum stood in the middle. Animal footprints molded into the mud testified to heat and desperate thirst. A stench of decay lay so heavy it was almost visible. Water bugs skated on the scum and devil's horses darted about the edge. On the far side of the pond, imbedded in sludge, the lost hog wallowed, emitting an occasional grunt of porcine ecstasy.

Willie Shoe cajoled, then threatened. The hog regarded him with beady eyes. The boy waded into the mud wrinkling his nose. "Now, Mr. Pig, suh—" Willie Shoe began. He pushed on the hog's ham section. "You just—"

Willie Shoe's feet suddenly shot out from under him and he fell face down. Sputtering and spitting, the boy shoved till both he and the porker stood on solid ground.

Wiping his mouth on his muddy shirt, Willie Shoe seized a stick. He struck Mr. Pig smartly on his ribs, steering the animal vaguely homeward.

Saree glanced at the sky. The likelihood of being missed increased by the minute. Saree quickened her steps.

"Whoa there, little missy!" Long legs covered with faded denim blocked Saree's path.

"Papa!" Willie Shoe shouted. The pig wheeled and fled back toward Holloway's pond, uttering delighted squeals in the distance. Saree's gaze traveled upward, coming to rest on the face of Plez Shoe.

"Where you been?" Plez demanded. "Your granny worried. She say even Miss Nellie don't know where you at!"

"Why, I—" Saree began. From the corner of her eye she glimpsed Willie Shoe waving frantically. "Willie Shoe said—"

"Naw, suh! I never said nothing. That hog done gone to the swamp by *hisself* and I done gone to find him by *myself.*"

"Lord, have mercy," Plez said, glancing upward. "There's snakes and no telling what all down there. I ought to whip you both." Plez turned to Saree. "Your grandma going take care of you.

Now get on home, before I change my mind. Go on now! Skedaddle!"

Little Granny Ballard tramped through the woods toward Turner's Landing straining for a glimpse of Saree. When she sighted the river she slowed her steps. At the water's edge cypress knees poised above the lilies like prima donnas.

Laura Ballard's father, Alec Moore, had carried her there in his arms. "A wee place where fairies dwell," he'd called it, in those artless days of childhood when her father was infallible. Granny stood a moment, perhaps recalling other times when a bitterness like acorns, was not yet tasted.

"You're a damn little liar!" A Yankee soldier stared into her face. "You're a lying little devil. There's a Johnny Reb hid out there. I'm a good mind to take that fine horse you're riding just to teach you a lesson!"

"Oh, no, sir! If you please, sir, Commodore Foote said I was to mention his name and you'd let me pass."

"Well, now, this is the army, not the navy, little gal. Besides, Commodore Foote ain't here, is he? Not that it'd matter." The soldier glanced toward the river then back to the child. "Where you been anyway?"

"My ma sent me. Missus Gish is ailing. My ma said to me, 'Laury, take this soup over there.' So I did."

"What Missus Gish? Ain't no house around here."

"Oh, no, sir. They ain't got a house. It got burnt. They took up down at the river."

The soldier clutched the white horse's bridle.

Tears brimmed in Laura Moore's eyes, threatening to overflow. "Commodore Foote said you'd let me pass."

"Let her go, Birdsong." Another soldier appeared out of the twilight. "She ain't nothing but a kid. How old are ye, honey?"

"Nine. I'm nine years old." Laura said. Two great tears tracked down her dirty cheeks.

"Well, that's a fine white horse she's riding," the first soldier said.

"Oh, let her go. It's probably all they got left." His companion

struck the horse's rump and it lunged away, almost unseating the
girl but she never looked back.

When she got home, Laura Moore told her mother, "Young
Alex is all right. He's got the cow and hogs hid at Turner's Landing.
He was proud to get the soup. Don't you worry, Ma. The Yankees
won't find him. I nearly didn't."

"Well, Laury," her mother said, "that livestock's all we've got
now. The Yankees came by again and took all that meat we hid in
the attic."

Little Granny turned from the river and headed back toward
the clearing. Saree skipped into view.

"I went to pick you these," Saree called. She thrust a handful
of wild flowers toward Granny's face. "Willie Shoe went by looking
for some old hog. Willie's daddy found him, so I just thought I'd
come on back."

"Two times in as many days! You'll be the death of me if you
don't quit running off, child."

Saree's smile faded and she lowered the bouquet to her side.
From the road came voices.

"Are you mad, Granny, like Willie Shoe's daddy?"

Plez was still chastising his son when they came face to face
with Paul Luke near the stable. Willie Shoe hung his head while
Plez recounted the boy's transgression. The errant pig, fettered with
a rope around its neck, appeared docile.

"The worst thing, Willie," Paul Luke said, stooping to the boy's
side, "is that you failed to inspect the fence before that hog got
away. The best thing is that you went after him. No harm done. But
if it happens again, we might not be so fortunate."

"Yes, sir, Mr. Paul Luke," Willie Shoe said. "If it happen again,
that old pig, he going have to *fly* out that pen!" Willie headed toward
the tool shed.

"I was aiming to whip that boy," Plez said, shaking his head.

"No need. He's learned his lesson." Paul Luke looked toward
the stable. "Plez, that bay mule in the last stall. He's quite sweaty.
Suppose he plowed too hard this morning? Got overheated?"

Plez laughed. "That old mule always foam that way. He the

one your daddy call Old Lather. Don't you recollect the first year when Mr. Lucas name him? Mr. Lucas, God rest his soul, he worry about Old Lather, too." Plez grinned. "Mr. Lucas, he come out here, and he study about it. He go over that mule from end to end. Then Mr. Lucas, he say, `Nah, he all right. That mule just got lots of water under his hide.'"

"Yes, Plez, I do remember. Well, he's got lots of gray on his old hide, too, since then."

"Mr. Lucas know his mules, all right," Plez said. He mopped his forehead. "Not much Mr.Lucas *didn't* know, I reckon."

Paul Luke turned and walked along the grassy road that ran between his tobacco fields. Fences stretched on either side, straight and taut. Fences guided and strengthened by his father's hands. Everything the old man touched absorbed his strength. Plez, Paul Luke's mother, even himself. And Mathelde, his sister. Lucas had made her strong, too. Strong enough to confront her father's wrath, to follow the man she loved along the river to another place.

Paul Luke stopped short. The north gate stood sagging on its hinges.

"Plez!" he shouted, pointing. "What's happened to that north gate?"

Behind him Plez led a mule along the road, ready to resume the afternoon plowing. Plez stopped.

"Ain't nothing *happen* to that north gate, Mr. Paul Luke," Plez said. "But if you wants to know what *wrong* with that north gate, I can tell you that. That north gate put up after your daddy passed. What wrong with that north gate is Mr. Lucas not here to oversee it hung."

Chapter 3

Saree hopped from foot to foot, a white bow in her hair fluttering with each bounce.

With unremarkable success she struggled to heed Little Granny's warning to stand still. Her grandmother's words after her escapade the previous day had drenched her with guilt. Probably hoping to escape another scolding, Saree turned her attention to executing ants with the toe of her shoe.

She was wearing the same camisole she wore the day she confronted Paul Luke, but it had been scrubbed and starched back to respectability. A new pink satin ribbon encircled her waist.

Little Granny wore the lemon-colored voile she reserved for church, summer funerals, and the festivities that infrequently dotted her life. One hand held a lard can. The other clutched a Bible with a wooden-handled fan protruding from its middle.

A wagon rounded the curve in the road and reached the spot where the two waited. Amid commands of "Whoa, Jason!" and "Hold up there, Saber!" the wagon lumbered to a halt. Its occupants, Ruby Gem, her husband Plez, and Willie Shoe, jumped to the ground.

"Mr.Paul Luke done lent me the good wagon this time," Plez said. He helped Little Granny aboard and into a low padded chair. Saree and Willie Shoe scrambled onto the rear. The boy's parents sat on a plank across the front.

"Was your ma mad about the mud?" Saree asked as the wagon moved forward.

"Yeah. She say I has to tend the pigs all by myself for a whole week."

Moments later the wagon passed in front of Corlew's General Store. The usual collection of idlers rested beneath the persimmon tree.

"Guess they going to the arbor meeting on the Illinois side," one said.

"I thought that arbor meeting was for Nigras," Eli Mayes remarked.

Eli Mayes raised patches of sorghum in the river bottoms; or rather, his wife, Vergie, and their eldest son raised sorghum. Eli fancied himself a political leader, not a farmer, an idea reinforced by his recent election to the three-man Hunt County School Board. Mayes attended sessions of the Grange and whatever other gatherings he found out about, scattering his opinions like dandelion chutes. Eli watched the wagon roll out of sight.

Another farmer hitched his overalls. "That ought to be seen to," he mumbled. "What say, Eli?"

Little Granny opened the lard can and handed out pieces of fried chicken dotted with spice and black pepper.

Ruby Gem produced a basket of tea cakes tasting of vanilla, and butter churned early that morning. Saree and Willie Shoe sat with the basket between them. Saree had been wondering what to expect ever since her grandmother first mentioned the evening's plans; she could leash her curiosity no longer.

"Willie Shoe, you ever been to an arbor meeting before now?"

"'Course I been. Pert near ever night for three weeks."

"Well, then, what do you *do* there?"

"They's singing and praying—lots of singing—and the preacher talk about Moses and all. Sometime he talk long. You can't go to sleep or nothing. Sometime it powerful slow." Saree felt crestfallen, but Willie added, "Except when they's a baptizing, but that's mostly on Sunday."

"What's that?" Prospects for the evening's entertainment still appeared pretty bleak.

"Baptizing is when all the folks that's lied and stole things, and sinned, and is willing to *say* they done it, goes down to the river, right in front of everybody. First the preacher pray, and then he jam 'em in the water, head and all."

Saree swallowed. "Don't nobody ever—ever—drown?"

"Naw. They just hold onto that preacher for dear life. Long as you got a-holt of that preacher, ain't nothing going happen. Guess God so happy he watch out." Willie Shoe added an afterthought.

"Come to think on it though, I ain't never hear of no *white* folks being baptized."

The wagon neared the Ohio River. Plez steered the mules into a clearing where other wagons and teams stood tied to cypress trees. At the water's edge a group waited to be set across the river on a makeshift ferry visible in the distance. Once on the Illinois side they would climb the riverbank a few hundred yards to reach the brush arbor, an open structure without sides. Its roof was saplings supported by an under-structure of scrap boards.

Saree looked around and reached for the woman's hand. She and Little Granny were the only white people there.

The raft ran aground. A rope was thrown to Plez, who wound it about a stump. Little Granny Ballard stepped forward, her hand outstretched toward one of the black ferrymen.

"Why, Tar Jack!" she exclaimed. "How good of you to oblige us!"

The man was one Saree had seen hoeing in Paul Luke's tobacco fields. Now he held a pole that he would use to push the raft to the other side of the Ohio.

Tar Jack was the reason Little Granny and Saree were there. Three days before he had cut a cord of wood and stacked it near the back door for Little Granny. Tar Jack had refused the dollar bill she offered him. He said shyly, "If you had any chicken and dumplings, though, I'd be much beholden to you for my dinner." Little Granny smiled. Early in the day he had watched her prepare a chicken to cook out of her own backyard.

Tar Jack leaned against the porch step while she brought forth bowls of food. Sitting in a rocking chair on the porch, Little Granny watched him eat in hungry gulps.

"That was a fine Christian thing for you to do. Not taking any pay for all that work." Tar Jack was not known for generous gestures. Neither was he known for sobriety. He customarily took whatever he was offered, spending it all on some form of illegal spirits.

The face he turned to her was shining. "Thankee, ma'am. Tar Jack is a changed man. Done joined the church. Been going to the arbor meeting near a month now." He reached for another biscuit. "You a fine Christian, too, Missus Ballard."

"Why I didn't know anything about an arbor meeting," she said. "Where's it at? I used to go all the time. Haven't been to one in years."

"Right over in Illinois. Across the Ohio there. Just colored peoples so far." His wet shirt clung to his back and shoulders. "Wish we could get some other respectable folks there. Like you, for instance. Be mighty hoped up to know we all could sit in front of the same God without no trouble amongst us." He scraped out a last bite of sweet potato pie and set the bowl aside.

Granny twisted in her chair. Tar Jack was smiling. Going to a black church service; there would be talk. Being the object of gossip was no new experience for Laura Ballard.

"Tell you what, Tar Jack," she said. "If I can find a way to get there, I'll bring Saree and we'll come one night."

The shallow spot selected for fording the Ohio was only a few miles upstream from Cairo, Illinois. A little south of Cairo the Ohio merged with the Mississippi.

Upon entering the arbor, Granny and Saree were ushered to seats on the second row, flanked by Ruby Gem, Plez, and Willie Shoe.

At one side of the lean-to stood two massive cypress trees, cracked and swollen with age, their branches interlaced. Crude teapots with wicks crammed into their snouts hung from poles, blowing opal flames into the twilight. Benches semicircled the space beneath the arbor. An occasional whirring of bats' wings, or a whipporwill's cry proclaimed that this territory belonged to nature. The church-goers sat on benches until they became crowded; late arrivals massed on the dewy grass barely outside the light. An odor of kerosene blanketed the still air.

"Folks, we only got us three song books." Reverend Antioch Pike said, commanding attention from the front. "They ain't even alike. But we all loves the Lord, and we sure enough can find us a way to sing his praise! Now all you all pay some mind here!"

Clad in a shirt so white it was near luminous, Reverend Pike held his songbook aloft. He shouted the first line. The hymn rolled out. Bodies swayed. Reverend Pike continued reciting the hymn line by line. After each prompting the congregation sang the words until the entire song had been completed.

"Deep river, I don't want to cross Jordan alone!"

Voices rose in wails and moans, stilling the wild things of the night. In one corner a Jew's harp and a guitar sounded out the notes. Finally Reverend Pike raised his hand and the crowd grew silent as he began his sermon.

"Some folks think as how we be *peculiar* people. Some folks wants to harry us because we just plain colored folk meeting to praise Jesus. Because we *colored* folk praising the Lord. But they be wrong, you see. Hear this word of scripture, little children of the Lord. 'Now God is no respecter of persons, but in every land, whoever fear God and work right is accepted.' Hear that, little children, it say whoever." Reverend Pike ran a handkerchief across his forehead and into his white hair. "Praise his holy name!"

Reverend Pike's gaze swept across the crowd and into the darkness. "Glory to the Lamb! *Whoever* fear the Lord God and do right!"

"Glory, praise the Lamb!" shouted those inside the arbor. Echoes rang from beyond the light. A low wailing arose from a few in the congregation.

Little Granny glanced toward the darkness. Her arm slid around Saree's shoulder.

The first indication that something was awry was a series of soft screams splitting the darkness. Running, some unexplained motion outside the arbor. People burst into the light. Those seated rose to their feet. Benches toppled.

Horses and figures stomped across the grass where moments before singing voices had rung out. The tail of a whip slithered around one of the supporting poles. Its tea kettle torch fell into the dirt. Angry curses erupted. Chaos prevailed outside the glow of light.

"Get the hell out of my way, nigger!"

"Shut up!" an anonymous voice ordered. "Remember, kick the black sonabitches but don't do no talking! Just get them goddamn Nigras!"

"Black sonabitches ought to stay here in Illinois permanent!"

"A couple whites, too!"

"Shut up! I said don't talk, damn it!"

"It's the Night Riders!" Ruby Gem screamed. "God A'mighty, it's the Ku Klux!"

Some of the congregation circled around Preacher Antioch Pike. Others fell to their knees where they were. Plez stood beside Little Granny.

"Under the bench, quick, child!" Little Granny ordered. A rock hurled from the darkness gashed Plez's forehead. Blood oozed. Saree stared. She had never seen a black person bleed. Little Granny pushed Saree and she fell under the plank seat almost atop Willie Shoe.

Little Granny's Bible lay in the dust. Just as Saree reached for it, feet appeared. She drew back her hand. Above the feet she could see white cloth like the sheets on her bed at home. From her cramped vantage point under the bench, Saree studied the man's shoes. They were of soft tan leather, emblazoned with some kind of metal buckle, not high laced work boots like most of the farmers wore. Somewhere in Saree's mind a spark of familiarity glimmered.

"Nigger lover!" the man flung the words at Little Granny. He swore as he strode into the concealing night.

"Fire! Fire!"

Plez, a bloody handkerchief tied across his forehead, jerked Saree to her feet. He shoved her, Little Granny, and his own small family toward the river, the safety of the raft. Behind them, flames from the blazing arbor leaped and cavorted, casting shadows across the silent water.

Chapter 4

"Preserving liberty is no easy task," Paul Luke said, concluding his customary July Fourth speech at Boatwright Park. "As Washington warned, `Government, like fire, is a dangerous servant and a fearful master.' Government must be contained, so our founders gave us a government of laws, not of men. They did well.

"Now, there's another matter close to the hearts of Hunt County folks. They think it's time we honor our own fallen hero, Cleveland Corlew. Our board of magistrates has proposed that a permanent monument be established in this community. I have contacted the United States War Department. It will take the efforts of many, but I am confident that such a memorial *will* exist before this day a year from now!" Paul Luke surveyed the crowd. "I thank you for your attention. Now, getting to the real reason for this gathering, let's all eat and enjoy ourselves."

Applause resounded as Paul Luke finished. The sun's reflection on the platform blinded him for a moment and he stumbled as he jumped to the ground. Grabbing the outstretched hand of Gabe Findley, a man he had known since childhood, he regained his balance.

Gabe's overalls emitted an odor of mildew and sweat mingled with Brilliantine hair cream. When he was a child Gabe's left eye had been caught by a fishhook, leaving it sightless and covered with a cloudy film. Gabe strained to get all the sight possible from his remaining eye, and it appeared larger than the blinded one.

Farmers lined up to wish Paul Luke well in his bid for another term in the state legislature. Assessing the aggregate mood he sensed that only a few were dissatisfied, including Eli Mayes.

"Now I'm of a mind that some kind of ruling ought to be made about these Nigras meeting around here in mobs," Eli said, not extending his hand.

"Mobs? Negroes?"

"You bound to know about that bunch meeting at the river.

27

Pert near a month now. Some whites been there too, I understand. Fifty-or-so Nigras. Yeah, I'd call that a mob."

"Oh, you mean the brush arbor meeting? I hear the Klan took care of that gathering a few nights ago."

"Took them long enough, too. I'd be in favor of some kind of law—"

"There's already a law, Eli. It's in the United States Constitution. Says people have the right to assemble peacefully. Ever any trouble over there at the river? Before the Klan I mean?"

"Must've been some. All them Nigras. And what about them whites that was there? A shame—"

"Eli, I never have favored mixing of the races anywhere. You know that. Bad judgment, in my opinion. But all that, what you're talking about, took place across the river in Illinois. People over there're a tad more liberal. Always have been."

"Damn it, Paul Luke, I know them facts. What I don't know is where in hell *you* stand on this."

"Eli, you can't wonder where I stand on anything. I stated it all in my debate with your friend Lail Stratton over there, during the last campaign. I believe the people in this district are in accord with me. They showed it in their voting."

The congregation of well-wishers dispersed. Paul Luke strolled about the area, letting his mind wander. Nobody knew how many years the Fourth Fest had marked the observance of Independence Day in Hunt County. It certainly was longer than anybody now living could remember.

Paul Luke flashed a smile toward Mae Dee Corlew and Georgia Rae Gardner, as he paused to chat with Reverend Wakerich from Mt. Pleasant Presbyterian Church.

Meandering through the crowd once more, Paul Luke recalled Fourth Fests he and Cleveland Corlew had attended in days past. The two of them would run in and out among their elders, teasing his sister, Mathelde, and pulling Nora Ballard's pigtails. Now Cleve lay in his soldier's grave at Mt. Pleasant Cemetery, but the Fourth Fest continued. And would continue, that being the order of things.

"Young Lanier! Young Lanier! I'd like a word—"

Paul Luke glanced around. Lail Stratton, out of breath, paddled his wheel chair toward him. Four years previously, kicks from a horse Stratton was shoeing shattered bones in his left leg. But worse, he suffered a bruised liver that would not heal. Paul Luke turned to face him.

"All formalities aside, Lanier, I've watched everything you've done since you beat me three years ago. Read the papers. Talked to my friends in Frankfort, my friends here." Stratton turned in his wheel chair and surveyed the scene. "Can't say you've done too bad, all told, for a young fellow just getting his feet wet in the politics of this state. Not bad at all." Stratton's eyes narrowed. Folding his hands into a tent he watched Paul Luke.

"From you, sir, that's a pleasant assessment."

"But, now you know, Lanier, if my health had gone a little better, I'd have come back for my seat this time. And I'd a-won it. Some folks around here, including myself, liked what the Tobacco Farmers' Protection Association was about. But, then, there went your very own daddy supporting the Grange. Some never believed the Grange had any answers to our farm problems, the way Lucas thought it did. A lot of people viewed it as a big social club."

For eighteen years Lail Stratton held the position in the General Assembly that Paul Luke won from him. Stratton had been violently opposed by Lucas Lanier, Paul Luke's father. Lucas resisted the rabid tactics of the renegade Planters' Protection Association, but supported the Grange Alliance. Paul Luke won his first election partly because of his father's status, even though the old man died seven years before.

"Of those two organizations, Mr. Stratton, my father believed only the Grange to be legitimate. He couldn't stomach midnight raids and crop burning under any guise, even your Planters' Protection Association.

"You have a host of friends in this district, and I hope that you regain your health. However, I don't believe that I'm representing these people only because of your inability to contest me."

Stratton spat into the dust. "When I get my health back, Lanier, I'm going to take you on again. And, by God, you'll be a beat man!" He spun his wheel chair toward Eli Mayes' group of observers.

Paul Luke walked in the opposite direction. Skirting the edge of the activities, he looked for his sister, Mathelde. She and her three children were expected to arrive from Cincinnati late yesterday. Hearing nothing from them, Paul Luke had waited as long as he dared before leaving home late that morning for the Fourth Fest.

He spotted Little Granny Ballard sitting with Nellie McCann in a circle of shade. Surely if the train had wrecked, Nellie with her notorious listening habits, would have heard.

"I'm expecting Mathelde," he said. "She should have come yesterday. Have either of you seen her here?"

Nellie McCann shook her head.

"What good news!" Little Granny exclaimed. "How long has it been? Six, eight years? And Fleming—will he be coming, too?"

Paul Luke winced. "Well, ah, not exactly. The children will be here, though. Fleming is—uh—Mathelde would prefer to tell you herself, I think."

Bidding a good afternoon to the women, Paul Luke resumed his walk.

Sixteen years ago Fleming Phelps had appeared in Hunt County with his survey crew. Now Paul Luke's sister, Mathelde, was returning home to face hardships ironically bound to Phelps' arrival. Sent from railroad headquarters in Cincinnati, Fleming Phelps had bought, coerced, and wheedled land for that iron monster, the steam engine. Lucas Lanier proceeded throughout Hunt County warning landholders. In Lucas' mind, railroad and contemptible became synonymous.

At that time Mathelde Lanier was seeing Silas Boatwright, surprising nobody in Hunt County with their engagement announcement. At an enormous celebration on Boatwright Lake, Fleming Phelps appeared, though probably not invited. That night Silas Boatwright lost Mathelde, the love of his life, to the Cincinnati railroad man.

Three weeks later Mathelde and Fleming Phelps eloped, leaving behind two heartbroken men, Silas Boatwright and Lucas Lanier. Mathelde returned only once, for the funeral of her father.

Paul Luke stopped beside a brick wall. A copper plaque attached to an aging post caught the sun's luster. "Silas Boatwright, 1885-1915. In Memoriam." Silas Boatwright went off to chase other dreams after he lost Mathelde. He learned how to fly airplanes

from Orville Wright. His recklessness, some said, put his mother Pearl in an early grave at Mt. Pleasant Cemetery. Long before the Zimmermann Papers or the sinking of the *Lucitania* forced American entry into the Great War, Silas flew clandestine missions mapping the German countryside for Great Britain. One of these cost him his life somewhere over Germany. His remains, like his dreams, were never recovered. Bartholemew Boatwright, Silas's father, commemorated the family's private lake as a monument to his son. With his wife and only child dead, Bartholemew found little to occupy himself. He eventually turned to hunting raccoons with his band of pedigreed bloodhounds in the Mississippi River bottoms. One snowy night the entire pack was destroyed while chasing an elusive coon down the railroad tracks, straight into an oncoming freight train. The old man brooded over damnable fate for a few months before finally surrendering to death himself. In his will he deeded Boatwright Lake and its adjoining territory to Hunt County.

At a distance Eli Mayes squatted against a tree, cleaning his fingernails with his pocketknife. A small group lounged around him.

Lail Stratton approached, sipping from a bottle of strawberry soda. "Going from a tobacco sticker to a legislator's no bad trick," he said, watching Paul Luke across the way. "I still say young Lanier is short shrifting the farmers around here. Them that's low on capital, and hard up for loans."

"Yeah, he ought to be up there in Frankfort right now," Eli said, "fighting them railroads that's taking all the public lands. Charging big fees to haul our goods to market."

"Well, now, Eli, you just go tell young Lucas what he ought to be doing," Gabe Findley said, squinting his good eye.

"I should," Mayes said.

"I don't recollect anybody ever telling his daddy what he ought to be doing," Gabe Findley continued, turning toward Eli. "Lucas always seemed to *know* what to do. Young Lanier's a heap like him, seems to me."

"I never did agree with Lucas," Stratton said.

"Plenty times I didn't neither," Bosh Tillson said. He had

walked up from the lake as the conversation began. "But you got to give him his due. Once old Lucas had his mind made up, a twenty-mule team couldn't budge him."

"Stubborn fellow, all right," Stratton said.

"I recall back when I worked at the saw mill," Gabe Findley said. "Old man Lucas Lanier used to come over ever year on the first day of August—regular as a almanake—to pick out his tobacco sticks. Talk about particular! That old man wouldn't have no stick lessen it was straight as a string."

"Cut from good oak, too," Tillson said. "Wouldn't have nothing to do with softwood."

"And honest as the day is long," Guy Childers said. "Why Lucas used to count them tobacco sticks three times just to make sure he paid for ever last one of them."

Childers straightened a cuff on the old brown coat he wore. Regardless of the temperature, he never appeared in public without it. Conjecture beneath the persimmon tree held that Childers had heired the coat from a deceased brother-in-law who had been a lawyer "up in St. Louie."

"Got to where, when we was cutting sticks, we'd find a perfect one, we'd say `that's a Lucas stick,' and put it in a pile to itself." Childers said. "Why, I recall the very day his daddy started making a tobacco man out of Paul Luke. Driest August I ever recollect. Driest summer, maybe. Well, old man Lucas told him, `Son, them sticks is little, but they got a big job to do.' Well, sir, that Paul Luke retch down and picked up one them little sticks. About knee high to a kadydid, he was." Childers smiled. "Looked at it like it was something holy. Taller than he was, I reckon.

"Next thing I knowed, old man Lucas threaded five or six big tobacco stalks onto that stick. Slung it over his shoulder like it weren't nothing. `See, son,' Lucas told him, `if them sticks ain't straight and strong, you put a little load on one, you done got you a problem.' Pretty soon the old man started sending Paul Luke over there to pick out the sticks. Well, he wouldn't take nothing but the best. Just like his daddy." Childers chuckled.

"Only Paul Luke went his daddy one better. He'd bring back any stick that broke, expecting us to give him another one."

"Well," Lail Stratton said, "since his daddy's gone, maybe

young Lanier's changed." He seemed not entertained with Childers' memories. "Everything could be going a lot better for us farmers, you know. Maybe Lanier's not so concerned any more about getting the best. At least not for the people he represents."

"Yeah, Lail's got that right," Eli Mayes agreed. He clicked his knife shut and crammed it into his pocket.

"Naw," Gabe Findley said softly. "I think you're both wrong. Old Roger Gilcrist, down at the mill, God rest his soul, he used to always say, `That young Lanier's just another Lucas stick.' May be the only time old Roger was ever right about anything in his whole life. Seems to me the old man got hisself one last Lucas stick."

A wagon clattered past. Bosh Tillson's grown sons, Daniel and Jack, waved from the plank seat. In the rear, Buck Junior Mabry, a dim-witted vagrant who slept in Bosh's cowshed, sat astride a board.

"Where them boys going, Bosh?" Guy Childers chided, exchanging a knowing glance with Eli Mayes. The Tillson boys' appetite for "white lightning" was perceived by everybody in Hunt County, although their father, Bosh, advocated total abstinence. The men watched the wagon weave through the park and turn onto the dirt road.

"Well, I got to be getting along," Childers said, rising from the stump he had occupied. "The old lady'll come looking for me. Or what's worse, send one of the young 'uns."

The group dispersed. Bosh Tillson stared after the disappearing wagon.

The most available supplier of illegal alcohol near Boatwright Park was Mad Molly Capps. She lived on the river in a shanty boat, skimming along the water and tying onto stumps wherever the demand for whiskey appeared. Molly concocted her supply in half a dozen stills hidden among the trees along the water's edge.

"Why you reckon she be called `Mad' Molly?" Buck Junior said as the three jostled along in Bosh's wagon. "I knowed one. At the hospital. In Hoptown. Name *Miss* Molly. She a nurse."

"Well, nit-wit, Mad Molly ain't no *nurse*. She ain't ever been one, either. Especially not in that place at Hoptown where you was at!" Daniel said, with contempt. "The way I heared it, she spent fifteen years or so in the pen. Criminal *insane*, so they say. Sent up for killing her man and some woman she caught him with. Shot them dead. Guess she was mad all right, dummy," Daniel laughed and flicked the reins.

Buck Junior scowled. "Don't call Junior no bad name," he said.

Mad Molly's shanty boat came into view, and Daniel stopped the mules. He tied the reins to the wagon seat.

An iron skillet of catfish fillets sizzled over a fire at the water's edge. Next to it was a sack of potatoes. A woman with flowing white hair, and wearing overalls, tended the meal preparation. She hurried into the woods when the wagon approached. Molly's sister, Gilly, lived on the boat with the bootlegger, some said. Others contended that Gilly stayed in the woods, and not on the boat at all. A recluse, Gilly was considered even stranger than Molly. Few of Molly's visitors ever caught a glimpse of Gilly as these three had.

Mad Molly pulled back a flowered cloth that hung across the door opening into the shanty boat. She wore a man's long-sleeved shirt tucked into a swaggering black skirt, tied at the waist with a length of rope. A felt fedora sat on her head.

"Who you be, and what you want?"

"We're the Tillson boys. You know us," Jack said. "We having a party at Boatwright Lake. Party got a little dull. Need something to liven it up. We got a dollar and a half."

"All three of you Tillsons?"

"Naw," Daniel said, "this here one's Buck Junior Mabry. He's a little short in the head. He's all right, though. Stays at my daddy's place."

Mad Molly tossed Buck Junior a look of contempt. "Yeah, I've seen him around here before. I don't sell to half-wits."

"Oh, he ain't buying," Daniel said hastily. "He just come along for the ride."

Mad Molly studied them. "All right, come on," she said. "But not him." She indicated Buck Junior with her thumb. "He'd best keep his distance."

Jack Tillson put his hand on Mabry's shoulder and shook his head. Glowering, Buck Junior watched the brothers walk onto the deck of the shanty.

The woman stepped through the curtain and reappeared, holding a jar of clear liquid.

"Here's your stuff," she said. "Now, when you leave, put the money on that tree stump over there." Her glance traveled from Daniel to Buck Junior sulking in the wagon. "And remember, don't give none to that silly-ass ninny you got with you." She set the jar down and turned back toward the rag-covered door.

Daniel picked up the jar, while Jack deposited a dollar and a half on the tree trunk Molly had indicated. The brothers climbed into the wagon. Daniel clicked his tongue to start the mules moving.

"Don't call Junior bad names no more," Buck Junior mumbled, glaring at the boat as they pulled away.

As Paul Luke concluded his stroll, his attention was drawn to the smell of hickory smoke and barbecue. Plez and his workers had cooked all night in a grove of locust trees and now dished out slabs of barbecued mutton, goat, and pork.

"Paul Luke Lanier, you do have a way of ignoring a lady!" A familiar voice spoke from behind Paul Luke.

He spun around. "Miss Lockett Lakewood, in the flesh!" His glance swept from her face to her feet, then upward again. "No man breathing could ignore you, ma'am."

"Well, you did!" Lowering her lashes she tugged on her lace-edged handkerchief. "You stared right at me and you ignored me, Paul Luke." A mass of curls had been created by the moisture at the nape of her neck. Her eyes were blue against milk-white skin.

"Lockett, if I didn't freeze in my tracks, you *know* I didn't see you. When was it that you fancy I ignored you?"

"When you drove up in your fine carriage."

"Did you holler at me?"

"Certainly not! A lady doesn't go about yelling at her gentlemen friends like that!" Her eyelashes fluttered. "And then during your speech. I was standing by the platform they set up. You looked right at my left ear."

"Surely I would have recognized that left ear."

"Paul Luke, you are *still* inside every bit a rascal."

"*Still* a rascal?"

"No, I take that back. I've never known you to be *still*. Not for a minute. But always a rascal."

Paul Luke chuckled.

"That man who introduced you?" she said. "He talked about your vigor and your—your fire. I believe I could have told them all more about that."

"It just may be a personal blessing for me that Judge Theed insisted on making the introduction himself." Aware of the scent of roses, he moved closer. "Tell me, what on earth are you doing here?"

"I came from Louisville yesterday to watch our trainer with the horses." She rested her hand on his arm. "Actually, that was more like an excuse. I wanted to be here today, to see you. I'm going back Sunday."

"So soon?"

"Oh, one thing more. The Jockey Club Charity Ball is next month. I'm to be Mistress of the Ball this year. I need an escort, and I was hoping that maybe you—"

"Ah, yes, Miss Lockett, the Mistress of the Ball. I'd be honored to escort you anywhere." He smiled. "But I do hope to see you again much sooner than that. At the dance here tonight?"

Before Lockett could reply, her mother, Letitia Marcom, swooped down on them. Letitia, married to Lockett's stepfather, Beech Marcom, was an older version of her daughter.

"How good to see you, Mrs. Marcom," Paul Luke said, taking her hand. "As I was about to tell Miss Lockett, I fear I am a little preoccupied today. I've been expecting my sister since late yesterday afternoon, and so far—"

"Mathelde is here?" Letitia's eyed widened.

"Well, not as yet, I suppose. She and the children are due. Fleming has been transferred to the railroad hospital in Paducah. Quite ill, I'm afraid."

A slender stranger approached them.

"Uncle? Uncle Paul Luke?"

He turned, unprepared for the tall, willowy young woman before him. Dark eyes tilted above a slender nose and even teeth. Wispy curls escaped the straw bowler she wore, and lay around her face like spirals of yellow ribbon.

"Rebecca? You can't be Rebecca! She couldn't be nearly so

tall." Even as he spoke Paul Luke pulled her against himself in a tight hug. "Thank God, you're here! Where's your mother? Let me look at you!" He leaned back to study her face.

Lockett and her mother, Letitia Marcom, retreated. Letitia brightened when Lockett whispered some tidbit in her ear.

"Mother sent me for you. She's with the luggage," Rebecca said, taking Paul Luke's hand and walking around the tables of food.

"Is everybody all right? Your sister and Will Roy? How's Fleming?" Paul Luke asked.

"Yes. My brother's bratty as ever. An authentic wart hog."

Paul Luke stopped. "You are so like my mother."

"That's what Mama always says," Rebecca gave his hand a tug to start him walking again. "We looked for Grandmother before I found you. Where is she?"

"On her annual trek to the continent I'm afraid. Somebody has to keep all Europe on its toes. If she'd known you were coming, nothing could have kept her away, though. You know that."

His expression grew serious. "How is your dad? You didn't say."

"Oh, I don't know. Mama beats around the bush. Maybe she'll tell you more than she tells us. She just keeps saying everything will be all right."

Rebecca's words were lost as Paul Luke spotted his sister a few yards away. "Mathelde!"

She rushed into his embrace. "Paul Luke! At last! I wanted to hear your speech. You can't imagine! There was a cow on the tracks. That delayed our train. Then when we got to Cairo it was too dark for a ferry. The telephone wasn't working. Finally today, a man at Wickliffe brought us here in his car. Oh, we had a time!"

"Never you mind. But I must admit, I was more than a bit worried." He studied her face. "How is Fleming?"

"Tell me, tell me—that you're all right. And Mama?"

"Fine."

Mathelde turned to Rebecca. "Go find your brother."

Mathelde looked at Paul Luke with tears in her eyes. "He's terribly ill, Paul Luke. They can't agree on a diagnosis. He's just wasting away. His doctors sent him to the Illinois Central Hospital in Paducah. Better facilities they said. But I'm—I'm afraid it's hopeless." He held her, stroking the back of her neck the way she had stroked his when he was a child.

Shortly, Rebecca returned holding the hand of her sister, Leighza. At nine, Leighza was awkward and homely. Huge freckles covered her face. Her front teeth were large. Auburn pigtails trailed down her back. In the short time since their arrival, Leighza had managed to spill grape soda on her stockings. The purple stains traveled down her legs into her shoes.

"Mama, I think you'd better come," Rebecca said. "Will Roy has gotten himself into a fight with some little girl."

"Let's go," Paul Luke said. "I'll tell Plez to put your luggage into my carriage."

They followed Rebecca to the back of the park where a group of children watched two small figures pushing and shoving each other.

"Oh, lord!" Paul Luke exclaimed in dismay.

Will Roy Phelps had indeed gotten himself into a fight with "some little girl," namely, Saree Ballard.

"Did, too, do it!" Saree cried with such vehemence that the dimple in her left cheek contracted. A pink straw hat with satin streamers tilted at a hazardous angle on the back of her head. Her dotted swiss dress was smudged with dirt. Pink bloomers peeked from beneath the full skirt. Her pink stockings and white patent shoes had been tossed against a tree trunk earlier in the afternoon. Old Puddin' stood guard over the abandoned footwear. Saree, with hands on her hips, glared at Will Roy.

"Did, too!" she repeated. Putting her hand on his shoulder Saree pushed so hard he fell back a step. Will Roy looked down at her bare feet, planted firmly in the dust.

Two steps and Paul Luke was at Saree's side. He touched her arm. "Well, now, I thought the fireworks were going to be tonight. What's the trouble?"

Saree pointed a finger so straight that Will Roy winced. "That boy—that *new* boy—he put a snake in the girls' outhouse!"

"A harmless little old garden snake," Will Roy mumbled. Paul Luke shot him a quick look.

"See there! I told you he did it!" Saree seemed ready to resume battle. Paul Luke stepped between the two, firmly taking each by the hand.

"Why don't we get some lemonade and work out a fitting apology?" Glancing at the other children crowded around, Paul Luke added, "There's lemonade for everybody. My treat." They fell in behind him.

Nora Ballard came running to them. "Is my daughter causing trouble?"

"No more than anybody else. We were just about to get some lemonade and work out a truce. Won't you join us?"

As they were leaving, a group of old friends gathered around Mathelde and her daughters. Enmeshed in conversation Mathelde waved her brother and the others on.

"Well. if that's not the beatenest thing!" Mae Dee Corlew said, jabbing Georgie Rae Gardner in the ribs. "After all the talk there's been, just look at them two!"

Twilight was not far off, and preparations for the evening's entertainment had been underway for some time.

Jars half full of kerosene, and holding rag wicks, had been strung up to provide light for dancing. A square of hard earth in the middle of the park formed a dance floor. Three musicians readied themselves, tuning fiddles and a guitar. Couples paired off. Children were being sent to stay the night with relatives or neighbors. Firefly lanterns blinked and the laments of mourning doves could be heard. A damp breeze swept across the lake, stirring the leaves and tousling hair. Heat lightning fluttered in the distance, and the smell of hickory smoke lingered in the air. The sound of laughter and happy voices echoed across Boatwright Lake. All was well.

Suddenly the musicians broke into a raucous tune, *You Gotta See Mama Every Night or You Can't See Mama at All.* Several laughing couples rose to dance on the hard earth.

Nora Ballard walked up to the edge of the merriment. She stood half in the shadows, her shoulders tense. Twisting the fringe hanging from her handbag she glanced back the way she had come. Amos McCann had apparently been watching for her, for he stepped forward immediately.

"My, you are looking nice tonight, Miss Nora," he said. Tucking his hand beneath her elbow he led her into the flickering light.

Nora smiled, appearing grateful for Amos' welcome. After a few moments they danced a fox trot, and the tension seemed to ease from Nora's body.

Paul Luke leaned against a tree in the semi-darkness. Lockett Lakewood prattled at his elbow. Detail after detail of society affairs in Louisville rolled off her tongue for half an hour. With that subject depleted she turned to discussing the Jockey Club Ball.

"And I do think smoked oysters are tastier than creamed salmon, don't you?"

"Oh, definitely." His concentration was so intense that she appeared to become flustered.

Paul Luke had been watching Nora on the dance pavilion with Amos McCann. Nora wore a candlelight-colored chemise that touched her body just enough to emphasize its slender curves. Tortoise shell combs, inherited from her grandmother, held the straight shining hair off her face. A strand of pearls gleamed against her creamy skin. Amos held her like a porcelain figurine.

After playing *Farewell, My Bluebell* and a number of other tunes, the music stopped. Rudell Babcock, the guitar player, announced a dance contest.

"Get you a partner. No matter who it is. Everybody got a chance, a chance to win. I don't care if it's Aunt Sal's old dog name of Ugly. You and old Ugly dance the best, you and old Ugly win the prize!"

Amos and Nora laughed and sat down.

A few yards away Lockett Lakewood continued her monologue. "I think a Cleopatra theme would be so original. Of course, I'll be Cleopatra, as Mistress of the Ball, with you as my escort. We'll be pulled across the ballroom floor in one of those Egyptian barge things."

Paul Luke's eyes shifted from the other side of the pavilion to Lockett. "The hell you say," he murmured. Then louder, "Please forgive me. I just remembered a previous commitment." He strode away. The dance contest was about to begin. Paul Luke walked straight to Nora.

"May I have the honor?" he asked, reaching for her hand. Nora stood hesitantly. Her glance traveled toward Amos, who bolted to his feet. Smiling, Paul Luke slid his arm about Nora's waist and turned her toward the music. Amos grasped Nora's chair, a raspberry scowl darkening his face.

The first dance was a fox trot.

Come be my rainbow, my beautiful rainbow,
And we'll have blue skies forevermore.

Paul Luke held Nora close, his breath ruffling her hair.

After each dance the crowd applauded to determine which couples deserved to remain in the competition. Paul Luke and Nora were selected each time, while spectators watched for a hint of intimacy between them. Amos McCann glared.

"We don't do this very often. I'm becoming tired," Nora gasped, laughing. "And my combs are coming loose."

"You're right, Nora. I don't see you often enough." Paul Luke pulled her closer.

Finally only two couples remained, Nora and Paul Luke; and Lockett Lakewood with her partner, Garland Adair. The band began *Over the Waves Waltz.*

"My comb!" Nora cried, reaching for the ornament as they entered a final whirl. But she was too late; the comb hit the hard-packed earth at her feet. In what appeared to be an accident Lockett Lakewood's foot stomped the middle of the tortoise shell shattering it into a hundred pieces.

At that moment loud bangs, booms, and whistles heralded the beginning of the fireworks display over the lake. Short explosions of light revealed the laughing revelers, and lit the frown that darkened Amos McCann's face.

Saree watched from the darkness of her attic window a mile away. The glowing sky looked the same as it had when the brush arbor church burned at the river.

Chapter 5

Gabe Findley hustled his wagon and mule team over the river road toward his cornfield. The sky threatened rain. Gloom pounced like a cat on a grasshopper.

Gabe waved to Plez Shoe walking in the opposite direction. Plez carried a string of catfish. He had gone out early.

"I should have been in the field two hours ago," Gabe remarked to Job, the collie dog standing spraddle-legged behind him. A sudden breeze blew dust devils in the road and cooled the sweat on Gabe's shirt. A dusty scent of rain weighted the air.

Job, with ears pricked, sprang forward, his attention riveted on the road ahead. He darted to the front of the wagon, barking and digging his claws into the boards.

"Fool!" Gabe muttered. He glanced ahead, and his good eye opened wider.

A woman clad in overalls ran toward them flailing the air with her arms, her white hair streaming. She screamed as she ran, but Gabe could not understand her above the clatter of the wagon.

"Whoa, 'Lasses! Whoa, Dogmeat!" Gabe shouted. He jumped to the ground.

The babbling woman caught the edge of the wagon with both hands. "My sister's dead! She's been kilt!"

Gabe stared at the woman.

"Molly Capps that lived on the shanty! Somebody's done cut her throat! Got to get the law!"

Slowly Gabe comprehended. Molly. Mad Molly. The white hair. The sister.

"You Gilly?"

The woman nodded, drawing her hand across her dirt-streaked face.

"Get in the wagon. We'll get the sheriff."

He turned the wagon around and whipped the mules into a run.

Corlew's Store had been open for an hour. Mae Dee watched

through the screen door as clouds roved across the sky. Nothing much had gone on since the Fourth Fest two days ago. Gabe Findley passed in his wagon.

"Getting a late start," Mae Dee mused. Taking her seat near the counter she began writing an order for the grocery supplier.

After a few minutes the screen door banged. Mae Dee looked up to find Plez Shoe. A string of catfish dangled at his side.

"Nice looking mess of fiddlers. Want to sell them?"

"No, ma'am. Ruby Gem going fry them up for dinner. I need a dime's worth of meal."

"Mighty pretty," Mae Dee eyed the fish while she measured cornmeal from a barrel. "Where'd you catch them at?"

"Why—er—down at the river." Plez shifted. Mae Dee figured he worried that at any moment she might ask the location of his lucky fishing spot. "Used some chicken guts for bait."

Plez laid a nickel and five pennies on the counter, picked up the sack of cornmeal and left. Mae Dee prepared to finish her grocery order. A sudden barage of shouts and the rattle of a wagon splintered the quiet. She scrambled to the screen door, reaching it just as Gabe Findley pulled on the handle. A strange woman followed him.

"Molly Capps is dead! Call the sheriff!" Gabe shouted, although Mae Dee stood only a few feet away.

"Molly?"

"Molly Capps, on the river! Mad Molly!" Gabe lowered his voice a little.

"The shanty boat woman? She dead?"

"Yes, dead! Throat cut. Call the sheriff, Mae Dee."

"No phone here. Nearest one is Nellie McCann's. Throat cut?" For the first time Mae Dee looked closely at the white-haired woman. She must be Gilly, sister of the notorious Mad Molly.

"Look after Gilly!" Gabe yelled running toward the wagon.

Mae Dee pivoted toward the interior of the store, not inviting Gilly to follow her inside. Instead, Gilly turned and began walking back the way she had come. Doubtless, on his return, Gabe would see her walking and pick her up, Mae Dee thought. Good riddance.

Amos McCann stood before a clothesline in his mother's back

yard. Raising a butterfly-shaped rug beater above his head, he whacked Nellie McCann's floral carpet. A cloud of dust flew into his face.

"What she wants with wool rugs in the country I'll never figure out," Amos muttered. Suddenly he froze with the rug beater in mid-air.

"What in thunder?" he cried.

Drawn by an ear-splitting commotion in the road, Amos ran into the front yard. A wagon peppered him with pebbles, and halted a few feet away with a jangling of harness. Amos, almost knocked off his feet by Gabe Findley, stood benumbed.

"Where's the telephone?" Gabe screamed. "Got to call the sheriff! Somebody's kilt Mad Molly!"

Amos pointed toward the screen door. Still holding the rug beater, he followed Gabe inside.

"Sheriff Meeks and the deputy are on the way," Gabe said, replacing the telephone receiver moments later. "Wants us to get some men together and meet him at the river. Take him about an hour to get there. He said don't bother nothing."

"Molly Capps murdered, I'll be thunder." Amos shook his head. "What else did Molly's sister say when you met her in the road? What'd you call her? Gilly? Dad-burned funny name."

"Not much. She'd been gone a couple days. Gilly has a shack somewheres in the woods. She come back early this morning, and there was Molly. Throat cut from ear to ear. Her money's gone, too."

Gabe looked toward Nellie seated in her rocking chair near the door, listening. "Much obliged for the use of the telephone."

Amos followed Gabe out the door. "I'll get Eli and the others. We'll go on down there," he said, heading toward his car.

Sheriff Claude Meeks and his deputy, Virgil Bigler, arrived at the shanty boat shortly after Amos and half a dozen other men. Meeks pulled his Model T Ford into the shade. Gilly sat in Gabe Findley's wagon, head bowed, her back to the river.

Meeks stepped from his car and glanced toward Mad Molly's shanty. More than once he had been summoned to quell a disturbance caused by somebody drunk on the moonshine she peddled. When he went to take her in custody she'd be gone, skimming over the water like a spider, defying arrest. Now Molly's evasion reached an abrupt and permanent end, yet Meeks himself still had not prevailed against her. Instead, he had been dealt another complication, the burden of apprehending whoever was responsible for her death. A distasteful business left for him to conclude.

Eli Mayes, Bosh Tillson and several others sat with Gabe Findley on a knoll.

"Where's the body?" Meeks called.

"Over there!" Eli Mayes nodded toward the boat. "I covered her up. The heat and all."

In the distance a mound of blue fabric lay on the deck, unmoving except when the breeze rumpled its edges.

Meeks stood looking down at his scruffy boots. The men all knew of his efforts to trap the bootlegger. They were probably wondering if he would pursue her killer with as much vigor, or simply shrug it off, a way to even an old score.

Sheriff Meeks hunched his shoulders and turned toward the shanty. His boots skidded along some uneven places. At the edge of the water Meeks wavered. It seemed inappropriate to assail Molly's boat while it stood powerless, tied at the bank with a knotted rope. Tucking his head, Sheriff Meeks passed into the dead woman's domain.

The rag covering the doorway fluttered in the breeze as if trying to escape the nail that held it. Newspapers weighted with rocks and chunks of tree roots littered the deck. Books could be glimpsed within.

Meeks lifted the corner of an old blue bedspread. A wooden-handled butcher knife lay next to Molly's body. Its long silver blade glinted in the light except where dried blood coated the metal. One of the woman's hands in death clutched a satin pillow partially beneath her head. The sheriff's eyes widened. Emblazoned on the pillow in bold green letters was the word "Sweetheart." Blood splotched the pillow and lay in patches on the deck.

Meeks ran his hand across his forehead. "What's that?" he asked Amos McCann, pointing to a gray pouch near the dead woman. The bag spotted with dirty stains lay open, its greasy drawstrings caught on the corner of a book.

"According to Gilly that's where Molly kept her money. It looks empty," Amos said. He and Eli Mayes had trailed behind the sheriff onto the boat. The other men approached.

"Anything else missing?" Meeks asked, squinting.

"Don't know," Eli said. "I don't reckon anybody's looked. We wouldn't know, anyhow." The others nodded agreement.

Sheriff Meeks walked to the wagon and touched Gilly's arm.

"I'm awful sorry about this, Miss Gilly. Terrible shock for you. Your sister dead. You finding her like that. We'll catch whoever did this. Don't you worry any." He gazed at the clouds before looking back toward Gilly. "I feel bad to ask you this, but since you're here—well, we sure need some help. Just a few questions. Maybe a look around."

Gilly sat with her head down. After a while she nodded and reached for the sheriff's hand.

Meeks walked Gilly toward the boat keeping himself between her and the still figure beneath the blue spread. The men watched, milling about on the river bank as though expecting some clue to materialize.

"Now, Miss Gilly, if you're up to it, I—I'd like us to have a look inside," Meeks said. He led the way into the shanty.

Unlike the deck, the interior appeared immaculate. Tasteful, framed artists' prints lined the walls. An exquisite silver service surrounded by packets of exotic tea stood on a table. Stacked near the door was a set of leather-bound reference books. Slivers of paper marked selected sections. Hanging on the back wall a number of fashionable gowns seemed to await a lady's whim. The scene was like a delayed dream, a fantasy waiting to be lived.

"Whew!" Meeks breathed, emerging from the dimness with Gilly, who had tears on her cheeks.

"The whiskey's missing," Gilly said dully.

Amos McCann and Eli Mayes, standing on the deck, moved closer to listen.

"How much? How do you know she didn't sell it?" Meeks asked.

"Ain't likely," Gilly said. "When I left about ten o'clock the night of the Fourth, Molly had four quart Mason jars—blue ones— left. They ain't there. Nobody hardly buys whiskey on the fifth of

July. Or the sixth, either. I think they was stole by whoever—"

"Hey, Sheriff, look what I found!" Gabe Findley shouted from the bank a few yards downstream. He held up a cluster of dollar bills. "Money!"

The men converged on Gabe.

"Well, I'll be a son of a gun! Where'd you find that?" Meeks asked.

"Molly had this old slick stump here. She'd always say,`put your money on the stump,'er— so I've been told. Wouldn't take no cash out of hand." Gabe glanced down. "I just walked by and there was these dollar bills with quarters laying on them, on top of the stump." Gabe handed the money to Deputy Virgil Bigler.

"So, the killer never robbed her, after all," the sheriff said. "But why? Why would he take the money out of that bag, then leave it here?" Meeks examined the stump, finding nothing more. Sheriff Meeks walked back to the dead woman's sister.

"Miss Gilly, you've been through an awful lot. I hate that. But there's still a little I need to ask. It might help a whole lot." Gilly bit her lower lip, eyeing Meeks as he went on. "Can you think of anything out of the usual? Did you see anybody around?"

Gilly turned away. "No, sheriff. Molly didn't have enemies, I don't reckon. Some teetotalers maybe didn't approve of her. But not—" She wiped her nose on her sleeve.

A thought seemed to occur to her. "Early this morning I was down fishing kind of close to Molly's boat. I seen a colored leaving the river down there. That's all."

"Did you know him?" Sheriff Meeks asked.

"No, don't reckon I ever seen him before. He had a string of catfish, fiddlers they was, and he left. It was real early. A little later on I went to the boat and found Molly."

"A colored, huh?" Amos McCann had walked up behind Meeks, intent on hearing Gilly's words. Eli Mayes stood behind Amos.

"Well, now, that's kind of funny," Gabe Findley said. "Just this morning early, I seen Plez Shoe—that works on the Lanier place?—coming from the river. He had a string of fiddlers."

Sheriff Meeks spoke, cutting off more conjecture.

"Miss Gilly, you come with me. We'll find you a place to stay. Bosh, you and your boys stay here with the corpse until Doc Haas and Crice's funeral wagon gets over here. My deputy'll keep you company. The rest of you men can go. I thank you for coming down."

As Meeks turned to leave, Gilly grabbed his arm. "Sheriff, if—if it's all right, I have a place in the woods. I'd like to go there a while. You can find me. I got to think about taking Molly back up the river to St. Louie."

The sheriff nodded and walked toward his car. Eli Mays and Amos McCann caught up with him.

"If you're going to do a little investigating about that Nigra," Eli said, "Amos and me are willing to go with you."

Meeks looked at his pocket watch and then at the two men. Today was his birthday. His mother expected him and his family for supper. Fried chicken, lemon meringue pie. This business might force his birthday dinner to be canceled.

The two cars pulled away from the river and soon passed Corlew's Store. The sheriff kept going, with Amos and Eli following, straight to the white Victorian Lanier mansion.

Paul Luke sat at his desk writing letters. Mathelde had gone to the hospital to visit Fleming Phelps, her husband, and would return late that evening. Ruby Gem and Rebecca, in charge of Leighza and Will Roy, worked in the kitchen making pecan tarts, their voices rising and falling in conversation. Paul Luke paused, listening to the pleasant cadence.

Noise of car motors and slamming doors intruded. Paul Luke pulled back the lace curtain and glanced toward the driveway. Three men, one of them Sheriff Claude Meeks, were walking toward his front door.

Paul Luke had known Claude Meeks since childhood. When Meeks tried to fulfill his lifelong dream of becoming a boxer, Paul Luke attended his pugilistic exhibitions in barns or on river barges every Sunday afternoon. Paul Luke, a companion of Meeks' younger brother, often watched the boxer "soak the tenderness" out of his hands. Using a mixture of white wine, vinegar, and rock salt, Meeks would submerge his hands for long periods. As they absorbed the concoction his hands became tough and hard, resembling boards. Meeks became known as "the toughest man in these parts."

Meeks married his childhood sweetheart and discarded his dream. He returned to work at his father's blacksmith shop where he had built his muscles as a youth. Prize fighting was an illegal activity, and even the lawful "exhibitions" of boxing likely would be stopped in a few years.

Paul Luke opened the French doors to admit the visitors. The three men—Eli Mayes, Amos McCann, and the sheriff—took their places on the high-backed velvet sofa while Meeks detailed Molly's murder.

Ruby Gem had headed to the door, but stopped at the sound of voices. No one noticed her standing in the hall.

"Now the reason we came here," Amos McCann said as Meeks finished, "is that Gilly saw a colored at the river right before she found Molly. We all think it was Plez Shoe. He was at the river this morning."

Paul Luke paled at the implication of Amos' words. "Oh, now, Amos, surely you can't mean—" He seemed to be mentally backing away even though seated in a chair in his own house. A fly buzzed behind the curtain. The grandfather clock ticked down the hall, next to the soundless figure of Ruby Gem.

The sheriff spoke.

"No, now, Amos, just hold your horses. We don't *all* think any such thing. Paul Luke, the fact is Plez was seen coming from the river with a string of fish early this morning. That don't mean I think he did it."

"Puts him at the scene of the crime, don't it?" Eli Mayes demanded, standing.

"Plez often fishes in that river," Paul Luke said. "And he did go this morning. We had his catch for lunch. Claude, you've known Plez for years. Surely you know he would be incapable of murder. Besides, what kind of motive would he have? Plez never drank a drop in his life. He probably never even laid eyes on Molly Capps."

"Pretty religious ain't he?" Eli asked. "Wasn't he one of them at that arbor meeting over in Illinois last month?"

Paul Luke looked at Eli.

"Why, yes, with his family." Rising from his chair Paul Luke

addressed Meeks. "Sheriff, I want this killer caught, and I'll help you any way I can. But I'll tell you one thing for sure. Plez had no part. He has to be left out of this."

"Now, now, Paul Luke, I understand you being a mite upset." Meeks said. "Frankly, I never thought twice about Plez myself. I guess with all the strain some of the men—well, it'll all blow over. Just tell Plez not to go off anywhere. I might want to talk to him later on." Meeks followed Paul Luke to the door.

Meeks got in his car and turned toward home. There was still time enough for supper with his mother. Pulling away from the Lanier house he hummed a few bars of *Camptown Races*.

Ruby Gem ran out the back door and found Plez with Willie Shoe hoeing in the garden.

After they left the Lanier house, Amos and Eli drove to Corlew's Store. A crowd milled about. Some stood under the persimmon tree, discussing Mad Molly's death.

"Dead. All for a few quarts of bootleg whiskey," Mae Dee said, shaking her head.

"I'm not so sure that's why," Amos said, leaning against the persimmon tree. A hush fell.

"What do you mean?" Gabe Findley asked.

"It wasn't for money. We found that on the stump. What else could it a-been? Though I can't figure how anybody in his right mind would kill for whiskey."

"That Nigra, Plez Shoe, was at the river," Eli said.

"Everybody knows Plez Shoe don't drink. Why he's got religion. Always been religious," Gabe said. Several agreed.

"Yeah, I think maybe a little too religious."

"What's that mean?"

"Well, look at it this way," Amos said. "Maybe somebody that don't drink gets to thinking how bad it is. Some folks make it and sell it. After while he might decide he'd do God a favor, so to speak. Now Plez Shoe went to the river a lot. No telling how many times he saw Mad Molly taking care of her trade. Who knows what he got to thinking?"

"Yeah," Eli said, "he'd been going over there to that arbor church ever night for a month. He might of got carried away with religion. It wouldn't be the first time something like that happened."

"Plez was in the store right early this morning," Mae Dee said. "I never seen him grinning so happy. He sure got to fidgeting, though, when I asked him about them fish he was carrying."

The crowd began to rustle about.

"This time it was Mad Molly," Amos said. "Who knows when he might get to thinking something evil about somebody else. Your wife, maybe. Or my mother."

Angry voices repeated Amos' words. A few of the men slipped away unnoticed.

The lights were still burning in Paul Luke's study when the grandfather clock struck twice.

A noise at the window caught his attention. He pulled back the curtain. Plez stood in the waning moonlight, tossing pebbles against the glass. Moiling clouds swirled across the sky. Paul Luke walked out into the darkness. He grasped Plez's arm.

"Man, what are you doing out in the night like this?"

"Mr. Paul Luke, I got to get away from here. Some folks think I kilt that white lady on the shanty. They done burn a cross down at the river tonight! I got to get away!"

"Plez, you're not guilty! You mustn't run away. If you do, you'll *look* guilty."

"No, sir, I never even see that lady. But the Ku Klux be after me. I got to go!"

"Where? How?" Paul Luke's grip tightened on Plez's arm.

"I figures I can get down the river to Memphis. I got people there. I can stay till they catch the one what done it. I couldn't go without telling you. Ruby Gem and Willie, they going stay here."

A black man had been burned at the stake in a little Texas town two or three years before. Perhaps he, too, had tried to escape an injustice.

"Here," Paul Luke said, pulling some bills from his pocket. "You'll need this." He took Plez's arm. "Now, there will likely be a hearing in a few weeks. Something like a trial. Promise me you'll come back for that. We can establish your innocence. I'll hire some legal help."

"Yes, sir, I will," Plez took the money. "Ruby Gem will keep in touch. You'll get all this back. I swear."

"Now, get to the river fast! If I took you in the buggy it would wake the whole county. Go, and God be with you!"

Plez turned and ran toward the river.

Three hours later Paul Luke, hearing the whir of a car motor, peered into the night. Sheriff Meeks had returned.

"I'm going to have to take your man into protective custody," Meeks called from the yard as Paul Luke opened the door. Instead of inviting the sheriff into the house Paul Luke joined him. "The Klan," Meeks continued. "There was a cross burning down at the river."

"Plez is not `my man.' He works for me. I know about the cross burning. Plez is gone, Claude. Ran away."

"Hell, Paul Luke! Do you know what this does to me?" Meeks belched. "They're going to want me to charge you with conspiracy. Or something like that. Hell!"

"No, Claude, I had nothing to do with it. Plez left against my advice. But I'll give you my word. He will be back if there's a hearing."

The rain that had threatened began suddenly. Meeks started to say something, but glanced toward the sky. Without a word he ducked his head and splashed through the raindrops to his car. Paul Luke stood in the rain watching the sheriff drive away.

Down at the river, raindrops pelted the smoldering cross, swirling ashes into the muddy yellow water. A small boat plunged through the waves churning toward Memphis. Inside crouched a solitary figure.

Chapter 6

Georgie Rae Gardner pressed the organ keys with all her strength. *Onward, Christian Soldiers,* the hymn that concluded every service at Mt. Pleasant Presbyterian Church, rolled forth.

Amos McCann led the singing, his hand moving to keep time with Georgie Rae. Cardboard fans waved farewell to mortal distresses. When the song ended, Bosh Tillson prayed for the congregation, and its members began to move.

Several women greeted Little Granny Ballard, and each made some reference to yesterday's murder.

"A woman bootlegging like that! She should've expected to come up dead."

"Them as live violent, die violent," Nellie McCann said, leaning on her walking stick.

Some who would not have spoken to Mad Molly if they had met her on the street talked as though she was an old friend. Most friendships cease with death; these unfolded like nightshade blossoms in the dark. Those who actually had been her customers said little.

Saree stared at the floor. Sometimes when she and Willie Shoe waded at the river's edge a woman would wave from a boat. Once she tossed them apples. Another time she warned against the current. Saree never knew her name. She was just "the boat lady."

Paul Luke, who stood in the aisle talking, turned to his sister. "Mathelde, we need to discuss some things. I'm going to be away the rest of the week."

"Yes, we do need to talk."

Will Roy, with his sister Leighza clasping Saree's hand, ran through the crowd to their mother. The fight between Will Roy and Saree at the Fourth Fest was now melding into that adverse friendship peculiar to children.

"Mama, Mama," Leighza said. "Can Saree come home with us?"

Mathelde glanced toward Paul Luke, perhaps thinking that with Saree occupying the children she and her brother might have an uninterrupted discussion.

"Why I think that's a lovely idea. But first see what Saree's mother has to say."

Nora Ballard stood at the rear of the building with Amos McCann, who hurried away to help his mother down the steps. With a smile Nora bent and whispered in Saree's ear.

The children darted away laughing. Nora waved to Mathelde.

The three were waiting in the carriage when Mathelde and Paul Luke emerged from the building.

"We want to have a picnic!" Will Roy shouted.

Paul Luke helped Mathelde into the buggy. Amos McCann was settling Nora Ballard and his mother into his Model T. Paul Luke's oblique glance followed Nora as the black mare trotted away.

"Are you ever going to get a motor car?" Mathelde asked.

"With these dirt roads? No, thank you. When that black mare gets stuck in the mud, then I'll consider it."

"'Becca, wouldn't you like to have a picnic?" Will Roy asked.

"Yes, but only if Mama comes, too. I'm not about to chase you all afternoon by myself."

"Tell you what," Paul Luke said. "We'll ask Ruby Gem if she'd be willing to go. After yesterday your mother needs a rest."

The children clapped. The black mare, not accustomed to so much energy at her heels, arched her neck and trotted faster, snorting a little. The world seemed fresh and newly cleansed after last night's downpour.

Ruby Gem and her friend Rejoice Tolliver waved to fellow worshippers as they left the sagging building where their grandfathers had worshipped as slaves.

Reverend Antioch Pike's sermon had been about love and forgiveness, concluding with the Klan's attack against the brush arbor meeting, and the cross burning last night.

When Reverend Pike sat on a bench, *The Old Rugged Cross* wailed from a harmonica. A guitar and drum picked up the cadence.

"I declare that Night Rider what tore down the brush arbor church be twelve feet high," Ruby Gem remarked, preceding

Rejoice down the path toward home.

"Go along with you, Ruby Gem! That Night Rider done look *twenty* feet tall sitting top on his horse!"

The two reached a cross path and stopped. Rejoice put her arm around Ruby Gem. "I know this worry about Plez done got you tore up. You try to take comfort from Reverend Pike's sermon. This thing going work out by and by."

Sighing, Ruby Gem turned toward the Lanier house.

Paul Luke met her at the kitchen door. "I thought you needed to know—Plez got away all right. Early this morning, right before the rain."

She said nothing, tears welling in her eyes.

"Ruby Gem, Mathelde and I need to go over some things. Would you take the children out to Boatwright Park? Rebecca refuses to go without someone to keep Will Roy in line. Pack a lunch. Take the buggy."

Ruby Gem nodded and soon produced a brimming picnic basket. She set out with the four children in the carriage.

Will Roy began to sing.

Oh my darling Nellie Gray,
They have taken you away,
And I'll never see my darling any more!

"Stop singing that song, Will Roy," Rebecca ordered. "It reminds me of that dead woman."

"You can't make me!"

"Ruby Gem can."

Saree and Leighza, laughing on the back seat next to Will Roy, became quiet.

"Who killed that lady, 'Becca?" Will Roy asked, stopping his song.

"Nobody knows," Rebecca said. "But I think it was the sister!" She narrowed her eyes and peered at the three.

"Uh-uh!" Leighza said. "At church this morning they said it was a man!"

"It was a man!" Will Roy said. "Maybe there's a wild man out there in the woods! Maybe her sister's a witch! A wild man and a witch!" Contorting his face he leaned toward Leighza, clawing the air with his fingers.

"I'm telling! You just wait, Will Roy Phelps! When my daddy gets out of the hospital, you're going to catch it!"

"My daddy." Saree appeared to turn the words over in her mind, like fingering pieces of a puzzle.

"Now you children stay away from the mud puddles," Ruby Gem warned, stopping the buggy beside a grassy mound. "Stay plumb away from that river, too. You hear?"

A game of "Blind Man's Bluff" got underway while Ruby Gem spread the picnic. In the distance Will Roy staggered about blindfolded. The girls stood, hardly breathing, trying not to be discovered.

"Dinner!" Ruby Gem called.

The only response was a crackle when Will Roy stumbled over a dry stick.

"Dinner!" Ruby Gem called again, her voice rising an octave. She began to mutter, but before she could complete her diatribe the game halted and the children scrambled to her side.

Will Roy sat next to Saree. His older sister began to tease him.

"Will Roy's got a sweetheart! Will Roy's got a sweetheart!" Leighza took up the chant and it echoed through the still afternoon.

Near the edge of the river a sleeping figure stirred.

Will Roy threw a pickle at Rebecca, hitting her on the nose. "Let's play Hide and Seek!" he shouted, jumping to his feet. Not it! Not it!"

The others took up the cry and the lot fell to Rebecca.

Ruby Gem cleared away the picnic, her thoughts flowing with the Mississippi toward Memphis.

Will Roy and Saree hid quickly, but Leighza hunted for an obscure place. Her search carried her to a bluff near the levee. She backed down the side and crouched behind a fallen tree.

A reclining figure turned, watching the little girl descend the bank.

Leighza squirmed. The yellow mud squished against the soles of her patent leather shoes. She wrinkled her nose. In the distance waves chased each other to the bank, murmuring at the river's edge.

Mathelde placed a glass of iced tea at Paul Luke's elbow. His study was dim, its blinds drawn against the afternoon heat. "I really feel uneasy letting the children go picnicking today after what happened. I'm glad Ruby Gem's with them."

"No need to worry about the children's safety. Whoever killed Molly Capps is miles away from here by now. Killers and such don't hang around. I only asked Ruby Gem to go because I thought it would get her mind off things. I really needed her here to pack for me. And to satisfy Rebecca." He changed the subject. "You heard about the Klan? That Plez left?"

Mathelde nodded.

"One reason I'm leaving tomorrow is to arrange help for Plez. It'll all work out. Right now my concern is for you. Have you thought about what you'll do if Fleming—?"

"Well, yes, and no. There are so many decisions." Mathelde twisted her wedding ring. "I feel like a burden. Barging into your life with my problems. Lord knows, you've got enough to think about—griping constituents, the General Assembly, your tobacco crop. I just can't put more on you—"

Paul Luke swung around in his chair.

"Mathelde, you didn't `barge' in! You're my sister, for God's sake!" He stood. "Looks like I'll be running unopposed. That removes some pressure. Besides, Mother will be home in early September. She's not going to let you take her grandchildren back to Ohio. Consider the thing settled. There's enough space and love right here."

Mathelde sprang to her feet. "Paul Luke, I see more of Lucas Lanier in you every day."

Footsteps were heard from the porch. He raised the blind.

"It's Nora Ballard and her mother. Were they to come for Saree?"

"Yes. I told her grandmother we'd send Saree home in the buggy, but she insisted on coming for her. You know how independent they are."

"Well, invite them in for iced tea and cake. The children should be back before long."

Fingers closed around Leighza's wrist. Her head jerked. A man crouched over her. Swaying, clenching her arm, he grabbed the tree with his free hand. Light and shallow like those of a bird, his eyes stared into her face. He grinned and mumbled words that meant nothing.

"Let me go!" Leighza screamed, kicking and squirming. "Let me go!" His grip tightened. She struggled harder.

The man laughed, like a delighted child winning a game. He lifted Leighza into the air and bounced her to the earth again.

She screamed louder. "Let me go!" Panic filled her voice.

Suddenly he slipped and fell into the mud, an incredulous expression crossing his face.

Leighza broke away and scrambled up the embankment. Her feet slid. She glanced back, trying to climb. Pain pierced her leg. Her knee, wedged in a fork of the tree where she hid moments before, would not budge. The man crept forward, almost touching her. Tears began to stream.

"Mother!" Leighza pulled and twisted her leg. Blood oozed from a scrape on her ankle. The man struggled along the bluff. Leighza grabbed an exposed root and wrenched loose.

Still she was not free. The man gripped her dress. Leighza grabbed the tree root and jabbed her foot toward his face. He fell back. Pulling herself away, Leighza heard the sound of ripping cloth. The man scrambled toward her. She clamored up the bank, barely eluding his grasping fingers.

Covered with mud, Leighza bolted across the grass to Saree and Will Roy.

"A man's down there! He almost got me!"

Will Roy and Saree gaped.

"There! See him?" Leighza pointed toward the river where a figure climbed into view over the top of the levee. Saree stared.

"Shoot, Leighza, that's just Buck Junior Mabry. He only wants to play. Amos McCann says he's a few pickles short of a barrel. Whatever that means. But my granny says he's not right in the head." Saree kicked a stump.

"But he scared me, and he smells funny! I don't want to play with him!" Leighza spit on her torn skirt and began to clean her bleeding ankle.

Saree and Will Roy gazed across the grass. Apparently unaware of the children, Buck Junior stumbled and got to his feet. Giggling, they began to imitate him.

"What you children think you be doing?" Ruby Gem demanded, running to them with Rebecca.

Ruby Gem, always avoiding the retarded man, knew Buck Junior only from a distance. She knew her role with other whites—politeness, a hint of subservience—but Mabry was an unknown quantity. Once on her way to Corlew's Ruby Gem had seen him enter the store. She turned back and attended to her errand another time.

"That boy be acting strange!" Ruby Gem exclaimed.

The children studied Mabry. Saree had seen the men at Corlew's laugh and wink and nudge each other when he came around.

Buck Junior, finally aware of their closeness, stopped to peer at them. He began to take uneven steps, covering the distance faster than any of them anticipated.

Will Roy seized a stick and waved it in the air. Leighza backed away.

"You children go for the buggy!" Ruby Gem cried. "When you all be ready to pull out, I'll come running!"

"Where you taking them?" Mabry demanded walking near. "Buck Junior be lonesome." He tottered and belched. Ruby Gem turned away from the stench of his breath.

"You hear Buck Junior?" He grabbed for Ruby Gem's shoulder, almost losing his balance. "Bring them back!"

Rebecca hesitated when the others ran to the buggy. Buck Junior reached for her arm but she jumped away.

Ruby Gem pushed him from behind. She grabbed Rebecca's hand and dashed toward the buggy. Buck Junior fell. As they raced away they heard him shouting, "You call Junior bad! No more! Don't call Junior no name! No more! You hear?"

Ruby Gem and Rebecca exchanged puzzled glances as the buggy picked up speed. The children held to the seat, hardly breathing.

Paul Luke and Mathelde chatted with Nora and Little Granny

over iced tea and coconut cake. Suddenly hearing the carriage the four jumped to their feet and hurried toward the door. Will Roy burst into the house.

"Ruby Gem had a fight! She pushed a man down! But Saree knew him! He's got pickles in a barrel!"

"What happened?" Paul Luke said as Ruby Gem ran inside. With the children supplying details she told of the day's peril.

"Mr. Paul Luke, I don't know what might happen to me, since I be a colored woman, and all. But when he reach for to grab hold Miss Rebecca, I push that white man! Lord have mercy! He fell down! What folks going say?"

"Ruby Gem, nobody could find fault in that. What you did was for the children's good. Don't you fret about color."

"Mr. Paul Luke, I ain't fretting about being colored. That's the good Lord's doing. It's just that sometimes, I— well—sometimes I wish—"

"You go on home now. Fix Willie some supper. Get yourself some rest. Mathelde's here to look after her children. I'll take the others home in the buggy." He patted her shoulder. "We're standing by you in this, Ruby Gem. Whatever comes up."

Ruby Gem left through the kitchen door. She trudged down the path to her little house behind the vegetable garden. Reaching the fence that enclosed her yard she walked inside. She sat in her chair by the fireplace for a long time, her brows knitted in thought. After a while Willie Shoe came in from repairing pig pens. She told him of the afternoon's episode.

"I just feel powerful oneasy," she concluded, rocking a little. "That boat woman kilt. The Night Riders all around, and now that white man, acting peculiar. Tetched in the head. Mad, too, like as not. Powerful oneasy, Willie."

"Now, Mama, don't you worry none. I going take care of you while my daddy be gone." He sat on the floor by her side.

Ruby Gem pulled herself erect and looked at him. "You nine years old, child."

Willie Shoe lowered his eyes and began running his finger along a crack in the floor. Perspiration stood on his lip like clear, tiny marbles.

"Willie, you build a big old fire in that fireplace. Bring in the wash kettle and full it with water."

The boy stared, his mouth agape. At her urging, he obeyed. Water sloshed over the sides of the iron kettle as he half-carried, half-dragged it to the fireplace.

With her back straight Ruby Gem walked to the windows. Closing each with a bang she secured them with lengths of broomstick, saving the longest piece for the door.

"You lay down over there on the floor. Go to sleep," she told Willie Shoe. "Anybody break into this house to do us dirt, going get a dipper of scalding water right in they face."

Willie Shoe lay on the floor. He turned his back to his mother, but his eyes did not close. Over and over he heard in his mind, *"White man tetched in the head! Night Riders all around! Stay away, Willie! Tetched in the head... Stay away, Willie!"*

Ruby Gem sat in her chair beside the fireplace all night. When the fluttery noises of the night creatures became silent, and the darkness faded into a lavender pink dawn, she fell asleep.

Chapter 7

A Model T puffed into the driveway of the Lanier mansion and stopped. Paul Luke emerged from the passenger side, pulling two valises behind him. He slammed the door and handed some coins to the driver.

"Much obliged, Whitsworth!"

Paul Luke watched the slow vehicle. Fortunately, Whitsworth Moseby, who with his wife, Mamie, owned the county's sole boarding house, had been available to drive him home from the train station at Wickliffe. Paul Luke was accustomed to having Plez meet him regardless of weather or time of day. Riding behind the black mare they would cover the three miles home while Plez reported the status of crops, and details of other farm business. After the serious discussion Plez would plunge into an account of whatever local events had happened during Paul Luke's absence. The custom was infused into the marrow of his existence.

"Well," Paul Luke mused, "this ordeal of Molly Capps' murder will be over in a week or two. It'll be good to have Plez back."

He surveyed the house. His "few days away" had stretched into two weeks at Frankfort. Exhaustion settled into his bones like summer dust. The house appeared forsaken, its blinds drawn, the French doors closed. The door glided open with a nudge of his shoulder.

Ruby Gem, wadding her apron into a knot, dashed toward him. The handkerchief that covered her hair was twisted to one side.

"Oh, Mr. Paul Luke, the sheriff done went off and got Plez. In the jail house, right now!"

"In jail? When—?" The suitcases clattered on the marble floor.

Mathelde hurried behind Ruby Gem. "The sheriff had him arrested in Memphis. They brought him back here. We didn't know anything about it until Sheriff Meeks came by yesterday."

"But—how?" Paul Luke walked toward the veranda. He rubbed his forehead. The children, still and subdued, were gathered on the porch.

Leighza and Rebecca sat on wicker chairs. Will Roy and Saree occupied the swing, moving it with their bare feet. Below them Willie Shoe leaned on the stair railing.

"Do you know what they've done to Willie Shoe's *daddy*?" Saree whispered. She moved to the steps near Willie Shoe.

Paul Luke nodded.

"Don't worry, children. Right now, let me think what I can do for Willie Shoe's daddy. We've depended on each other for a long time, you know." Paul Luke turned toward the door. He had taken half a dozen steps when he stopped, shook his head, and returned to the children. He removed his tie, stuffed it into his pocket, and loosened his collar. Sitting on the top step he encircled Saree's shoulders with his arm.

"Things like this happen." His words were slow, a long time coming. "But all we have to do is show that Plez hasn't done anything wrong. Before long, he'll be right back here with us."

"But what if the men in the sheets won't let him come back?" Saree said, rubbing her eyes with dirt-stained fists. "What if they won't, Paul Luke?"

He looked at the girl. Even in her green years she could pose questions beyond the ken of some in the General Assembly.

"You know that Plez is colored, Saree. Those men who wore the sheets want to hide what they are, so they cover themselves up. I guess they're like bats. They only come out at night, when it's dark." He leaned against the step. "And you'll learn, bats aren't really birds. They just sometimes appear to be. They can fool people. When we rip their sheets off, those men will have to hunt some other place to hide. Somebody else to fool. They won't be able to bother Plez anymore."

He ruffled Saree's hair.

Rebecca, Leighza, and Will Roy stole into the house leaving Saree on the steps, with Willie Shoe still standing beside the rail. After a few minutes Willie Shoe sighed and walked toward the hog pens.

The boy looked around to find Paul Luke strolling at his side.

"They going do something bad to my papa."

"They'll have to do something bad to me first." Paul Luke

hoped his words did not sound hollow. Who could predict what the Klan might be capable of, anonymous as bats, behind their concealing shrouds? Could they amass enough bravado among themselves to harm Plez? Paul Luke glanced toward the horizon.

"Willie, your papa was like a part of my family before I was even born. And your grandpa before that, and his papa, and on and on, away back."

"You means like forever, Mr. Paul Luke? Forever, like it say about God in the Bible?"

Paul Luke gazed at the trees in the distance. Trees that had stood for a century, maybe more. Green grass rose with the breeze, turning blue. It rippled green, blue again, like a Gypsy's skirt whirling across the limestone fields.

"No man has control over forever, like God does." He put his hand on the boy's shoulder. "But you hold on tight to that Bible, Willie Shoe. We're going to need it, no matter what happens."

Paul Luke left the boy and went to his study where he sat for a long time. Finally, he reached for the telephone and called Sheriff Claude Meeks.

"Paul Luke! I been expecting to hear from you. Went over to your place last evening. They said you'd be in today."

"What's going on, Claude? I understand you've got Plez Shoe locked up. How'd that happen?"

"Yeah. Molly Capps' sister came down. Swore out a complaint against Plez. I didn't have any choice. Got a lead on Plez's whereabouts from a colored boy we picked up drunk off a towboat. The Shelby County sheriff down there took Plez in for us. Went to Memphis myself and brought him back on the train couple days ago. Plez came right on back here, just as easy. Ought to bear some weight at the trial."

"*Trial!*" Paul Luke shouted. "What trial?"

"Grand jury indictment. Circuit judge due in next week, if I'm not mistaken. That's when the trial is set for, I reckon. You might ought to check with the commonwealth attorney though. I'd never of picked Plez for the killer myself. But he's safe here. Never any trouble in my jail. Told his wife she can see him anytime."

"By damn, he'd better be safe, or there'll be hell to pay!" Paul Luke slammed the receiver on its hook.

Later, he placed two additional calls: one to Zacharias Renfrow, the family lawyer he had known all his life; the other to Frankfort, the state capital.

Four days later, for the second time in less than a week, Whitsworth Moseby's Ford sputtered into the Lanier driveway. The driver was a short heavy-set man, not Whitsworth. He stepped to the ground, handling his stiff, unmoving right leg like baggage that had somehow become attached to his body.

The man leaned against the Ford surveying his surroundings. The house sprawled white and imposing. Stretching out on either side of the lawn as far as the eye could see, rose fields of tobacco. The man seemed about to topple forward as he hobbled to the front door. As he approached, it opened and Paul Luke extended his hand.

"Nursie Baltz! Man, you don't know how relieved I am to see you at my door!"

"You did send for me," Karl Ludwig Baltz, commonly known as Nursie, reminded him. "What's this big investigation you need done over here in this little hole in the woods?"

Baltz's status as an investigator approached fable. His sense of integrity was credited with ending more than one scurrilous political career. Some were aborted at the state house in Frankfort; others at the capitol in Washington.

"I need a favor from you, my friend. There's been a killing down on the river, a white woman. Bootlegger. The only fact anybody seems to be interested in is that my workman, a Negro, was fishing down there. Attested to by several of our staunch, and vocal, citizens. Nothing about this thing fits." Paul Luke pushed a chair toward Baltz, who shook his head.

"The grand jury met last week. Just on that shred of circumstantial evidence, it up and indicted him for murder. Trial's already set for next week. I need you to do some smelling around, my friend. And fast."

Nursie propped on the edge of Paul Luke's desk. Amusement glinted in his eyes.

"Me go smelling around to free a colored man that's killed a white woman? That's a new role for an old Kraut like myself."

Whistling a German military tune through his teeth, Nursie hobbled to the window. Studying the rustling leaves, he continued to whistle, ignoring Paul Luke.

Baltz had grown up in pre-war Germany. Europe, roughly divided into two camps, steamed in a cauldron of distrust and ambition. The turmoil erupted into the assassination of Austria's Ferdinand by a citizen of adjoining Serbia. Germany seized the assassination as an excuse to rise against her old foe, France, who joined forces with Serbia. German troops marched through "Little Belgium," disregarding an 1839 Treaty with France that promised no invasion of Belgium, situated between the two powers. France stopped Germany only twenty miles from Paris, at a little stream called the Marne.

When Germany marched through Belgium, Baltz himself, at age twenty-eight, felt personally betrayed. However, his career as a hospital administrator diverted his attention from politics. Perhaps Baltz would have spent all his days absorbed in this occupation had not chemical warfare been first used by his homeland.

Baltz turned to Paul Luke. "I'm not sure what you're asking me to do. If the Negro murdered her—"

"Nursie, I'm not trying to impede justice. The man isn't getting a fair deal. There's more to this, I tell you. But nobody's looking." Paul Luke raised his upturned palms in frustration. "The man's entitled to fairness. That's all I ask."

Baltz left the windows, limped to the desk chair and sat. Without looking up he began flipping through Paul Luke's appointment book.

When Germany released chlorine gas against enemy troops at Passchendaele Ridge in the Battle of Ypres, Baltz had not been able to keep himself from criticizing his nation's leaders.

"A barbaric abomination," Baltz called it, speaking at a public meeting in Bremen."Where will it stop? A whole nation destroyed in one attack? The air that wraps this globe will become a sea of poisonous gases. Everything that breathes will drop dead. Man will invent something a million times stronger than dynamite. And that will snuff out this little spark off the sun."

Baltz's outspoken assault at the Bremen meeting had earned him a reprimand from high German officials. It also brought him, in time, to the attention of the Allied Forces. Their intelligence agents contacted him at his hospital post. Because of the betrayal of his ideals he capitulated to the Allies, "But not for wealth, you understand."

Rolling the chair away from the desk, Baltz turned to Paul Luke. "I'll do it. In the interest of justice, I'll do this investigation you want."

Paul Luke grabbed Nursie's arm. "I never thought you'd walk away from this." He reached for a tablet. "Now, here's a list of people you might want to see, along with their—connection—to the incident."

Nursie took the tablet. "I'll report back in a day or two."

"Take whatever time you need," Paul Luke waved his hand. "But there are some hot-headed people around here. I don't want Plez—he's the accused—to get hurt. By the way, you're welcome to sleep here if you like."

Nursie looked him straight in the eye. "Paul Luke, you paying for this?"

He nodded.

"Well, then, I'm staying at the boarding house over by the depot. Already rented Moseby's car. I work better on my own. Don't like to apologize for odd hours, companions I've been known to keep. If it's all the same with you, that is."

Paul Luke nodded, the tenseness leaving his shoulders.

"Do you want a map of the area? I sketched one here, just in case." He handed Baltz a rolled parchment.

Baltz unfurled it and studied the map. "That's the road to the river, eh? All right, I'll report back in a day or so."

Paul Luke watched the investigator pull himself into the Ford. He closed the door and went to tell Ruby Gem and Willie Shoe what Baltz would be doing for Plez. He heard the sizzle of frying pork chops and smelled cornbread baking. He felt hungry, and good.

After their evening meal Paul Luke and Mathelde sat on the veranda watching twilight descend across the tobacco fields. Paul Luke related the details of his transaction with Nursie Baltz.

"Well, it sounds as if you've hired a capable man," Mathelde said. "Certainly a fascinating one. But why in the world do you call him Nursie? Surely his parents didn't name him that!"

"Hardly. When he escaped Germany just as the war ended somebody began calling him Nursie as a joke."

"Because of his hospital connection?"

Paul Luke nodded."He hated the name so much that it stuck. Or so the story goes."

"What's his real name?"

"I have no idea. If I heard it I doubt I'd remember. Nursie is such a misnomer. It really fits him, in a reverse sort of way."

Leighza and Will Roy, sweaty and cross, came running to their mother, arguing over a croquet game just completed on the front lawn. Further conversation about Nursie Baltz became impossible.

"Gilly! Gilly!"

Nursie Baltz entered a small clearing enclosed by trees. A shack stood in the center. He carried a cane, using it as much to frighten snakes as for support. A mockingbird trilled its symphony into the early morning.

"Gilly! Gilly, I need to talk to you! It's about your sister!"

A white-haired woman appeared at the side of the hut, a shot gun aimed at the detective's chest.

"Who the hell are *you*?"

"My name is Baltz. I'm an investigator."

"Did you kill my sister? You get the hell out of here, you son of a bitch! You ain't going to cut my throat!" Gilly raised the gun to eye level.

"No, no, nothing like that. I just want to ask you some questions." Turning his back to her, Baltz looked for a stump to lean against.

She came closer and sat on a mound of dirt, the gun pointed at the ground, her finger resting on the trigger.

"You don't *know* who killed your sister, do you, Gilly?"

"That nigger over yonder in the jail house—he done it!" Venom

tainted her voice like blood reddens water.

"But you just asked me if I killed your sister. If you're so sure, why'd you ask me if I did it?"

She raised her gun. "If I thought for a minute—"

"Lower that, now. I'm trying to find out who *did* kill Molly."

"Well, be about it then."

After almost an hour of verbal sparring, Baltz gained Gilly's trust. She provided him the information she had.

"My sister never took no money direct from nobody. She'd always say `put your money on the stump.' She didn't aim for no revenuers to cotch her changing whiskey for money."

A squirrel sat in a tree, scolding and chattering. Gilly appeared to contemplate shooting it for her breakfast. She glanced at Nursie, and decided against it.

"Now you last saw your sister alive on the night of July Fourth." Baltz wrote in the tablet Paul Luke had provided. "I don't suppose you'd know the names of any—er—visitors—she might have had that day?"

"I was there seldom—didn't really see nobody much—" Gilly gazed at the squirrel. "By damn! I do remember! I was cooking supper about dark that night. I seen them before. Come down there in a wagon. Molly was laughing at them. Brothers, I think she said. Name of Tolver, Tolson—no—Tillson! That's it! The Tillson boys. Looked like grown men to me."

Nursie unfolded Paul Luke's map and showed it to her, but the woman had no knowledge of the area beyond the river.

The investigator was barely out of the clearing when the crack of a shot echoed behind him. The squirrel ceased its chattering. Baltz stopped in his tracks. He had heard the same crackle the day a bootlegger's bullet shattered the thighbone in his right leg.

Rhode Island Red and white Plymouth Rock chickens knelt in coops along the front of Corlew's Store, their beaks open, wings spread against the heat of the sun. A number of farmers lounged in the persimmon tree's shade. When Whitsworth Moseby's Model T pulled up to the store they became motionless, watching the stranger who was driving.

Nursie Baltz bought a grape soda and a Moon Pie. He

mentioned that he was looking for the Tillson place.

Mae Dee Corlew volunteered directions. Baltz left, almost bumping into Georgie Rae Gardner entering through the screen door with a basket of beans.

"Gabe just heared on his crystal set where President Harding is awful sick. He mayn't live," one of the men remarked as Baltz left the store.

"Just who was that?" Georgie Rae inquired, looking after the disappearing figure.

"Land o' Goshen, woman! I don't know," Mae Dee said, wringing her hands, "but I wish I'd of found out before I went and told him how to get to Bosh Tillson's place!"

She opened the screen door and questioned the idlers. "Any of you all know that fellow?" Two shook their heads, the others stared at her.

She turned back to Georgie Rae.

"He talked a little funny—you know, like a foreigner come from overseas. You don't reckon he's got it in for Bosh's boys? Was they ever in the war?"

Gabe Findley shook his head. "Naw, Mae Dee. It ain't nothing. Ain't much a fellow crippled like that could do anyway, come to think about it."

Daniel and Jack Tillson leaned against Whitsworth Moseby's Model T conversing with Nursie Baltz. Several children watched from the house through screenless open windows.

"You boys drinking any at the Fourth Fest?" Nursie asked suddenly, catching them off guard.

"Uh, yeah. Yeah, we was," Daniel mumbled. Jack nodded.

"Where'd you get the whiskey?"

"Down—down there at the river."

"Who from?"

"Uh—ah—Molly—"

"You just drink only at Fourth Fests?"

"Naw, uh—naw," Daniel said.

"Did you run out of whiskey the night of the Fourth?"

"Well, yeah, we did. We give a right smart of it away. We run out. Yeah."

"Did you go back down there for more that night?"

"We was plumb broke—" Jack said.

"Where were you on the fifth of July?"

"Why, I don't recollect, not rightful. We was sick. Say, why you asking us them questions for anyway?"

Nursie, bringing his interrogation to a conclusion, relented a bit. "So, you left Molly alive and well, around dark. The two of you?"

Jack Tillson smiled and looked down at his bare feet. Putting his hand under his dingy white undershirt he scratched his ribs.

"Me and Daniel. And the half-wit. He was with us."

"The half-wit?"

"Yeah, Buck Junior Mabry. Lives in my daddy's old cow shed. He's tetched. Not right. You know," Jack winked and pointed to his head.

"Could I talk with him?"

"Yeah, if you can find him. Don't expect much from him though. Not much there."

"Well, you two think about it. I'll be back."

Nursie shook hands with the men and left.

Half an hour later he again pulled into the Lanier driveway. By-passing the front he went straight to the kitchen door and knocked. Ruby Gem appeared, holding a mixing bowl and a wooden spoon.

Nursie stepped inside. "Are you the Lanier housekeeper? My name is Baltz. Investigator. Do you have time to answer a few questions?"

Ruby Gem set the mixing bowl down with a clank and faced him. "Did somebody done send you down here on account I pushed that white man? I ain't no trouble-maker. That white man be batty. He about to hurt the children."

It was Nursie's turn to be startled. After an instant he realized that her fright stemmed from some kind of misconception. He gradually dispelled her fear, convincing her that Paul Luke had hired him to help defend Plez.

"What did your husband say that day when he came in from fishing?"

"Well, he say it powerful hot. Then he say Missus Corlew down at the store try to buy them fish off of him—"

Nursie waved his hand.

"Does your husband drink? I mean whiskey. Did he ever work for the deceased?"

"Nah, sir, Plez never been sick a day in his life. He never taste no whiskey, neither. That be the stomp-down truth, Mr. Boss."

Baltz stifled a smile.

"Did your husband ever have any *dealings* with the dead woman?" He gazed at her, eyes narrowed. She shook her head.

"Now, about the man you pushed. Tell me more. Whose children were with you? Where did it happen? When?"

A little later Nursie chugged onto the road in Whitsworth's car. Swirls of dust almost obliterated Corlew's Store as Baltz passed it heading toward Boatwright Park.

The next afternoon at five-thirty Baltz showed up at Paul Luke's front door. "I'm here to eat supper with you."

Paul Luke clapped the detective on his shoulder. "Come in!" he closed the door. "What've you found out?"

"We'll get to that in time. Right now, you're the next person I need to interview on this thing."

Paul Luke laughed. "Am I the suspect now?"

Nursie's eyes squinted against the afternoon sun. "You are a source of information, just like the others I've talked to. You gave me a tablet that lists everybody's connection to this case. Yet your name isn't on it anywhere. You're the man who hired me. Don't tell me you have no link!"

"Paul Luke!" Mathelde called coming down the hall."Dinner is waiting. The children are already seated. Are you—?" She peered around the corner and stopped.

"It's all right. This is Nursie Baltz. He's staying. Tell Ruby Gem to set another place. Fast as she can."

Dinner began quietly. The children stole quick looks at the stranger.

Ruby Gem had prepared chicken and dumplings for the family tonight, a meal she described,"not fine enough for comp'ny." Particularly company like "Mr. Boss," for whom she had developed great esteem after one meeting. Meanwhile, Baltz was telling the children about his birthplace, Bremen, Germany.

"Someday very soon I'll tell you the story of how my little village came to have a very famous statue of a donkey, a cat and a rooster," Baltz concluded.

"Now! Now! Tell us now!" Will Roy shouted.

"Oh, there's not nearly enough time tonight. Tell you what! I saw a nice park up the road apiece. What would you say if we took lemonade and cookies there some afternoon for a kind of story-telling party? You must play there quite often, eh?"

A pall fell over the children.

"Well—" Will Roy said. "We haven't been *there* in a long time. There was a daffy man, and—and—Ruby Gem pushed him down. But maybe if *you* went—"

"U-m-m-, I see," Baltz stared at Paul Luke. "What do you know about this?"

"According to Ruby Gem and Saree Ballard, a neighbor's child who was with them, it was Buck Junior Mabry. He's retarded. A big stout fellow." Paul Luke sipped his coffee. "Wanted to play with the children. There was a little set-to between him and Ruby Gem, although I think he meant no harm." Nursie dug into his peach cobbler. The thick cream could have come from cows on a green hillside in Germany.

"His family?"

"Doesn't have one. Bosh Tillson sort of looks after him to some extent. A tragic, though colorful story, according to hearsay. His father was a preacher. Red-haired Irishman. Always rode a snow white horse. The family had been on an outing. They got on a riverboat, *The Pittsburgh*, at Paducah, to return here. Afterwards, people swore they saw rats by droves leaving down the anchor rope in Paducah."

An expression of alarm crossed Mathelde's face. Rebecca shuddered. Leighza scooted her chair closer to her mother. Will Roy poked his finger at a crumb on the tablecloth. Watching Paul Luke, Baltz put the last bite of cobbler into his mouth.

Before any more of the tale could be told Mathelde rose. "Well, children, why don't we go into the parlor and sing some songs before bedtime. Rebecca, will you play for us? Please excuse us,

Mr. Baltz."

The children, murmuring goodnight, stood and followed their mother. Will Roy looked back over his shoulder.

"And—?" Nursie prompted, watching the departing brood.

"To make a long story short, there was an explosion just before they docked at Cairo. *The Pittsburgh* burned in the middle of the Ohio River. Thirty-one people died, including Buck Junior's parents. He was saved. One of the lucky ones."

Silence engulfed the two. Ruby Gem poured more coffee and removed the dessert plates.

"Well," Nursie said, after she left. "Those Tillsons really stick together on their story. Practically word for word. But I think I may be onto something. Do you have a lawyer representing Plez?"

"Well, I guess! I've contacted Zacharias Renfrow. He'll defend. You know him?"

"Only by reputation." Nursie set his coffee cup in its saucer. "Tell him I'll be by to see him tomorrow afternoon. Might also want to see if he can get a continuance on the case. Don't believe we could be ready by Monday, even if we hurried." Baltz chuckled. "Or `lit a shuck,' as you Kentuckians say."

Through a gap in the lace curtains, while his sisters sang a hymn about bringing in the sheaves, Will Roy watched Baltz leave. Later, when he said his prayers at bedtime, his thoughts kept straying. A donkey, a cat, and a rooster, cast in unchanging stone, beckoned from some faraway part of the world.

Chapter 8

Darkness settled and the crowd at Corlew's was no less somber than the August night.

The president was dead.

Word of the nation's loss had trickled into the community early that morning. Most households had little access to news outside of what they could glean second or third hand beneath the persimmon tree. Mae Dee Corlew, in a burst of good will, volunteered her store as a gathering place to distribute information. Gabe Findley, every bit as charitable as Mae Dee, bustled onto the scene bearing his crystal radio set with all its appurtenances. A grounding wire from the radio soon spiraled around the end of a lead pipe.

He tinkered with some metal bands, while the mute crowd watched. After some time, Gabe nodded. His radio base was operating. Earphones in place, Gabe installed himself on an empty chicken crate. He occupied the limelight and his throne atop the chicken crate for most of the day.

"Warren G. Harding, twenty-ninth President of the United States, died today at the age of fifty-eight, of a res—respi—well, he had the grippe!" Gabe said.

Adults exchanged glances. Children chased each other, banging Corlew's screen door, evading Gypsy moths that danced in the circles of lantern light. The world shifts; history evolves; men die; but the artless moth endures.

"Who'll it be, now? Another Republican, I guess," Bosh Tillson said. "I never voted for but one danged Republican in my life. My coffee ain't tasted right since. And that's been twenty years."

"Why, of course, the vice president will take his place," Amos McCann said, walking up with Eli Mayes. "That's Coolidge."

Gabe Findley raised his hand for silence.

"He'd been to Alasker. Took sick out West somewhere. Died in Californie. Coolidge took over already."

"Well, if you want *my* opinion," Mae Dee said from the doorway, "the President of the United States got no business running around in them foreign countries over there no way."

The crowd stirred, moved by an ill-defined awareness of the heat, of life's continuity, and of a man's vulnerability. A few left. Others went into the store. Using the persimmon tree for home base the children began a tag game.

"Kids tired of homemade biscuits, been wanting light bread for a week," Bosh Tillson said, walking inside the store with Eli Mayes. "What do you think all this is going to mean, Eli?"

Eli removed his hat and scratched his head. "I ain't no Republican, but I liked Harding some. He never had much truck with that League of Nations idea Wilson pushed for. Harding thought the best way to keep us out of war is stay to ourself. `Get everything back to normal here,' he always said. Don't know much about Coolidge, though. I did hear tell he don't cotton to giving the veterans much benefits. I don't know about that. If there's anybody we owe something to, it's them, seems to me."

Bosh nodded to Sheriff Meeks who was leaving the store.

"Give me a pound of that dog, too, Mae Dee," he said, pointing to a stick of bologna, "and some of them cheese and crackers over there." He winked. "Going to take the old lady a treat tonight."

Outside, Lail Stratton sat in his wheel chair near the door.

"Sheriff Meeks!" he called. "Been wanting to ask about that murder down on the river." The sheriff went closer. "That nigger that works for young Lanier? He still locked up?"

"Yeah, Plez is sitting in the jail right now."

Stratton leaned forward and cocked one eye. "He ever going to trial? What's the hold-up?"

The sheriff fumbled with his keys. His glance swept across Stratton's withered frame.

"Zacharias Renfrow's defending. Asked for a continuance. Circuit judge reset the trial for next month."

Stratton's expression became shrewd.

"Guess it don't hurt to have influence. My understanding's young Lanier's up and hired some big investigator to come in here and muddy the water. That right, Sheriff?"

"Aw, hell, Lail! The law gives the man a chance at a fair trial, even if he *is* colored. You wouldn't take that away from him, would you?"

Stratton lowered his eyes.

"Well, I have to be going," Meeks said. "You just rest easy the court's going to do the right thing, Lail."

The Louisville and Atlantic locomotive steamed away from the Louisville depot pulling its cars like toy blocks. Paul Luke strolled into the bright August sunshine.

Stopping on the brick sidewalk he gazed across the Ohio River to where the land was not Kentucky anymore, but Ohio. Boundaries were painfully arbitrary. This is Kentucky, that is Ohio; all one in the universe. Paul Luke stared into the water.

At length he heard a voice. Lockett Lakewood sat behind the wheel of her Jones Motor Car.

"Well! If only you found me *half* that captivating, I'd be tickled to death! I came for you. Get in!"

"Lockett! What are you doing here? How'd you—?" He opened the door and sat beside her.

"How'd I know when to meet you?" She prepared to release the brake. "There're only two daily arrivals from your neck of the woods. All I had to do was meet both of them."

"*Our* neck of the woods." Putting his hands on her shoulder he kissed her mouth. Then, leaning back, he took in every inch of her, from the pleats in her skirt to the creamy glow of her bare arms.

"Staying at the Galt House?" Lockett moved away, as if to bypass the intensity of his eyes.

"Yes, the governor's committee on the economy meets there tonight. You look ravishing. How I wish the governor would cancel his meeting! But that's not going to happen. Big decisions to be made. I need to get my two cents worth in. Unfortunate timing, though."

Lockett clutched his arm, keeping her eyes on the street. "But there's the Jockey Club Ball tomorrow night! You didn't forget about that?"

"Forget the ball? My dear Lockett, that's why I'm here! The governor's committee is only an inconvenient coincidence.

Governor Morrow knew most of his committee would be here for the ball anyway. Right crafty of him."

Lockett turned on Broadway and stopped before the burgundy canopy of the Galt House.

"Well, I wanted to see that you got to your hotel." She bent toward him and kissed his mouth. "If you finish with your committee by nine tonight, call me."

He kissed her, and would have again, had the wind not whipped her gauzy neckerchief across his face, filling his mouth with silk.

"I will." He cupped her chin in his hand, tilting her face to his. "But don't expect it. We won't finish early. There's a lot to discuss. Then there's certain to be some talk about Harding's death. Its implications."

She lowered her head, a disappointed look on her face. He reached for his bag behind the seat.

"Oh, by the way, I'm sending the car back to the hotel later on. It'll be on the street here, and the key will be at the desk. I'm expecting you to be prompt when you pick me up for the ball tomorrow."

With a smile and a wave she left. The beige roadster turned a corner and vanished.

Paul Luke descended the marble staircase at the Galt House. Above the lobby rose a three-story atrium. Rows of iron reeds, flowers, and cattails, painted in lifelike colors, formed guardrails on the upper floors. Green Rookwood pelicans stared into the lobby from atop marble columns. In the background a waterfall plinked. A brass clock struck half past seven.

The doors to the Limestone Room stood ajar and Governor Ed P. Morrow sat at a Chippendale desk. His hand picked committee members talked in groups, only a few listening.

The Limestone Room was elliptical in shape. Picture-frame paneling throughout the room enclosed leaves, flowers, and seedpod replicas of tobacco plants, created from inlaid copper, brass, and iron. A chandelier said to be two centuries old hung above.

"Gentlemen!" The governor stood, ready to open the meeting.

Shard McFadden of Bond County hiccuped, and tried to cover the sound with a cough. Paul Luke suppressed a smile. The

Chickasaws were said to have bestowed the sobriquet "Big Drunk" on McFadden's grandfather. The old man gained political notice because of his efforts in setting up the Kentucky state constitution of 1891. Since then, successive McFaddens slid into office on the old fellow's unsteady coattails. Shard McFadden won election because he appeared oblivious to the bootlegging that made Bond County notorious; McFadden also exerted influence with the sheriff of his home county.

Opposite McFadden, Howard McDougal of Marshall County relaxed. McDougal never took a position on any issue, a policy that earned him the by-name of "Both Sides" McDougal among his contemporaries. He probably was selected for the committee because his lack of commitment would take him in whatever direction the governor led.

Governor Morrow read a eulogy to the late president and jumped into the committee's task.

"Gentlemen, with a record budget projected for this great commonwealth of ours, I urge you, with all sobriety—" His eyes turned toward Shard McFadden. "—with *all* sobriety, to consider every revenue-raising option we have open. Acceptable to your constituents, of course."

Silence stood with the governor like another presence. He cleared his throat.

Beech Marcom rose. "Governor Morrow, and legislative friends," Marcom began, spreading his hands on the table before him. "The reputation this state enjoys as the absolute paragon of horse racing perfection must not be tampered with. To tax the tracks would be foolhardy to the point of creating chaos. To do so would pull down the wrath of every man, woman, and child in the Bluegrass!"

"Both Sides" McDougal nodded and scanned the room.

A millionaire horse breeder, Marcom owned farms at Lexington and in Paul Luke's home county. He also was Lockett Lakewood's stepfather. Not a member of the General Assembly, the man wielded power because he was the state racing commissioner, as well as head of the autocratic Jockey Club. A conflict of interest by any measure. It had been said of Marcom that he valued four things in life; horses, women, money, and power. But not necessarily in that

order.

A. Dixon Murphy, from Garland County, rose to speak. He was campaigning for governor and had more than likely exerted pressure to be appointed to the committee. Murphy favored levying a five-cent per ton severance fee on coal to relieve farm taxes. Against Beech Marcom's vocal objections Murphy also wanted to eliminate pari-mutuel betting. Such an uproar ensued that the governor struck his pewter water pitcher with a spoon to restore order. Paul Luke watched, saying nothing.

A suggestion to lobby for the repeal of prohibition followed, to which Shard McFadden hiccuped a loud, "No!" Representatives from poverty-stricken regions proposed raising taxes on automobiles and gasoline; others thought a solution lay in trying to influence Congress to increase the duties on imported farm goods. Another group, certain that immigrants coming into the country caused the unprecedented budgetary growth, decided it would lobby Congress to end immigration.

After an hour of haranguing, Gattis Todd, from the Eastern Kentucky coal mining region, stood. He and Paul Luke had entered the General Assembly at the same time, but disagreed on most topics. No one doubted that Gattis Todd intended to be governor one day.

"The senator from the Ohio River Valley has not given us the privilege of hearing his thoughts," Todd said, gesturing toward Paul Luke. "I suggest he might do that at this time. If indeed, he has any!"

Paul Luke's good-humored expression never wavered. His gaze swept across the table, scrutinizing the committee, and came to rest for a full minute on Gattis Todd. Paul Luke stood and walked to the front, stopping near the governor's lectern.

"Gentlemen," he began, "I am vexed, as you all are, with the budget crisis we must address. But my greater concern is the division and partisanship here, among us, the solution finders. The arguing has become more tedious than a tired horse. We must put it aside and work for the good of every Kentuckian.

"To my coal mining friends, let me point backward to the Federal Highway Act passed just two years ago. Clearly an intent to `soak the rich,' it is already becoming a system of political patronage through the highway department."

Beech Marcom and "Both Sides" McDougal nodded approval.

"I disagree categorically with the Bond County representative, Mr. McFadden. The Eighteenth Amendment is costing this nation, this state, millions in lost taxes through the prohibition of legal alcohol. Even industrial alcohol is being poisoned to prevent its consumption. Some of the finest lawmen ever to wear a badge have died trying to enforce this nightmare. Mobsters are becoming millionaires running rum and other whiskeys from overseas. Bootleggers and their `blind tiger' establishments multiply. Where is the sanity, my friends?"

A commotion erupted, led by Shard McFadden, whose hiccups had diminished during the evening. Paul Luke glanced about the room. Well over half the men sat contemplating his words in silence.

"With due respect to Mr. Marcom," he continued, "I say that the Jockey Club must divest itself of its track control in this state. A racing commission has to be independent to insure honesty and integrity."

Beech Marcom scowled, puffing dark cigar smoke in spurts. "Both Sides" McDougal looked confused. Taking his cue from Marcom he shook his head. Shard McFadden watched, appearing pleased that Paul Luke's scrutiny had traveled past his own pet interest—Prohibition—into Marcom's racing and gambling domain.

"Now I believe in the integrity of this committee, and of this governor," Paul Luke went on. "I believe we can cast away our regional differences and work together. I believe that nothing makes a man more suspicious than knowing too little. Government was not created to make a few men rich, but to assure the well being of all. There comes a time in every man's life when he watches the world go by and complains, or he gets up and does something to change it. This is that time.

"Concerning our common challenge, the budget, may I remind you, gentlemen: When it rains in Kentucky, we all get wet."

None of the committee members moved. The governor began to applaud and others joined, even Beech Marcom and Shard McFadden. In the back of the room an empty chair creaked. It had been vacated by Gattis Todd, the would-be governor, in the seconds following the speech.

Governor Morrow set the date for a second meeting and adjourned. Most of the men rushed to shake Paul Luke's hand, praising his insight and unifying appeal. Quotes from "The Kentucky Rain Speech," as it came to be known, would be heard in the months that followed.

Gattis Todd regretted his own political bungling. Had he remained quiet, Paul Luke would have said nothing. On such the threads of fate are strung.

Closing Beech Marcom's front door Paul Luke guided Marcom's stepdaughter, Lockett, to the Jones roadster parked just beyond the white pillars of the porch.

Lockett's raven hair was swept to the crown of her head, where it tumbled in curls to her shoulders. A diamond crested band, the special insignia reserved for the Mistress of The Jockey Club Ball, arched across her forehead. Scarlet silk floated around her, which, with the scent of her perfume, left an impression of rose petals fluttering in the twilight. The muscles above Paul Luke's elbow tightened where her fingers rested.

"You didn't call last night," she reproached, settling into the seat at his side.

"Well, no, I didn't. It was after ten when the meeting ended." He pulled onto the road from the private lane that led to Beechwood Farm.

"That wasn't too late to call."

"But you said nine."

"You know I didn't mean that."

"My dear Lockett, I always take a lady only at her word." He tweaked a curl. "Besides, you must have needed every hour of the last twenty-four to create that hair style.Tell me, do you have little sausages wrapped up inside all those curls?"

Lockett scooted away from him. "You're impossible," she fumed, reaching to protect her hair-do. "And if you don't slow down, I'll look like Mama's wash woman when we get there! Just how would you like that?"

"Depends on the wash woman."

Electric lanterns blazed atop the six-foot wall that circled the Seelbach Hotel. An attendant parked their car; then the two were obliged to stand still for photographers. Paul Luke visualized the watchers at Corlew's Store, tongues clicking, heads wagging. A smile lifted the corners of his mouth, but fled when an inexplicable likeness of Nora presented itself. For a fleeting second Nora stood at his side. The image of her elegance, more seductive than Lockett's finery, flitted through his mind. It was Nora's hair, brushed into a smooth halo that he looked down upon, not Lockett's curls.

"That's enough," he said brusquely, leading Lockett past the photographers, through the beveled glass and brass doors of the Seelbach.

When they reached the main ballroom, Beech Marcom, head of the Jockey Club, announced them. Accompanied by applause, the wooly beam of a spotlight followed them to their table. Cold sparks glittered from the diamonds on Lockett's forehead, becoming less defined when the spotlight died. As other couples were introduced, *My Old Kentucky Home* played in the background. Paul Luke and Lockett sat at a table with her mother, Letitia, waiting to be joined by Lockett's stepfather when he finished as Master of Ceremonies.

Paul Luke felt uneasy about Beech Marcom. In his speech last night he had spared no factions, condemning Marcom's own position in the state racing industry. Although the man appeared to accept Paul Luke's judgement concerning the state budget woes, who could predict his behavior in a purely social setting?

Aware that his name was being called, Paul Luke turned to find Beech Marcom, his hand outstretched in greeting. With him was another couple. Paul Luke soon discovered that Marcom's interest tonight lay not in the tangled knot of the state's racing management. Marcom was consumed with his own wish to negotiate the purchase of a horse farm belonging to the couple that accompanied him.

"You *could* invite me to dance," Lockett pouted. He jumped to his feet and took her hand.

"Would you give me the pleasure?"

They swirled onto the dance floor, his attention focused on the woman in his arms. He pulled her close, one hand holding the nape of her neck.Their lips almost touched.

"Do you realize that I've hardly seen you since the Fourth Fest? Such absence is not to be tolerated."

Her eyes filled with astonishment. "You know that Fourth Fest is a tender subject with me! Whatever made you bring that up tonight?"

He spun her away from a near collision with another couple. He leaned back and the space between them increased.

"What's the matter? Has something come between us?"

"No! But I *am* distracted, at the moment. I just happen to be looking at that nibbly left ear of yours. It affects me in some dark, mysterious way."

She peered into his face. His hand tightened on her waist.

"Dark and mysterious indeed! You are a genuine fleshed-out devil, Paul Luke Lanier! The way you treated me at that Fourth Fest! You were nothing short of rude!" Contrary to her words her expression lacked animosity. She smiled and waved to friends.

"My dearest Lockett, what are you talking about?"

"Why, is your memory so short? You left me standing there by myself, and *you* went to Nora Ballard!" The orchestra changed tunes and without missing a step he led her into a fox trot.

"Nora and I had already scheduled that dance earlier," he lied, "and I felt obliged to honor it. I was over-tired. A lot on my mind, as you must recall. Besides you didn't lack attention for very long I noticed!"

"No-o-o, as I *recall*." She stepped from the path of another couple. "It appeared that I was boring you with my conversation about this very ball. In fact, I'm wondering right now if you really want to be here." Her eyes sparkled.

"Absolutely! Being at this ball right now with you is more important than anything else in the world." He pulled her to him. "If ever I hurt you, even one jot, my dearest Lockett, please accept my most contrite apology."

"Well, I do wonder about you and her." Lockett tucked her head beneath his chin. "Maybe I have no reason, but sometimes I can't help it."

When the music ended Paul Luke turned toward their table but Lockett took his hand. She guided him to a door that exited onto an intimate veranda.

"Enough about that. As you said, this is the ball. You're here with me. Let's talk about us."

"Yes." His breath ruffled her hair. "Let's talk about you and me."

"Oh, there you are, Paul Luke!" With a feeling of dismay Paul Luke turned to face Letitia Marcom, Lockett's mother, who said, "I simply must take you to meet Judge Willis! He just this minute arrived from Cleveland." She took his arm. "Lockett, dear, you must pay your respects to the judge again, too!"

"Mother, I don't want to visit with that stodgy old judge this evening! I'll just go back to the table with my friends. And please don't let him monopolize Paul Luke too long. You know how the judge can talk!"

A group of well wishers swept Lockett away while Paul Luke allowed himself to be taken like a prize stallion and introduced.

"Senator Lanier," the judge said after a short conversation, "I want you to meet my niece, Miss Beatrice Washburn, granddaughter of your state's own Colonel Washburn." He reached into the shadows behind him and fished out a flustered young woman.

"Beatrice, Mr. Lanier is in the General Assembly at Frankfort. Been mentioned for governor a few years down the pike, if I may so say."

Miss Washburn squealed. "O-h-h-h, I must hear more about that! If—if you'll just ask me to dance." She blinked behind thick spectacles.

Paul Luke bowed. "Miss Washburn, fortune smiles. May I?"

They glided onto the floor, her arm coiled around his neck, pulling him close. She peered about for acquaintances, holding her transient prize like a trophy.

At a table near the judge, Gaddis Todd sat with his wife and Shard McFadden. Todd, still smarting over his blunder the night before, sipped from a flask supplied by McFadden. It contained the best "dew" Bond County had to offer. Watching Paul Luke from the corner of his eye, Todd frowned. He stood as the crowd of dancers started back to their tables.

"How many votes you reckon he's picked up on the dance floor tonight?" Todd growled. He headed toward the aisle Paul Luke would take returning Beatrice Washburn to her uncle, the judge.

"Now, now, Gattis," McFadden soothed, following Todd. "Lanier's liked. Respected. If you faced him tomorrow for governor, he'd probably take you. But nothing's lost. There's plenty of time."

Gattis Todd strode into Paul Luke's path, jostling some of the crowd, pushing into its midst.

"Well, there's no doubt about it," Todd said, his voice loud. "*Mister* Lanier from the Ohio Valley may very well become governor of Kentucky some day—if he *continues* to spawn *bastard* constituents to vote for him!"

Shocked silence fell over those near enough to hear. It stretched across the room as Todd's words were repeated. The violinists, preparing to play a waltz, froze, instruments perched under their chins. Beatrice Washburn clapped her hand against her mouth. All eyes focused on her companion. Paul Luke's fists clenched at his sides.

"That's cheap talk for this ballroom," Paul Luke's voice rang through the quiet. "In the presence of these ladies. Todd, those words belong in the dirt of that street out there! Along with your filthy mouth!"

He moved toward Todd, but Shard McFadden stepped between them. Lockett Lakewood hurried to Paul Luke's side.

"No, Lanier," McFadden pleaded, walking so close that only Paul Luke could hear. "He's already wounded his career tonight. Drunk. Attacking you. Let him go, for God's sake!"

Paul Luke hesitated. Lockett tugged at his elbow and he turned to face her. The orchestra began its delayed waltz. The crowd around them thinned. Shard McFadden put his arm about Gattis Todd's shoulders and led the man who burned to be governor from the room.

"I don't believe Gattis Todd's talk," Lockett said, steering Paul Luke away. "I want you to know that I was not the source of that gossip in this town. I don't believe it for a minute, and I wasn't— I wouldn't—"

Paul Luke gazed into her face, his mind still on the confrontation with Gattis Todd. Lockett took his face in her hands and repeated what she had said.

"Lockett, I know that. You wouldn't say those things. Besides, there's no way in this world that your mother would let you be the first to tell such a tale as that!"

Lockett stiffened. "Paul Luke, you don't *know* that!"

"Well, your mother does have an ear for gossip. But that's not a quality reserved to women only I've noticed."

"This conversation isn't going to get more unpleasant, is it? There's been enough of that already."

"No, I'm concentrating on an entirely different matter for the rest of the evening." He took her in his arms."Let's dance."

"I noticed how close you danced with the judge's niece."

"I did, didn't I? The judge's niece is not as—reticent—as you might suppose."

"The judge's niece is a stuffy bore, just like he is!"

Lockett took his hand, and led him through the French doors onto the moonlit veranda.

"It seems ages ago, but we were going to talk about you and me before—" She raised her head.

His kiss sent her dancing on a string. Lockett pushed against him like a shameless barmaid, but after one reeling moment she pulled away. She withdrew from his arms and strolled into the moonlight. Paul Luke followed her, his eyes reflecting the moon. Moving against her, he lifted her chin with his hand.

"No, wait." Lockett avoided his lips. "We must get back now. The ball's almost over."

"I'm not exactly sure where you Louisville women get your charm," he said as he took her elbow, "but you do have a way of making a stranger feel welcome."

"Oh? Well, some strangers are more welcome than others."

"And, by the same token, it takes more—welcoming—for some than it does for others."

"You're no stranger here!" Lockett turned away. Leaning against the iron banister, she watched the moon slide in and out among the clouds. "Is your room at the Galt House satisfactory?"

"Yes, quite," he traced the outline of her ear with his finger. "Quite satisfactory."

Lockett whirled to face him. "You'd say that, even if it weren't!

Paul Luke, you are too easy to please. How can you be so—so—I think I must inspect it myself."

He raised an eyebrow.

"Yes." She folded her hands beneath her chin. "I think that's *exactly* what I must do, in the interest of hospitality. It's going to be quite convenient. After all, you *do* have a car."

"There might be talk. You may have gathered that I'm not exactly regarded as Prince Valiant."

"Of course, there'll be talk! There's been some already. What do you think they'll do, kick us out of the Jockey Club? Take my title away? The ball's over. Besides, they wouldn't dare." She laughed. "Not with Beech Marcom to face. Oh, they'll whisper behind my back. But I'll still be Beech Marcom's stepdaughter, after all is said and done." She reached for his hand.

Waving to departing friends they returned to their table. Lockett engaged in a whispered conversation with her mother before turning to Beech Marcom.

He was in an expansive mood, having consummated his deal for the horse farm. He put his arm across Paul Luke's shoulders. "This state needs more men like yourself," Marcom told him.

The orchestra played *My Old Kentucky Home* once more and the ball ended.

"Come." Lockett headed toward the veranda. Paul Luke followed her down the steps and across Main Street to their car near Belvedere Park. Facing the waterfront they sat in the Jones roadster.

Lockett moved closer to Paul Luke. He took her in his arms and bent toward her. Then abruptly pushing her away he sat up.

"Lockett, I must get you home. This is no place for us."

"But I haven't inspected your room yet. Remember?" She ran her fingers along his thigh.

"Lockett!" He brushed his hand across his forehead. "All right, then. As you wish. But I must take you home and arrange to return the car. I have to leave tomorrow." Paul Luke got the roadster started and headed toward the Galt House.

"You know I really intend to take the car back myself. But I just don't drive at night. Now would you please look in the back and bring that little valise with you?"

He stared at her, one eyebrow lifted. Then, retrieving her bag, he followed her through the discreet side entry of the Galt House.

The mid-morning sun reached across Talbott Tavern greens. Paul Luke, sipping coffee in the shade of a century-old oak, watched Lockett pinch pieces from a hot bun.

Talbott Tavern, once a stagecoach stop and Indian outpost, nestled in a valley three miles north of Louisville. During pleasant weather patrons preferred the lawn, where a contented sheep or haughty peacock might wander between the tables.

Lockett reached across the table. "Paul Luke, I can't tell you how happy I've been these last few hours with you. At the ball— it's all like a dream."

"Lockett, you must know how it's been for me."

She dropped his hand and lowered her eyes, her expression wistful. "Yet, I went through last evening knowing it was probably our last time together. I think—I wish I hadn't known."

Concern ruffled his thoughts. "Known what? That's morbid, Lockett. I'm afraid I don't understand."

She twisted the cameo pendant at her throat. "It's Nora Ballard." Words emerged fast. "I absolutely adore being with you, but I feel like—like I'm stealing from—no, *substituting* for her every time we have a moment together."

"Lockett, I hardly spend time with Nora at all, seldom see her, even."

"I don't understand that. Not at all. At the Fourth Fest I thought about it. Seeing her, even from a distance. I felt, well, like you were at her side, not mine. Whatever has been—is—between you two, I'm afraid there's nothing for us, Paul Luke." Her voice trembled with tears.

"Lockett—don't—" He reached for her hand, but she drew it away.

"Something happened that last night we were together with Cleve Corlew. That I know. But what? I guess I'll never know that. Things have been different ever since. Even before he died. Oh, I've tried to come to terms with it. But whatever the circumstance, you and Nora—to one extent or another—the two of you do share that child."

"That little girl is dear to me."

"And I suspect her mother as well is—`dear' to you." Lowering her lashes, Lockett swallowed. She twined her hands together in her lap and glanced obliquely at Paul Luke. She seemed to find whatever expression she sought on his face because she picked up her fork after a time and began to eat. Paul Luke followed suit, lifting his orange juice in a mock toast. They sometimes laughed during the rest of their meal. Perhaps concluding that they had received news of some very good fortune, people around them smiled.

"Well, Paul Luke," Lockett said after she swallowed her last bit of Eggs Benedict, "you do have a train to catch."

He nodded and placed several silver dollars on the tablecloth.

The car waited, its motor started by an attendant. They sat for a time in the sun-streaked shade. The blue grass fell like a velvet drape across the hills. Clusters of oak and black walnut trees huddled in the valleys. After a time Paul Luke released the brake and turned toward Louisville. Neither spoke until they reached the train station.

"You're sure you don't mind my leaving you with the car like this?"

"Of course not." Lockett removed her wide-brimmed hat and placed it on the seat beside her. "But since the breakfast and the relationship seem to have ended at the same time, I do have one final question to ask. You might not answer, but I must ask."

He raised an eyebrow and waited.

"Would you—could you—tell me that you have never been close with Nora, in the way you've been with me?"

A train steamed into the station and a few flecks of soot settled on his shirt. He looked into her face, his eyes wide and dark.

"Well." She slid behind the wheel. "The whole thing has been lovely, as they say. A lovely affair. But it's over."

He reached into the back for his suitcase. "We'll take that up later. Good-bye, Lockett." His lips brushed her forehead.

"Good-bye, Paul Luke," she whispered into the breeze that teased her hair and swept away the final trace of his kiss. "Don't believe everything you're told."

Chapter 9

Zacharias Renfrow walked into the Hunt County Jail and set a wicker basket on the sheriff's desk.

"I'm here to see Plez. His wife sent some victuals. I'd like for you to sort of search through this basket, Tom."

Tom Scott, the jailer, regarded the lawyer with mild curiosity. Zach was wearing his "going-to-court" suit, but there was no trial today.

"Aw, counselor, I don't need to inspect that. Plez ain't going to try nothing." Scott closed his knife and slid it into his pocket.

"All the same, I'd appreciate it if you would. I know it's a formality, but let's go by the rules. You know you're doing your duty. Just a quick check."

Scott lifted the white napkin with his forefinger and perused the basket, sniffing. "Looks fine. Smells even better. Come on, Zach."

He led Renfrow down a narrow corridor to the last cell, the only one occupied. Plez stood when the men approached.

"Be half an hour or so." The lawyer pulled a cane-bottomed chair into the cell as he entered. Tom Scott nodded and locked the cell behind him.

Plez brightened at the sight of Ruby Gem's basket. More white dotted Plez's hair now than a month earlier.

"Your wife fixed up a nice meal for you here, Plez. You're fortunate I didn't eat it myself, it smells so good. Go ahead. Eat while it's hot. We'll just talk a bit."

"Yes, sir!" Sitting on a stool Plez opened the basket.

"Thought I'd let you know, we're working up a good defense for you. I guess Ruby Gem told you about the investigator Paul Luke hired?" Renfrow watched Plez devour a fried chicken wing. "You do know about him?"

Plez nodded. "Yes, sir. Him and Mr.Paul Luke done been here

to see me."

"Good man, Baltz. Peeked through every knothole in the fence, so to speak. Judge set the trial for the middle of next month. We'll be ready."

Plez sprang to his feet, the basket clattering to the floor.

"They ain't ever going to find a colored man innocent." Turning his back he looked through the bars. "White folks' jury. White lady dead. No chance. Cross burning down at the river done told Plez what to expect." After a few moments he walked back to the stool, staring at the contents of the overturned basket.

Renfrow righted the basket, recovering scattered pieces of chicken.

"Now, Plez, that cross burning was done by a handful of riffraff in the heat of the moment. There's hardly anybody in Hunt County that wouldn't give you a chance in a sane situation. They know the kind of life you've lived in this community. What you did here years ago."

"People has a habit of forgetting the good at a time like this." Plez picked up a biscuit and brushed away dirt.

"Nonsense! You know those Laniers. Paul Luke, his mother. All of them have looked after you like family. But nobody in Hunt County ever called those folks `nigger lovers.' Everybody knows why the Laniers have so much regard for you, Plez. I certainly don't have to tell *you* why."

"No, sir." Plez looked at the scars he had borne on his hands for more than thirty years. Instantly his fingers were like doors and windows, with flames on the other side.

"You've been decent. Church-going. Good family man. Besides all that, those Laniers will never forget how you went into that fire. It was a brave thing you did, Plez. Folks in this community haven't forgotten it, either."

Plez leaned forward.

"No, sir. Nobody could ever convince Paul Luke or his mother that you're guilty of what you're accused of. In this world *or* the next." Renfrow scooted his chair closer to Plez."You know, I've never heard it from you, Plez." He peered over his spectacles. "What exactly did happen that day of the fire?"

Again Plez looked at his hands. His thoughts slipped through the iron bars and traveled back into the past. *The hot September sun on his back, the red birds calling, the scent of sweat and wilted tobacco.*

"Guess I near on to fifteen year old," he began after a while, his voice low, muted by the distance of years. "My mama, Maw-Maw, we call her, she done the cooking for Miss Naomi Ruth and Mr. Lucas Lanier. She move here with them from Tennessee after they first marry with each other. All my kin before me, they all belong to Mr. Lucas' family, and proud of it. They stayed on, working for wages, even after the freeing.

"On this day, it be tobacco cutting time. Maw-Maw be fixing dinner for the workers. Frying chicken over by the stove. Miss Naomi Ruth stand in the door. Miss Naomi Ruth say the grease flame up. The curtain, it blow out and catch a-fire.

"I be toting water to the tobacco field. I see the fire blow out the window. Miss Naomi Ruth, she be screaming. I retch in for to pull her out the door." Plez wrung his hands. "But I never touch no white lady before. I be trying to think where best to grab onto Miss Naomi Ruth.

"But Miss Naomi Ruth, she grab me 'round the neck. Her dress be on fire, all over. I jump back out the flames, and her holding on. I beat that fire off Miss Naomi Ruth with my hands. But I never feel no hurt, or nothing."

"You must have felt something after that. Like some kind of hero. Proud."

"No, sir, Mr. Zacharias. There weren't no time. My Maw-Maw still stand there in that fire, screaming and crying, `Plez! I'm here, Plez!' And screaming and crying. 'Plez!' The fire all the time go higher, and she holler,`Plez! Help me!'" He raised his head. "*But I couldn't reach her, Mr. Zach! Lord Jesus I try!* She scream and cry till the rafters done fall in. And I couldn't —`Here, Plez!' Screaming till the rafters fall." Tears streamed down his face. "And Plez couldn't—"

The lawyer scrutinized the scars on the man's hands and forearms.

"Plez, the people in Hunt County know you did that. They respect you for it. I don't believe there's a man who wouldn't take you onto his own place if you needed it. There's no reason you can't get a fair hearing. Most folks were shocked that you'd been accused of that killing."

"Yes, sir, I reckon that cross just set down there by the river and burn itself."

"Tell me, Plez, that day of the fire. Where were Bosh Tillson and Eli Mayes and all the others? How do they fit into this?"

"Oh, they live here, and down there by the river. They all come running to the fire. Trying to help. Except Mr. Amos McCann. Him and his mama move in after that happen."

"You got burned on your hands and arms, didn't you? Who looked after you?"

"Some of the colored folk help me. Then Mr.Gabe Findley, he say, `Fetch the doctor over here.' Doctor Haas, he take a look. He say, `Get some grease and wrap this boy's hands. And arms, too.' He have to see after Miss Naomi Ruth. She be in a family way, and all."

Zacharias' eyes widened. He leaned forward.

"In a family way?"

"Yes, sir. Few months after the fire, Mr. Paul Luke, he be born."

"What about now, Plez? How do most white people around here treat you? Before this killing came up, I mean. Friendly?"

"Oh, yes, they always hollers at me, `How you, Plez?' or `Ain't this a fine day, Plez?'"

"Plez, that jury over there in the courthouse will be made up partly of these same folks. Now, there *is* a percentage of people who are rather emotional. About a lot of things in general. But I just don't believe that cross burning was aimed solely at you. The Klan never came into your house or yard and bothered you. Now did they?"

Plez shook his head.

"When we get into your trial, I will likely be looking at some of those same people. I am persuaded in my mind, that they respect you as a person. But at the same time, if they think you killed Molly Capps after all is said and done, certainly there's no feeling so deep that they would rise up and forgive you. If I can show them there's just a real good chance you didn't do it, I think...." A burst of energy seemed to overtake Renfrow. He shuffled his feet.

"I have to put my hope on those people, and you're going to have to lay your hope on these same people. Now Paul Luke hired Baltz to help build up what he can." Renfrow stood. "And if you don't have faith in *anything* else at this point, Plez, you know you've got me, doing my damndest to get you out of this mess!"

"I sure wish Miss Naomi Ruth was here."

"Why? Don't you think Paul Luke is doing all he can?"

"Yes, sir. But if Miss Naomi Ruth come tearing down to that courthouse with steel in her eye, folks going to think hard before they hand Plez any rotten apple."

Tom Scott appeared at the cell door and Zacharias followed him down the hall.

Renfrow stopped on the small porch in front of the jail. Tom Scott joined him.

"Did you ever know of Plez Shoe to take a drink?" Renfrow asked.

"That's funny. Commonwealth's attorney Milton Harp asked me that last week. No, Plez Shoe don't drink. I told Milton the same thing."

"Are you sure?"

"Zach, I been part of the law here for twenty years." Scott turned around and hung his jail keys on a nail inside the door. "I know everybody that drinks. And I know all them that don't."

"I'm going to have to sit down and have a long talk with you about who drinks in this county and who doesn't." Renfrow glanced toward the street. "Sort of compare your records with mine."

"Now you sound just like that Baltz fellow. Took half a day of my time asking the same thing," Scott sounded none too pleased.

"Oh, then that'll do." Zacharias put his thumbs under his suspenders. "Tell me, Tom, what's the talk concerning this case? Heard anything?"

Scott, scratching his shoulder, took his time answering.

"People always excited when they's a murder trial, especially a case like this. But ain't been much said about a hanging. Not like you might of thought."

Renfrow touched his hand to his forehead in a farewell gesture and left. The jailer picked up a broom and began to sweep. He had the rest of the afternoon to finish.

Paul Luke stared out the open window of the train. A curl of smoke floated behind the engine like a widow's veil, partially obscuring the landscape. A great deal had happened since he passed this scenery two days before. He had a lot to think about.

Enchanting, sophisticated, Lockett was a woman of the world. Take it or leave it. Then there was Nora. At the Fourth Fest she had been soft in his arms. Yielding; yet, aloof, with a reserve that seemed—uncertain?

Not so with Lockett. She knew precisely where she was going, and she pulled whatever she wanted along with her. But the peril, the excitement, like hanging from the edge of a heartbeat, was worth it. Was Lockett trying to push him into Nora's arms? Not likely that she'd retreat. Still, he'd have to analyze those remarks she'd made that morning.

Nora stood like a besieged regiment with only her mother to sustain her. On the other hand, all Lockett's battles had been won before she marched onto the field. She had only to make a triumphal entry. Yet, Lockett had implied that she was withdrawing. Was he ready to let her go?

Paul Luke thought of the governor's committee on the economy, of Gattis Todd's words at the ball. Of Saree, and Nora. Glad those words did not fall on their ears. Why? He was fond of Saree. Of Nora. Lockett said so. What could Lockett know, or guess?

The engine heaved to a stop. He looked beyond the courthouse lawn to the jail where Plez waited not knowing his fate.

Paul Luke pulled his thoughts together, steeling himself for the pandemonium at the depot. Whole families were gathered to watch the train disgorge its passengers and freight like a fettered black dragon. "More always comes out to watch on Sundays," the conductor observed, standing at Paul Luke's elbow.

"Nora!" Paul Luke shouted, spotting her in the distance, like a ghost emerging from his thoughts: Then subdued, "Nora?"

She waved. The black mare and his carriage waited beside the shady courthouse.

"I would have sworn that was my horse and buggy," he teased as Nora approached. She lowered her head. Perhaps her remoteness was a guise. A ploy to hide doubt. She was a blossom in his hand, one he could shield or crush. Or could he?

Nora's hair curved against her cheeks like the whorls of a finger painting. Black lashes fringed her eyes. She wore a long-sleeved dress of lavender batiste topped by a lace collar, products of Little Granny's fingers.

"I brought Mathelde to the train. She asked if I'd mind waiting to give you a ride. Only an hour."

He breathed deeply. Her scent, clean, unsophisticated, was like soap. His pulse quickened. Having her alone for the ride home presented an appealing prospect. But her next words gave him to understand that would not be the case.

"The children are here. They're over by the roses." She pointed to an area near the sidewalk.

"Has there been a change in Fleming's condition?"

"No, not that I know of. Mathelde just felt that she needed to spend some time at the hospital. She thinks they may be going to try another diagnosis. A doctor from St. Louis." Shading her eyes she beckoned to the children.

Will Roy ran ahead of the others. He greeted Paul Luke in a manner suggesting an absence more like two months than two days. Paul Luke grabbed a post, saving himself from being jostled to the platform. His suitcase went flying, giving Nora a sharp blow to the shin.

"Nora, I'm sorry!" Feeling himself turning slightly crimson, he retrieved the bag and headed toward the buggy. Nora followed behind the girls, walking with a slight limp.

"Oh, it's bleeding!" Paul Luke said, as he prepared to help Nora into the carriage.

"No, it's all right." She dabbed at the scratch with her handkerchief. A bruise was forming under her ruined stockings.

At a loss for words, Paul Luke climbed into the driver's seat and clucked to the black mare. Will Roy sat quietly. From her position in the back seat, Saree leaned forward and stretched her neck to assess her mother's injury.

"How was Louisville? I suppose you got a lot of business done?"

"There was one very important committee meeting. Other than

that, not much accomplished." Nora knew about the ball. She was in all likelihood dying to hear what happened. He gave her an oblique glance.

"And the ball?"

"I wondered if you'd forgotten that. Yes, the ball was a suitably august affair. Successful to the point that there'll probably be another one next year."

"And what of Lockett?"

"Lockett gives you her kindest regards," he lied, stealing another glance at her face. "Along with hugs and kisses."

"Oh? Is she going to mail them? Or did she send them with your baggage?"

The remark sounded like that of a suspicious woman. Paul Luke again found himself thrown off balance. He squirmed. The black mare quickened her pace.

"Mother said to tell you Mr. Renfrow came by." Rebecca said from the back seat, unwittingly coming to his aid. "He wants you to telephone. Something about Plez."

"Ah, yes."

"I'd like a picnic next time, like those other people," Will Roy said, sitting between his sisters. "Wouldn't you?"

"Picnics are among my favorite things." His gaze fell on Nora. "Especially if there's a dance contest."

They reached the Ballard house. Paul Luke pulled the mare to a stop and jumped down to assist Nora. Ignoring her outstretched hand he encircled her waist and lifted her to the ground. "I'm sorry about the accident. Let me help you inside."

"No need, thanks. It couldn't be helped. I'm sorry, too."

"You smell nice. Like pine and some kind of flower. Violets, maybe."

Smiling, she removed his fingers from her waist. The children shouted good-byes. Nora and Saree walked onto the packed earth that was their yard. Old Puddin' came out from under the house, tail wagging. An oil lamp glowed in the window.

"You got a letter from Grandmother," Leighza announced, as Paul Luke picked up the reins.

"Yeah, a big fat one," Will Roy added. "It must be l-o-n-n-g."

Nora watched Paul Luke's carriage pull away. Opening the door, she followed Saree into the lamplight.

Laura Ballard arose from her chair when she saw her daughter's face. "What's wrong?" she said.

"Nothing. Just a small accident." Nora bent to examine the spot of dried blood. "Paul Luke's valise hit me on the shin. He hated it."

"I imagine he did. Do you need a bandage?"

"No, just let me sit here for a moment."

Little Granny disappeared and returned with a bottle of iodine.

"Nora, I just don't understand." She dabbed at the scratch. "You seem happy to be with him. Then you change, like you're resisting. Or like it's wrong for you to have feelings. I know you think a lot of Paul Luke. But you—" She looked into Nora's face."Nora, why? For Saree's sake, Nora—"

Nora jumped to her feet, the pain forgotten.

"Mama, I know. He thinks a lot of me, you say, and I of him. I know what you mean. But I can't be any different, Mama! I just can't! Don't you—can't you—understand how I *feel*?"

Nora began to sob. Laura Ballard sat on the chair arm, and cradled Nora against her shoulder.

Paul Luke took his mother's letter from the desk in his study. He turned it over, smiling at her clear angular script. Just like his mother—no curlicues, no wasted strokes.

He opened a walnut cabinet beside his desk. Pushing aside some books and papers, he removed a decanter and felt around until he touched a silver goblet.

He poured a glass of the brandy his mother had smuggled in from France on her last foray abroad. *What could be more fitting than to drink of Mother's contraband while I endure this letter of hers*, he mused, unfolding the onion-skin sheets.

Dear Paul Luke,

"You're probably going to need some fortification
for this ordeal of a letter. If you'll look in the cabinet by
your desk, you'll find a cache of brandy. Feel free to help
yourself. I will renew the supply upon my return. You'll
forgive my stashing it in your study. That did seem a secure

place, and close enough to be handy.

"What a long time I've been without news from home! Your last letter was dated July third, and I've hardly been in one place long enough to receive another.

"I have news! Expect me home September fourth. You should meet me at the train yourself; but knowing that erratic schedule you keep, I will count on Plez to be there. Send the wagon, too. I have become attached to additional baggage since I left in June. Oh, the money I've spent! Your father is whirling in his grave. He always said I judged the value of a thing strictly by what it cost—and nice things *do* cost.

"Your July letter mentioned you were expecting Mathelde. I was happily stunned, though sorry about her misfortune. Well do I recall her last visit. Your father's funeral. Do give Mathelde my love. I can't wait to see the children. I have presents for all. It's high time Rebecca be introduced to French perfume, so I bought her some. I trust Fleming is getting on well; perhaps out of the hospital by now. This has been a trying ordeal.

"Your father would say 'what can you expect from a railroad man', but he always was narrow about some things. Thank God, ill feelings don't reach from beyond the grave.

"Tell Laura Ballard I bought bolts of fabric in Paris, so she may soon be busy on my winter wardrobe. I got extra to give her for Nora and Saree.

"You'll never guess who I ran into in Rome. Charlotte Randolph, from Virginia. She asked if you are governor yet. She was broken-hearted when I said you haven't shown much interest so far. I told her I first want a grandson to carry on the Lanier name. She has two daughters of age."

Wincing, Paul Luke poured himself another glass of brandy.

"How is precious Lockett? I imagine she invited you to the charity ball. The most beautiful couple there. She is such a fine young woman—exemplary character, respected family, no scandal. I can hardly wait to hear whom Letitia cut and quartered with her sharp remarks this time. I'm sure Beech Marcom conducted himself in grand style, as usual. I've always lamented that he has no son.

Wouldn't 'son of Beech' be a delectable term?"

He chuckled and turned to the last page.

"There's oodles more, but it will have to wait until I see you, or I won't get this posted before we sail.

"I did catch a cold in London, but cured it in France. The medicinal value of brandy is an unsung story, another argument against Prohibition. I must bring this up to Governor Morrow when I see him next."

She ended with the usual endearing phrases. He could imagine her eyes sparkling as she sealed the envelope. Those eyes that revealed her soul.

He was replacing the brandy, moving the books to conceal it, when the telephone jangled.

"Zacharias! I was just about to call you. How's the defense shaping up?"

The lawyer hesitated before answering.

"Hard to say. Plez is well-liked. The Klan has cooled down. I think we have a chance. That's about all I can say. Wish I could call up a little divine guidance. Intervention. Something. I'd rest a lot easier."

"What about Nursie Baltz? Is he still poking around?"

"Baltz had to go back to Frankfort, but he'll be here for the trial. He did a lot of good work, though. A lot of good work. By the way, trial starts September seventeenth. That's `Court Monday.' Went by to see Plez. Told him we'll be ready."

"I'll get down there again myself. By the way, Zach, you can start expecting a little of that divine intervention you were looking for. According to a letter I just received, Mother's due back on September fourth."

Renfrow chuckled. "That might be just what we need to do the trick."

Chapter 10

Saree tugged on the slat gate that opened into Willie Shoe's yard. Old Puddin' followed.

Willie Shoe sat on a three-legged stool beneath a tree, his back to the girl. The brim of the straw hat pulled over his ears resembled an axis around a globe.

"Willie Shoe! Guess what! My mama got a letter. In the mail." The boy did not look up. "What you doing, Willie Shoe?"

"Cutting out new gourd dippers. Mr. Paul Luke say they needed for the water barrels."

"Did your mama get a letter?"

"Lordy, I don't reckon! My ma didn't get no letter. What would she want with any letter? She couldn't read it no way. I never knowed any folks like us what could read."

"Granny said my mama's letter said I'm to go to school this year. Wouldn't you like to go to school, Willie Shoe?"

He stuck his knife into the dirt and looked across the fields. "What'd I want to go to school for? Don't need no learning to tend hogs. Don't make them little pigs no difference. Just if they's slop in the trough all they care."

"Well, I guess," Saree left the yard, sounding doubtful.

From her attic window Saree had watched children walking along the road. They carried tin dinner buckets and books fastened together with leather belts. Saree slowed her pace. How would she feel if a letter had come for Willie Shoe, but not for her? There might never be a letter for Willie Shoe. At least, Willie Shoe could talk to his daddy about it. Maybe he really didn't care about not getting a letter.

She looked ahead, shading her eyes with one hand. Leighza, Will Roy, and Rebecca were sitting under the locust trees in front of Paul Luke's house.

In a few moments Saree joined them with news of her mother's letter. Rebecca, holding a half-eaten apple, looked up from her book and yawned.

"Mother signed us up for school weeks ago," she said in a bored voice.

"We've been to school before now. In Cincinnati," Leighza said.

"Yeah, I thought when we moved here, maybe they wouldn't have school," Will Roy said.

In the distance Willie Shoe was coming down the path. Little Granny had instructed Saree to be home in time for the noon meal. She took leave, with Old Puddin' trotting behind her.

A short time later Willie Shoe stepped into the big white Lanier kitchen. His mother dried the last dish and stacked it in the china cabinet. Removing his hat, he sat down before a square table in the corner. Ruby Gem put two filled plates on the table. She sat opposite him.

"Ma, you ever knowed anybody what could read?" Willie Shoe asked as the meal neared its end. "Besides white folks?"

"Why of course! Reverend Antioch Pike can read. He reads the Bible to all of us. And, and—well, there's other colored people that can read."

"Where they learn it?"

A frown creased her forehead. "Why I guess somebody learn them. School maybe. Some places has schools for colored. One here, over at Kevil."

"Kevil! How far that be?" Willie Shoe's fork stopped halfway to his mouth.

"I never been over there. I think your daddy say it take 'bout three, four hour in the wagon."

"You ever wish you could?"

"What, read?" Ruby Gem swallowed a bite of boiled cabbage. "I always look at it like this. The Lord want me to learn reading, he make a way for it. Your papa, now—" She put her fork down. "He want to learn it bad. Ain't said nothing lately, though."

"Ma, it seem funny to me why the Lord always make a way for white folks. Why you reckon the Lord don't want us to learn reading?"

Ruby Gem, casting about for an answer, seemed relieved to find Paul Luke observing them from the doorway.

"Mr. Paul Luke," Willie said, his gaze following his mother's. "I got all them dippers hollowed out. They out by the hog pen. I take them to the field directly."

"Good." Paul Luke looked at the boy closely. "You were asking your mother just now if she ever wished she could read. What about you, Willie? Are you wishing you could read?"

Willie Shoe lowered his head. "Yes, sir, I wish I could learn it sometime."

One afternoon a few days later Paul Luke found Eli Mayes sitting in the shade, giving his horses a rest from plowing.

"Eli, I need to talk to you in your capacity as a county school trustee."

Mayes nodded. He pushed his sweaty felt hat to the back of his head.

"There's a nine-year-old boy I know of who should be enrolled in school. But he isn't."

"Well, turn that young man in to the truant officer when school starts. We'll fix him up."

"The boy is colored."

"Damn it, Paul Luke, you know as well as I do, the Nigra school's over at Kevil. Lucky to have it, too. We can't hardly afford the schools we got for whites."

"You know Kevil is a good fifteen miles away, Eli. Bad roads, too. But it did occur to me that our own school right here isn't full yet."

Mayes gave him an incredulous look.

"Man, are you plumb out of your mind? Take a Nigra into *our* school? Why the people'd never allow it! They'd shut down the school to get rid of him! Why—who is it, anyway?"

"His name is Willie Shoe. His par—"

"You talking about that one his daddy's up for murder?"

Paul Luke nodded. "Right now, he happens to be the only colored child of school age right in this community."

"Now, Paul Luke, I know that you—being our state senator

and all—know all about that 'separate but equal' ruling. Happened long about 1900, I believe. Over in Louisiana. Some Nigra wanted to ride the white street car. Plessey or Blessy, something or other. The court ruling provides them education and all, I reckon, but not with *our* children. That's why we got that school for them over at Kevil."

"That's exactly my point!" Paul Luke jabbed the air with his finger. "Seems some people think that ruling reads 'separate but separate.' What about the *equal* part? No way on God's green earth can this child get to Kevil and back every day. Yet the law provides that he be educated. There's room for him here."

"Ain't no way people'd stand for that! Nigras ain't like us. They got funny ways. They're different. Besides, that one's tainted already. His daddy and all." Eli kicked a lump of damp earth. "Even if they was saints, you'd have a hard time."

"I agree. Colored people are different, and some of their ways seem odd to us. I'm not trying to change anybody from being what they are. I am simply saying it won't hurt anything for this boy to go to school. Since he's 'tainted,' as you say, that seems all the more reason to help him—"

Eli interrupted again, stomping nervously about in the plowed dirt. "Help, hell! You realize you don't have to take the guff I'd have to take. You're not on the school board."

An eyebrow shot up and Paul Luke smiled. "I'm no stranger to guff, Eli."

"Paul Luke, you told me less than a month ago, you don't favor mixing the races. Is your memory so short you don't recollect saying it?"

"Eli, for God's sake, going to school in the same building is hardly mixing the races, any more than walking on the same road, or fishing in the same river." Paul Luke daubed his face with a crumpled handkerchief.

"I won't allow it. I can't."

Paul Luke looked away. "I'd hoped it wouldn't come to this, Eli." He turned and faced the man. "That school building is on my property. Through some freak oversight the land title was never transferred to the school board. I had this confirmed last week. Zacharias Renfrow went through the records at the courthouse for

me. Now, of course, I'll get this deed changed right away. But—"

"You never stop, do you? Well, maybe the school *could* use somebody to do a few chores, cut wood, tend the fire in winter. Stuff like that, in return for a little learning. Don't imagine the idee's going to set too well in this community. I ain't about to make any promises, you understand. I ain't the only school trustee, but I'll think on bringing it up at the meeting Thursday night. I'm sure as hell telling the whole county who come out here pushing to let a Nigra in! Damn!"

Eli turned his back to Paul Luke, untwisted the lines from the plow handle and shouted, "Giddap!"

Paul Luke stepped across the wire fence to where the black mare waited in the shady river road. He picked up the reins and tapped the horse's flank. With that little piece of business all but settled, it might be a good time to stop at Corlew's for his mail.

As he drew near Corlew's Store, Little Granny Ballard opened the door on her way out, disturbing an assemblage of flies clustered on the screen. The woman wore a grim expression, as she always did after an encounter with Mae Dee. Today's skirmish must have been particularly harsh since an unnatural hush hovered over the farmers gathered under the persimmon tree. Little Granny walked along muttering to herself.

"I had to buy cloth to make Saree some dresses." Little Granny said when he stopped the black mare. "She's starting school, you know."

As Granny left, Mae Dee opened the screen door of her store and shooed a fly out. "I don't see how in tarnation Laury Ballard can be so civil to them Laniers, after the way Paul Luke's done," she mumbled. "And her taking that little gal off with a wagon load of coloreds like that. A wonder she didn't get that young 'un hurt."

Although the reasons for the allegiance between Laura Ballard and the Lanier family were well known in Hunt County, Mae Dee seldom bothered with facts against her own assumptions.

At eighteen Laura White had married Crawford Ballard, owner of the Hunt County newspaper, *The Yeoman-Gazette*, which he himself had founded. The newspaper barely supported its own publication costs so Crawford Ballard farmed tobacco for a living, sustained by his dream of onr day becoming a prominent and prosperous publisher. Married to a man she loved and respected, Laura Ballard would reiterate her own contentment, "I'm happy with you now, Crawford. Let's hold today in our hands and be glad."

Crawford Ballard continued to rely on tobacco for available cash, although now he traded with sharecroppers to do the actual labor. The price remained stationary until marketplace changes dropped the price to four cents per pound. The downward spiral continued but production costs increased. Then Congress passed an awesome tax on tobacco products. Consumer demand fell. But the primary cause of the difficulty, in the minds of many tobacco farmers was the vilified "Duke Trust."

James B. Duke, son of an impoverished tobacco grower in North Carolina, rose to head the American Tobacco Company, which by 1900 controlled virtually all the American tobacco trade. Joining forces with competitors, Duke created a monopoly. This done, the conglomerate would send one lone buyer who would offer the tobacco farmers a take-it-or-leave-it price. Within five years the offer dropped to three cents a pound for prime leaf and downward to a penny for "trash." In September, five years after Duke's take-over, the Planters' Protection Association was formed to lawfully fight the "Duke Trust." The Association planned to keep all tobacco off the market through a growers' boycott until the conglomerate made a decent offer.

Crawford Ballard, seconded by Lucas Lanier, Hunt County's most powerful grower, blasted the Planters' Protection Association's planned boycott. Fiercely independent, Ballard wrote an editorial that the Association was proposing to sabotage the independence of the tobacco farmer in the same way that the "Duke Trust" had done. He continued his rhetoric in *Yeoman-Gazette* editorials.

Some clandestine members of the Planters' Protection Association began to pay nocturnal visits to farmers who opposed the boycott, destroying crops, burning barns, sometimes even beating the dissenters. These militants called themselves "coon hunters" because they struck at night. Some wore hoods and became better known as "Night Riders," frequently attacking black workers whose only offense was hauling tobacco crops for a day's pay.

In the middle of one moonless night, Crawford Ballard's crop was targeted for destruction. Upon his attempt to intervene he received an unmerciful beating and was left bleeding in his yard. Ballard never fully recovered. He died a year later, without regaining the ability to stand upright. Had Lucas Lanier not hired a dozen armed "rabbit hunters" to protect his fields at night, he too, would have undergone the Night Riders' wrath.

Crawford and Laura Ballard, with Nora, who turned five that year, fled to Tennessee. Nursing her husband, Laura Ballard watched him die, broken in body and spirit. She determined to avenge his death.

A week after Crawford's burial, Laura Ballard returned to Kentucky and called on an attorney in Paducah to file a civil suit against her husband's assailants. In the dim glow of her lantern she had recognized and could name them all. Because Crawford and his little family had been living in Tennessee months before his death, the crafty attorney filed the lawsuit in federal district court at Paducah, under diversity of citizenship. This was to prevent the offenders from being tried in Hunt County where a jury of peers was almost certain to contain some secret sympathizers to the Planters' Protection Association, and its "coon hunters."

Laura and Nora were awarded eighteen thousand dollars to be paid equally by those named in the lawsuit, although little was ever received. To the astonishment of none who had witnessed Laura Ballard's unflinching courage, she and Nora moved back into the very homestead where their tragedy had occurred. The violent movement against the tobacco farmers floundered to near death as news of Laura Ballard's court settlement spread. Her stand gave heart to others who opposed the masked vandals, so that orderliness was restored and satisfactory marketing practices again emerged. As for the *Yeoman-Gazette*, Laura Ballard had nothing more to do with it.

A week after Paul Luke's discussion with Eli Mayes, the Hunt County School Board, led by Mayes, appeared at the Lanier door. Paul Luke had been expecting their visit. He set his coffee cup aside and ushered them into the parlor.

They sat stiff as clothespins in a row on the maroon sofa. John Dowdy and Dr. Aaron Haas, the other two members, looked first at Paul Luke then at Eli.

"We, uh, the three of us, had a little unofficial meeting to go over what you and me talked about last Monday," Eli said, leaning forward.

Paul Luke sat opposite him in a gold velvet chair. "And?"

"Well, Dr. Haas here, he—" Eli nudged the man on his left with his elbow. "You tell him, Doc."

Paul Luke regarded Dr. Haas with some affection. He had been the Lanier family physician for years. Paul Luke thought of his black pill bag; the way he always warmed his hands in winter before touching a patient; the cough syrup he concocted from his own formula. "Yellow and slick, but it does the trick," Mathelde would say over Paul Luke's childish objections, urging him to swallow. When anybody asked how many lives he had saved, the doctor always replied with a chuckle, "Only one that I know of for sure. I grabbed a lady ready to jump into a cistern once, and held on till her family got there."

"Well, Paul Luke, it's like this," Dr. Haas said in his soft drawl. "I'm sure you know about the Day Law. Prohibits mixing of the races in Kentucky schools, no matter how we feel personally about the situation."

They had acted fast. But, of course, Dr. Haas would know what to do. Paul Luke studied him for a moment before replying.

"Carl Day, Breathitt County. 1904. Judge William Reed's ruling." Paul Luke said, leaning back in his chair. "But you do know that when state law and federal law conflict, the federal law takes precedent?"

"You talk like some dad-burned gibble-gabbling lawyer," John Dowdy said. "Why can't that little nigger boy just live with somebody over at Kevil and go on to school? No good reason I can think of. Except maybe you'd miss working him on your land here."

Paul Luke's temper flared. "So, you all favor taking him from his family?"

"Hell no, that ain't it!" Eli exclaimed, pounding the sofa arm with his fist. "What we all favor is trying to keep from having the whole school shut down. The law's the law! People are getting hopping mad over this, Paul Luke, and there's no telling when the Klan might—"

"The building is on my property."

"That's no argument, Paul Luke," the doctor said. "That building can be hoisted and moved on down the road to somebody else's land."

Paul Luke nodded. "That won't be necessary. We are deeding the land to the school, in any case." He sat loosely in his chair. "Now, federal law based on the Fourteenth Amendment does say separate, but equal, facilities. This child has a right to attend school. And not have to leave his family to do it."

John Dowdy bolted upright. "By damn, Paul Luke, you don't get to paint the world, you just get to *live* in it. What you Laniers think ain't *all* that matters."

Eli scrambled to his feet and the others followed. "We still got a little time. You try to figure something out. I'm not sure where this is headed."

Only Dr. Haas shook hands with Paul Luke as they left.

The school board had been gone less than an hour when Reverend Wakerich appeared at the door. Ruby Gem directed him into Paul Luke's study. Despite the heat he wore his clerical collar. This was more than a social call.

"I've had people in and out of my house for two days. The whole congregation's disturbed." He extended his hands, palms up. "What are you trying to do?"

Paul Luke swiveled in his chair. "Trying to resolve a conflict."

"*Resolve* one? Seems to me you're *creating* one."

"The conflict is in the law, Reverend, which I had nothing to do with creating. The child should be in school. The available school is *here*, not fifteen miles or three hours away. What would you do?" Paul Luke looked closely at the minister.

"Well, I—" Reverend Wakerich moved his feet from side to side. "A lot of people are uncomfortable with the matter."

"That's to be expected." Paul Luke tapped his chin with a pencil. He fastened an amused gaze on Reverend Wakerich. "Doesn't your congregation, some of it, at least, see this as a humanitarian issue— as doing good?"

Wakerich stared through the lace curtains at the shadows

flickering on the grass. A rain crow called in the distance, and hens cackled behind the house.

"Sometimes it's not easy, doing good. But then it's not easy for decent folks to do bad, either. People who are downright evil to the bone have the easiest time on this earth. No qualms. No choices to make." Wakerich leaned back in his chair, eyes fixed on the ceiling. "The fellow who doesn't have a strong leaning in either direction; the man pulled from one pole to the other over every decision—he's the one with troubles. Problem is, almost every last one of us finds himself in this spot at one time or another. Not sure which way to go. Not too exactly sure where we are at the moment. That's how some folks feel about this school business. They want *me* to figure out where *they* stand." After a moment Wakerich looked down and smiled."Doing good? Yes, I think so. But costly."

"Costly? How, reverend?"

"Children will be confused. Some yanked out of school. It may even be closed."

"I'll never let that happen. It can be prevented. At least, the closing can."

"Maybe so," the reverend rose from his chair. "But it could be costly to you." He walked toward the door and stopped. "Talk is, you may get an opponent. Have a hard race on your hands. There's a lot being said."

"Talk's inevitable." Paul Luke shrugged. His manner was grim as he closed the door behind Reverend Wakerich.

Thursday night Eli Mayes unlocked the schoolhouse door. He struck a match, found the kerosene lamp, and lit it. Dr. Aaron Haas and John Dowdy followed Eli inside.

They set to work appointing teachers and setting up a budget ledger. Miss Janelee Meriwether would be in her second year and so would get a twelve dollar raise. A tentative schedule was established, listing families who would take turns boarding the county's teachers during the term. A few janitorial duties were assigned; textbooks and supplies discussed. When the budget had been finalized John Dowdy peered over his bifocals.

"What we going to do about the nigger?"

"I've been thinking this thing out," Dr. Aaron Haas said. Laying

his pencil down, he tilted his chair on its rear legs. "I believe the whole thing will handle itself."

"Handle itself!" Eli said, blinking. The kerosene fumes burned his eyes. He wiped tears away with his fingers.

"Now, now, Eli, hear me out," the doctor said, lowering his chair. "If we don't let the boy in, the court could get into it. We *are* breaking the law, in one way."

"What do you mean?" Mayes asked. "You don't think Lanier would stoop to that?"

"No, not really. But there could be others. They could come crawling out of the wood pile like possums."

"If we do let him in we're breaking that state law you all was talking about," John Dowdy said. "We might as well eat the devil as to drink his broth. I don't see any difference in it myself. I say let's keep the nigger out. He can go to school at Kevil. It ain't our fault he lives here instead of over there." Dowdy glanced toward Eli for support.

"Let the boy start school," Haas said."You mark my words. The whole mess will come to a head and we won't have to do another thing." He leaned back again. The other two looked dumbfounded.

"If you know something we don't, spill it!" John Dowdy said.

"The key to it all is Lanier himself. You'll see. He's brash at times, but a fool he's not."

"I'm not so sure I understand, Doc," Eli said. He leaned forward, elbows on his knees.

The doctor set his chair down on all four legs. "Paul Luke Lanier is basically an idealist," Haas said."And he hasn't lived quite long enough to understand why all his high faluting ideas won't work. But, on the other hand, he's a realist, too.

"Today he thinks we all three ought to be in here cheering for his little colored boy. But now, in a week or two, when school opens, he'll see what's happening. A school in turmoil. His colored boy facing a lot of strain. People talking about Lanier losing his senate seat."

Haas pulled a pipe from his shirt pocket. He lit it slowly. "I tell you this. Young Senator Lanier's going to do whatever he has to do to get things back where they ought to be. For us, and for him. The way I see it, we got no worry."

Another weary week dragged its length out before August ended. Paul Luke, true to his promise, transferred the school property to the county board. The trustees met again, and in a volatile four-hour session voted two to one to allow Willie Shoe's attendance on a trial basis.

On the great morning of the first day of school Saree was to meet the Phelps children at the wye in front of Corlew's so they could walk together.

A number of children dawdled in front of Corlew's as Saree joined the group. But a common thread knotted their conversations. A black boy was being permitted to experience their learning in their environment, their world.

"My pa said don't look at him. Let on like he ain't even there," Ann Findley said.

"You don't hardly come to school enough to know who's there anyways," Ellen Childers said, sliding her dinner pail into the crook of her elbow.

"Hey, it's Snake Man," D.D. Dowdy called, recognizing Will Roy. "You the one put a snake in the outhouse, ain't you? Don't that nigger boy live on your uncle's place?"

Will Roy frowned. D.D. Dowdy was a big boy, probably a sixth grader, and he sounded ominous. Will Roy glanced around for some kind of diversion but escape came from another source.

Hearing an approaching wagon, the children stopped in the road and turned around to look.

It was Eli Mayes transporting the teacher, Miss Janelee Meriwether, to school for the first day of classes.

"Crowd's awful small," Eli said, taking in the group. "Lot of folks keeping their young 'uns home on account of the Nigra. Now, Miss Meriwether, you just go right on and act like it's the naturalest thing in the world to have him sitting there. Just like we talked about. It'll work out."

Children scampered as the wagon rolled past. It pulled up in front of the schoolhouse with what amounted to a flourish. After helping Miss Meriwether to the ground Eli unlocked the building and entered alone.

Willie Shoe with his mother stood apart from the others near a mass of pink, white, and lavender hollyhocks. Saree focused her attention on the ceremony just in time to see Eli present a brand new flag to Miss Meriwether.

"For the school," he said. "Bought it myself." Shooting a quick glance toward the hollyhocks Eli left.

Ruby Gem squeezed Willie Shoe's hand. He walked to the end of the line, looking back at his mother. She stood smiling. On her next visit to the jail Plez would hear every detail.

The first order of business was to assign seats, with the seventh and eighth graders in the rear. Saree tried to sit by Willie Shoe, but Miss Meriwether said no, she'd have to sit up front with the beginners. Then Miss Meriwether stuck Willie Shoe away in the very back.

"But he's—" Saree began, and was immediately shushed.

Next Miss Meriwether led a prayer. After some singing and a few words to Eli's new flag it was time to get down to business.

The first and second graders sat together at little tables near the teacher's desk beside the blackboard. Those beyond second grade got to sit at individual desks that were bolted to the wooden floor. Tall open windows, unencumbered with screens, faced each other in rows down both sides of the building. A cool crossdraft rustled papers on Miss Meriwether's desk.

After Miss Meriwether handed out books to the older children, she turned her attention to the little ones. She talked about brushing teeth, and gold stars, and names on a chart.

"I smell a goat."

Miss Meriwether stopped in mid-sentence and turned toward the voice in the back of the room. The voice belonged to D.D. Dowdy.

"Why Daniel David, there are no goats for miles." Miss Meriwether chuckled. "That's not possible."

"I smell a goat," D.D persisted.

"Now Daniel David," Miss Meriwether said, "at the end of last term, you and I agreed that you had grown up. That this year, you would be polite and considerate. Now, I'm afraid—"

"I smell a black goat," he interrupted.

Two or three girls giggled. Miss Meriwether fingered the wooden dowel she used for a pointer. Fifteen pairs of eyes watched every move.

"Daniel David, there are *no* goats!" she said. She held the dowel firmly across her middle.

"Well, I smell one. A black he goat."

Scattered laughter rippled through the class. Miss Meriwether tapped on her desk. "Very well, then." She glanced around the room, her gaze coming to rest on Willie Shoe. "Willie," she said, "would you go outside and give a good look all about the school? Look under the building. See if there is any sign, whatsoever, of a goat anywhere. Would you, Willie?"

His mouth curved into a wide grin. "Yes'm, I'd be much obliged to."

D.D. Dowdy, hiding behind his new geography book, grinned and made an occasional sniffing sound. Miss Meriwether ignored him. Walking to the window, she stared out so intently that the children peered about. Finally she closed her eyes and began to speak.

"Children do you smell the jasmine? I smell the jasmine blooming there." She opened her eyes. "Right outside that window. See?"

Eyes shifted to the window and heads nodded.

"Daniel David, do *you* smell the jasmine?"

The boy closed his geography book, a surprised look on his face. He squirmed and glanced self-consciously at the watching children.

"Yes'm."

"Wonderful!" Miss Meriwether walked to the blackboard. She laid her pointer in the chalk tray. "Sometimes our minds play tricks on us. We imagine that we see—or hear—or smell—a thing that isn't there at all. Like billy goats instead of jasmine. Terrible mistakes can be made if someone allows himself to be tricked."

She turned back to the young faces. "In addition to what folks call `book learning,' that is reading, arithmetic, spelling, geography—all those subjects—we must learn an another important lesson here. A number of important lessons. Tolerance. Compassion.

Big words, aren't they, children? What those words mean..." She searched for an explanation. "What they mean is that—that we must try hard to smell the jasmine when it's there. And if there is none, why then, what? Let us plant some!"

The children regarded her curiously.

"These are hard lessons, children. You don't understand what I'm saying. Very well. This is a beginning. Oh, it will take the whole year, and longer, much longer, to understand it all. Maybe even a lifetime. But today, we must deal with this day only." She spoke softly, to herself.

"What can I teach you this day?" Miss Meriwether walked to the window beside the jasmine. The children stole puzzled glances at each other. Red faced, Daniel David slipped down as far as he could in his seat and opened his geography book. When Willie Shoe closed the screen door Miss Meriwether turned.

"Well, Willie, did you find a goat out there?"

"No,'m."

"Did you smell anything?"

"No,'m."

"Nothing?"

"No,'m. Just that jasmine."

"Good for you! Please take your seat, Willie." Miss Merriwether sighed and smiled. "Now, you eighth graders, take out your spelling books. The rest of you get your tablets and copy from the board. See if you can smell a little arithmetic, while I work with the first and second graders."

After that, the morning improved. Last year's pupils had retained most of the basics Miss Meriwether left with them. The incoming students appeared inquisitive and eager. The year held promise.

Noon brought a welcome interlude. The children gathered their tin buckets and newspaper-wrapped biscuits and trudged outside, plopping down in shady spots around the trees.

Saree joined Willie Shoe who sat eating biscuits and bacon in the seat Miss Meriwether assigned him that morning. Half an hour later Miss Meriwether rang the bell, signifying the end of noon recess.

Thirty minutes before school ended Miss Meriwether assigned penmanship practice to the older children, and allotted counting sticks to the beginners.

"While you are working," she said with a smile, "I'll call each of you to my desk to fill out your enrollment card. Then the whole world will know you are a pupil in our school."

Taking them alphabetically, she soon finished with the Babcocks, Hershall and Richie, who were cousins.

"Saree Ballard."

Saree stood and walked to the teacher's desk.

Miss Meriwether beamed at Saree when she said the "birthday facts" Little Granny had taught her. Miss Meriwether's eyes were green up close, and her auburn hair, like ripened cornsilks, curled against her cheeks.

Most of the children, hot and tired, abandoned their assignments and sat, half listening to the teacher's questions. Some of the youngest laid their heads against the table, eyes almost closed. The older pupils labored over their penmanship guides.

"Almost finished," Miss Meriwether said. "Names of parents. Father's name first." Miss Meriwether's pencil poised above the enrollment card. "Saree?"

Saree felt her face pale, and her eyes widened. Breathing rapidly, she was ready to flee.

"Now, now," Miss Meriwether said, apparently misinterpreting Saree's panic. "You only have to *tell* me. I don't expect you to *spell* it." She waited expectantly.

Saree's fingers clenched the edge of the teacher's desk, her knuckles white and hard. Her eyes darted about. Rebecca's head was bent over her penmanship guide. Leighza appeared to be half asleep, her pen loose in relaxed fingers. Will Roy slumped in his seat, staring out the window as if mesmerized. Wisps of smoky clouds slipped across the blue September sky. In the back of the room Willie Shoe counted thin little sticks.

"She's a bastard, teacher! She ain't got a daddy."

Attention flared among the children as if lightning had arched through the open windows. Miss Meriwether froze. Without hesitation Saree flew into the face of Cull Tillson, whose mouth had spoken those despicable words. The closest children scrambled, falling back. Others, on the periphery, stood transfixed, watching Cull's attempts to protect himself.

By the time Miss Meriwether regained her perspective, blood seeped from a long scratch on Cull's face. Two buttons from his shirt careened across the floor. Only Rebecca, by putting her arms around the sobbing girl and drawing her close, was able to subdue Saree. Cull Tillson, a husky, swarthy fourth-grader, obviously shaken, was dismissed.

"Go on home, Cull," Miss Meriwether said. "There are only a few minutes left."

An apology might be appropriate, but from which child? That Cull genuinely regretted his mistake went without saying. He sniffled, wiping his eyes with his fist as he left.

"Children! Take your seats at once!" Miss Meriwether stood straight and still until they quieted.

"Children, do you remember the words I used this morning when we were talking about jasmine?" She went to the blackboard and wrote in large letters: t-o-l-e-r-a-n-c-e; c-o-m-p-a-s-s-i-o-n. "For tomorrow I want all the fourth through eighth graders to know the meanings, and the spellings, of these two words. But especially the meanings.

"Now, class, when children first start school, they don't know answers to all the questions. Sometimes they don't know their ages, or their birthdays, or even the names of relatives. When this happens I make a note to contact the parents. This is a private matter. You children are not to get involved. There will be no more outbursts.

"Oh, and add one other word to that list on the board. Respect. R-e-s-p-e-c-t. You need to know that word, because we're going to have it in this classroom; for you, for me, for yourselves, and for each other." Her glance covered every corner of the room, pausing for an instant on Willie Shoe, and again on Saree. "Good afternoon, class. Remember tomorrow's assignment."

The children filed from the building toward the freedom that was finally theirs. Only Saree hung back, walking slowly. Once again her world had been twisted, disfigured, blemished with dark permanent splotches not of her making.

Ruby Gem, by the hollyhocks, scanned the noisy group until

Willie Shoe emerged, last in line.

"Did the day go good, Willie?"

"Yes, Ma," he took her hand. "Didn't nothing happen that wasn't supposed to."

Miss Meriwether stood in the door watching. When the voices died out in the distance, she went to her desk. It was a momentous occasion deserving some kind of recognition, this day of integration. Miss Merriwether took out a note pad, and began to write.

Dear Ruby Gem:

She stopped to think for a moment. She tore the page from the pad, folded it, and stuck it into her handbag. Then she started writing again.

Dear Mrs. Shoe:

Miss Merriwether frowned, examining the end of her pen. Again she tore the page away, folded it, and put it in her purse. Finally she began once more.

To the Parents of Willie Shoe:

I am pleased that you are sending your son to school here.
I will strive to teach him what the school officials think
he needs to know. I will look after him while he is in my
care. I anticipate no problems.

Miss Meriwether read the note thoughtfully. Had any teacher before her confronted a class like this? Would one ever again? She stared through the open door into the empty schoolyard. Biting her lip she folded the note and slipped it into her handbag with the others.

A shadow fell over the patch of sunlight facing Miss Merriwether's desk. She looked up to find that Eli Mayes had come for her.

"Any trouble today?" Eli asked as she settled herself on the spring seat of the wagon. He clucked to the horses."You know what I mean."

"It was an unusual first day," she hedged.

"People are awful upset. Been a big to-do at Corlew's. There's talk of closing the school."

"Permanently?"

"Till we do something. John Dowdy and me got them to wait a couple days till the board can meet. Doc Haas'll be back tomorrow."

"Just a minute!" Paul Luke called, awakening at dawn from a sound sleep that had not come easily. A muffled thumping grew louder, coming from the front of the house.

"Just a minute!" he called again. He pulled on his robe as he rushed to the front door. He yanked it open and stared sleepily into the gray light, seeing nothing. The thumping continued louder, close. Feeling a warm wetness strike his hand, he glanced down. Blood.

Two shapeless forms jerked and flopped at his feet. Blood splattered the porch, the door, his face. Huge globs and drops and streaks. He stared, frozen. Minutes passed. Finally the forms stopped floundering and lay twitching at his feet.

"My God!" he cried, stumbling backward.

Ruby Gem ran up behind him from the kitchen.

"Chickens!" she screamed. In the throes of death one of the birds lurched, showering blood across her white apron. She shrank back.

"Look, there!" Paul Luke pointed. Two chicken heads lay next to the steps, severed from the carcasses on the porch. Slits in the soft earth appeared to be from an ax blade. Thin streaks of blood smeared the dewy grass. A piece of paper fluttered from the door post. Paul Luke seized it. Pencil marks covered the paper like discolored bruises. "Niger not wilcum." Viciously Paul Luke wadded the paper into a ball, and wheeling, turned toward his study. He was shaking as he brushed past Mathelde in the hallway. "Keep the children back," he snapped.

From his study Paul Luke dialed the sheriff.

"There's been an incident here, Claude. Some chickens slaughtered. Blood all over the place."

"Some son-of-a-bitch did the same thing at the jail." Meeks' voice crackled. "We just found it. No clues yet. Virgil's gone to work on it, though."

"Did they do anything else? I mean, is Plez all right?"

"Left some kind of note's all. Yeah, Plez never heard a thing.

Guess Tom Scott and me will be sleeping at the jail for a spell."

Shortly before sunset the next afternoon Paul Luke knocked on Dr. Haas' office door. It opened immediately.

"Come in, come in, Paul Luke. I watched you coming up the walk. You look pretty chipper. Plain to see you've come for some reason other than medical attention. Have a seat." The doctor pushed newspapers from a chair onto the floor. "I gather you're here to talk about the school dilemma."

"A precise diagnosis, Doc. There are other things on my mind, too. Prejudice. Hate. The violence that can spew from seemingly decent folks. But I can't stop that. What I can do is admit defeat. Tuck tail and run, so to speak."

The doctor stood rubbing his chin. He peered down at Paul Luke.

"Run? From what?"

"From the turmoil. The disruption. Not just disruption of the school, but of life in this community." Paul Luke paced about the cluttered room, which smelled faintly of ether. "The children don't deserve this. I was wrong to think it would work. It was poor judgment to push this as I have. I won't have a part in the closing of that school. The children are not to blame." Paul Luke sank back into his chair.

Dr. Haas perched atop his desk. "Paul Luke, you were right in your goal, but wrong in your expectation. I think most people know deep down that what you want is right. But they're just not willing to admit it."

"The whole thing blew up in my face." Paul Luke's shoulders slumped. "The lawyers in the assembly speak of an old law school adage," he said, after a while. "'If the law doesn't support you, argue the facts. If the facts don't support you, argue the law. If neither supports you, attack the person.' That's been played out here pretty graphically these last few days. The law is on my side. Some of the people agree. Others use fear as a stopgap. But one thing is crystal clear. Willie Shoe can't continue at the school."

"You're fully convinced?"

"Aren't you? This morning there was an incident. Chickens slaughtered at my door. At the jail, too, the sheriff said." Paul Luke rose and touched the doctor's shoulder. "Dr. Haas, that was a threat. The school, Molly Capps' murder, Plez Shoe in jail. I should be thankful it wasn't worse. I'm dropping the school issue. What might be next, if I don't?"

"Will he go to Kevil?"

"No. Ruby Gem and I talked. She understands. Mathelde volunteered to tutor him for now. I know Mother will help, too." Paul Luke turned toward the door. "I trust you will pass this on to the board?"

"We're having a meeting here in half an hour. Will you stay?"

"No, thanks, I'd best get on home before dark."

At seven o'clock John Dowdy and Eli Mayes entered Dr. Haas' office. The school board had secretly changed the location for its emergency meeting to avoid confronting an angry crowd.

Dr. Haas closed his medical bag and shoved it under his desk. Mayes pushed some utensils aside and sat on the examining table. John Dowdy lingered by the door.

"I told you all it was a mistake to let that little nigger in," Dowdy said. "Now see what's happened. Set the school back twenty years."

"Nothing's happened," Haas said. He sat down behind his desk.

"Plenty's happened! You wasn't even here, Doc!" Eli shouted. "I talked myself blue in the face yesterday at Corlew's. And how much good did it do? I'll tell you how much." Eli kicked the table leg. "None! Not one piddling bit!"

"I warned you," Dowdy said. "I warned the both of you."

"Yes, and I told you it would all be settled without us having to do a thing," the doctor said. "And the court didn't get into it, either." He opened the bottom drawer of his desk and propped his feet on the edge. "Paul Luke just left here thirty minutes ago. He's pulling the boy out."

"Out of the school?"

"How come? Laniers ain't known for giving up."

"Said it was a matter of conscience. Said he couldn't see `sacrificing the many for the one,' or some such. He couldn't stand to see the school closed."

"Is Lanier sending him to Kevil?" Dowdy asked, easing away

from the door.

"No. He felt bad about it. Said his sister and Naomi Ruth could teach the boy for a while, till he works out something."

"Well I'll have to give you credit, Doc," Eli said, examining a splinter in his thumb. "You said Lanier's no fool. Turned out just like you thought it would."

"He may not be a fool," Dowdy said, "but he may not be a state senator much longer, either. He's lost hisself some votes over this little deal."

"That may be so," Haas said. "But Lanier knows he's right, and deep down, well—sometimes that's enough."

Chapter 11

On the second Monday in September—Court Monday—all Hunt County flocked to Wickliffe, its county seat. The wooden sidewalks creaked. Surrounded by its two acre lawn the courthouse faced Front Street like a Nordic warrior.

The gaiety of Court Monday could never be matched: not by the showboats that docked at Nine Toes Landing on the Mississippi; not by Bailey Brothers' Circus; not even by Bisbee's Colossal Tent Show that set up right after strawberry picking. Today's proceedings would come closest of all to fulfilling the universal dream of something for nothing.

Uppermost was Plez Shoe's trial for the murder of Molly Capps. Women bobbed babies on their hips and some told stories of encounters.

"My Maudie and my William met him right in the road—face to face, mind you—on their way to Corlew's! They said he was toting fish. I don't recollect for certain—it might of been the day that poor woman was kilt."

No one seemed willing to convict Plez outright. Gabe Findley squinted and recalled how Plez "helped widder women fix fences, or dug a grave when somebody passed."

Whitsworth Moseby walked across the street from his boarding house and stopped near the iron fence that enclosed the courthouse. Lail Stratton sat in his wheelchair beneath a beech tree.

"Well, Lail," Whitsworth said, "There's one thing I ain't heard mentioned about this here business. Do you reckon it's liable to hurt Lanier's politicking? What do you think, you having been in politics and all yourself? He shore jumped in with both feet to defend that nigger. Some folks—well, you know."

Stratton studied his fingernails. "Young Lanier couldn't hardly do anything else. He owed him that. You recollect that fire, don't you? Burned the nigger pretty bad. I was there myself." Stratton's glance traveled to the jail behind the courthouse. "Some have a pretty high regard for Plez. Besides, if fathering a bastard didn't stop Lanier, I don't rightly see how this would."

Moseby turned back toward the boarding house. When he walked into the sitting room that served as a lobby he discovered Nursie Baltz standing inside the door.

"Why, howdy," Moseby said. "You going to be wanting a room?" He nodded toward the valise the investigator carried. "I thought you finished poking around here some time back."

"Yes, I need a room for ever how long the trial takes. Finished my investigation, all right, but the job isn't done until this trial's over."

Jury selection for the murder case had begun at eight that morning. Tension cloaked the courtroom like an invisible fleece.

The attorney for the commonwealth, Milton Harp from Hickman County, jotted an occasional note on the tablet before him. Confidence clothed him like the pin-striped suit he wore.

Zacharias Renfrow attempted to dissect the minds of the potential jurors. How did each regard Prohibition? The murder of a bootlegger? What if the bootlegger was a white woman? The accused murderer a black man? Zacharias mopped his face with a damp bandanna.

Harp was the third commonwealth's attorney to be appointed in five years. His two predecessors had been removed from office by a pair of bizarre happenings—each committed suicide. One shot himself while traveling between circuit court convenings, and the other jumped off a boat into the swollen waters of the Mississippi during a spring flood. A motive was never established for either, although everybody knew that one, "with his robes of office, dabbled in intoxication." The other, purportedly, was in love with a quadroon madam, Kizzy Cortlandt, who ran a whorehouse in Cairo, on the Illinois side of the river.

After his appointment, Milton Harp wasted no time speculating about his predecessors. He would have to campaign for election. To keep the job, he needed some well-publicized victories, one of which would be the case of Molly Capps' murder. What jury would fail to convict an accused black man of so foul a deed?

On the lawn below, schoolboys—Court Monday being an

unsanctioned holiday from lessons—flung a dried coon skin at each other. Laughter and shouts taunted those who shrank back.

Paul Luke stopped his buggy in front of the courthouse. He helped his mother and sister to the sidewalk. Half an hour later, after tethering the black mare, Paul Luke met Zacharias Renfrow. He was headed toward his office next to Crice's Funeral Home.

"Jury selection's over," the lawyer told him. Wrinkles wreathed his eyes. "Went as well as could be expected. I'd like to see your mother this morning, if she's here."

"She's here, all right." Paul Luke chuckled. "I'd like to see her, too. She's been back from Europe ten days, and at home hardly one. Although she did ride in with me a while ago."

"Been in my office most of those days. Lot of help she was, too, sifting through Baltz's notes. Court convenes at twelve-thirty. Ask your mother to stop by if you see her before then."

"You're not thinking of putting her on the witness stand?"

"No, oh no. I want her sitting on the front row, looking at the jury. Those eyes of hers can make a fellow feel like he's facing a mirror."

The arrival of a Model T drew their attention to the street. Amos McCann had been in town earlier, but had gone home to get his mother. Not only was Nellie McCann in the car, but Nora, Little Granny, and Saree sat on the back seat. The canning factory was already operating on its winter schedule, two days a week. Still, it was a surprise to see Nora in Wickliffe today with Amos. Saree clutched her mother's hand, her eyes missing nothing.

To the left, the Presbyterian Ladies' Christian Aid Society had set up a booth between Hall's Dry Goods and Domestics, and Clark's Sundries. With a stick dipped in India ink, Mae Dee Corlew lettered a sign: PIE AND COFFEE 15 CENTS NOON DINNER 50 CENTS.

Nellie McCann, carrying a cigar box, headed toward a chair where she would collect quarters and dimes and dispense change. Other Society members hustled from side to side stacking plates, moving cups, rearranging. Reverend Wakerich hovered near the chocolate pies.

At the low end of Front Street, away from the horse traders,

Paul Luke's tobacco workers gathered under the shade of a brush arbor. A prayer for their friend frequently broke forth. Some gatherings had ended with a lynching. But this time there seemed reason to hope. Sometimes a hymn floated across the expanse. The absence of Plez's silver baritone left a void in the melodies.

The sound of a harmonica came from the nearest corner. A man with no legs sat on a wooden platform with wheels. One hand curled around a mouth organ, from which he coaxed melodious sounds. The other hand held a pair of polished chicken bones. A red cloth strip with sleigh bells sewed to it was tied around his wrist, so that he could clack the bones and jingle the bells with the same motion. A tin cup sat on the sidewalk.

Saree, never having seen such an arrangement, much less a legless man, stared. He was like Lazarus in the Bible whose friends carried him to beg on the streets.

Some members of the Ladies' Christian Aid Society looked at the musician. Somebody should tell him to move to a different corner. His competition for nickels and dimes could affect their day's receipts. They had charitable pledges to fulfill in foreign lands.

Down the street a wagon stopped near Moseby's Boarding House. Willie Shoe wrapped the mules' hame strings around a stake on the wagon front. Mathelde's three children and Ruby Gem jumped to the ground. Saree ran to join her friends.

In the Ladies' Christian Aid Society booth, Mae Dee Corlew turned to Mathelde and smiled.

"I think it's just wonderful how your children and their little cousin get along together."

"Oh, they're not cousins. They've just become great friends."

Mae Dee clapped her hand across her mouth. "Well, I *am* sorry! I—everybody—just always thought you knew."

"Knew what?" Mathelde served a slice of lemon pie.

"About—about—" Mae Dee fingered the lace jabot at her throat. "I myself never have been one to gossip, or carry tales out of school." Her thin eyebrows lifted like the wings of a startled dove; her voice whirred. "Um—you might ask your ma. She must know what everybody says—"

Mathelde glared at Mae Dee, then whirled with such force that the stacked cups rattled along the plank table. Nellie McCann, in the process of changing a quarter, gawked.

Paul Luke entered the circuit courtroom twenty minutes before time for the trial to begin, and found a vacant space on the last bench.

The Hunt County courthouse, one of the newest in the state, was built eight years before, after the county's first courthouse mysteriously burned. Whether foresight or vanity prompted its size, this circuit courtroom was the largest Paul Luke had seen in his travels about the state. In winter, heat steamed from radiators, an uncommon luxury. Along the rear wall and up the left side, tall windows reached almost to the floor. Outside the second story room, trees scraped the glass.

"Seems kind of odd putting a nigger on trial," a farmer in front of Paul Luke remarked to his neighbor.

"Yeah, most of the time I remember, it's been a necktie party."

Paul Luke watched the jury file in. Only two, Lail Stratton, at the end of the jury box, and Guy Childers, wearing his familiar brown suit coat, caused apprehension. Stratton could be fair-minded. But if he harbored a grudge because of his election loss to Paul Luke; and if he decided to talk against Plez in the jury room, Guy Childers might well follow Stratton's lead. Paul Luke looked toward Zach Renfrow.

The defense lawyer sat half turned from the counsel table, studying the faces of the crowd. Renfrow had wrung victories out of hopeless cases before. But a survey of this courtroom might chill even Renfrow to his fingertips with fears of disaster. When Zacharias spotted Naomi Ruth Lanier in the third row his expression brightened. Her gaze could engage the eye of any juror, sending whatever message she intended.

Members of the black community were not allowed to sit on the benches, so they stood along the walls like dark fringe edging a cape. Zacharias began straightening a pile of calfskin law books on his table.

On the other side of the enclosure, attorney for the commonwealth Milton Harp sat with his assistant, Leotis Newton. The latter had a face resembling a mole, and he appeared pale enough to have spent his life underground. Newton leaned over the table studying his notes through thick spectacles. Milton Harp swung around in his swivel chair and made a show of conferring with Newton. Both wore well-cut suits, in contrast to Zacharias' wrinkled white shirt, and bow tie, twisted down at one corner.

The double doors to the right swung open. Handcuffed, Plez entered followed by Sheriff Meeks. Voices rose. Bailiff Marbles Rickman, strutting about like a Bantam cock, threatened expulsion of the crowd. Then the door to the judge's chamber opened, and Rickman ordered "All rise!"

Judge Standish Theed strode in, followed by his clerk, and the court reporter Decker Landiss, a frail man with protruding eyes. Landiss nearly obscured himself when he sat at a table below the judge.

Judge Theed was an amicable man, with white hair above a face the color of fresh sunburn. He had a habit of resting both elbows on his desk with hands raised, so that he looked like a praying mantis about to pounce on the court reporter. Judge Theed's detractors, particularly members of the Anti-Saloon League, bestowed upon him the nickname "Outlandish Standish" because he refused to support Prohibition. His position so humiliated his wife Margaret, and their daughter, Pansy, that the two rarely showed their faces in public.

"The First Circuit Court of the Commonwealth of Kentucky is now convened to hear the charge of murder in the first degree against Plez Shoe, accused in the death of Molly Capps, on or about July Fourth last," Marbles Rickman announced, sounding more like an auctioneer than a bailiff.

The judge turned to the lawyers and inquired if both sides were ready. They nodded.

"Your honor," Zacharias said, standing. "I request that you invoke the rule that allows for witnesses to be removed from the courtroom. If it please the court."

Judge Theed looked at Milton Harp.

"I have no argument with that," Harp said. The judge waved, and Marbles Rickman ushered the two front rows of witnesses from the room.

"How does the defendant plead?"

Judge Theed waved toward Zacharias Renfrow, who jumped to his feet. Zach clapped Plez on the shoulder, signalling him to rise, but the defendant looked puzzled. Renfrow bent down and whispered to his client. Plez rose from his chair.

"Not guilty, your honor," Plez said, after a nudge from Renfrow. The judge called on Milton Harp.

Harp stood and strolled around the enclosure. His figure swelled, expanding out his expensive suit. The on-lookers nudged each other. Some darted glances toward Zacharias. Plez, seated next to Zach, ducked his head. Nursie Baltz, on the other side of Renfrow, studied Harp with the detachment of a scientist.

"Gentlemen of the jury," Harp said. "There has been a murder in Hunt County. A suspect—" Harp eyed Plez. "A suspect who fled this county, yea, this very *state,* was picked up and indicted. The purpose of the prosecution today is to offer testimony that will place this defendant, this suspect—" Harp indicated Plez, "at the *scene* of the crime, at the *time* of the crime. There is no evidence that any other person was involved. The commonwealth will ask you, gentlemen of the jury," his voice rose, "to do your duty and find the accused, Plez Shoe..." Sharp flung his outstretched fingers toward Plez, then gathered them together in a fist. "...guilty of murdering Molly Capps!"

Chapter 12

The crowd gasped. Plez Shoe a killer? In cold blood? Judge Theed called for the defense counsel's opening statement.

Zacharias Renfrow stood, watching the jury through his gold-rimmed glasses.

"The prosecution has told you what he aims to do, and that should come as no surprise to any of you.

"That's his job. His job is not to go out and try to find evidence of innocence. No, Mr. Harp has to represent the commonwealth, not the accused, and, by George, that's what he's going to do."

Renfrow removed his glasses and rubbed them with a crumpled handkerchief.

"My friends, to this point in time, the commonwealth has *not* said Plez Shoe is guilty. The commonwealth has said, `h-m-m, reckon we ought to have a trial, search out the facts on this.' And that's why we're here today." Renfrow replaced his spectacles.

"Oh, yes, there *has* been a crime in Hunt County. A...citizen...has been murdered." Zacharias drew his mouth down. "And Plez Shoe, a Negro, lives, works, and fishes in Hunt County. I'll grant you that. But those facts alone do not make the commonwealth's case. You will have to grant *me* that. My friends, you must insist on hard evidence. You must require the commonwealth to present *bonafide* proof against Plez Shoe. The fact is, the commonwealth can't do any such thing. Members of the jury, no such proof exists!

"Let me tell you what I intend to show here. I will demonstrate over and over, that of all the people who ever visited that crime scene Plez Shoe was not one of them. Plez Shoe never had any reason to go to that boat down there on the river. Plez Shoe had no motive to kill Molly Capps! He did not then, and does not now, have the inclination to do violence to anybody.

"There is more *than* the shadow of a doubt here. Plez Shoe is

not guilty of that killing. All I ask for is your undivided attention."

He took a few steps and turned back to the jury. "And I know I can count on that."

Zacharias dropped into his chair, and nodded toward Harp, who called Gabe Findley, the commonwealth's first witness.

"Mr.Findley," Harp began, his voice cordial, "would you be so kind as to tell the court what you know personally about the discovery of the murder?"

Settling into the witness chair Gabe watched Harp with his good eye. "Yeh. I see this lady running at me lickity-split, screaming like a banshee. Skeered my mules." Gabe grinned self-consciously. "Skeered me a mite, too, I reckon."

"Who was this lady?"

"Found out later it was Mad Molly's—er—Molly Capps' sister. Miss Gilly, I believe they call her."

"U-m-m. You say she was screaming. Did you talk to her? Find out about the screaming?" Harp, puffed out his chest, looking like a rooster about to crow.

"Yeah, she'd found the dead body down there at the river."

"The body? What body?"

"Molly's dead body. Weren't no other dead body down there."

"What did you do next?"

"I left Miss Gilly at the store for a few minutes and went and called Claude and he come on down to the river."

"Claude?"

"Claude Meeks, the sheriff of this here county."

"Now, Mr. Findley, will you tell the court of a meeting you happened into with the defendant," Harp nodded toward Plez."That same morning last July?"

"Objection!" Renfrow bounded to his feet. "Your honor, what meeting in July is counsel talking about here? He can't assume his own evidence. The evidence has to come from the witnesses, not from the prosecutor! Exactly what meeting is Mr. Harp talking about?"

"Sustained," Judge Theed said. "Now, counsel, nothing's taken for granted in this court. You're going to have to build your case here."

"All right, your honor." Harp glanced toward Renfrow. "Mr.

Findley, did you have occasion to be on the river road the Saturday following July Fourth of this year?"

"I told you I was going down to the bottoms to tend my corn crop."

"Did you meet anybody else on that road? Did you happen to come upon the defendant," Harp pointed toward Plez. "Face to face?"

Gabe Findley scratched his head with a thumbnail, that through some injury, had taken on the appearance of a thick Brazil nut. Harp frowned.

"Yeah, I seen Plez on the road before I met that lady running towards me. About half a mile from the river. Had some fish. Little fiddlers, they was."

"When you say Plez, are you talking about the defendant?"

Gabe stared at the prosecutor. "Yeah, it was him."

"How did he look?"

"Well," Gabe stopped scratching and motioned with his thumb. "Plez always looks about like he does now over there. Maybe in a bit of a hurry—"

"In a *hurry*?" Raising an eyebrow Harp glanced sidelong at the jury. "No further questions."

Zacharias approached the witness.

"Gabe—Mr. Findley, where did you say you were heading that morning? The day Molly Capps' body was found?"

"I was going to the river bottoms to work my corn crop."

"Now, you said you saw Plez Shoe on the river road." Zacharias stared at the floor, calculating. "You put him within half a mile of the crime scene. That right?"

Gabe nodded."Yeh, I reckon so."

"And, Mr. Findley, that also puts *you* within half a mile of the crime scene, doesn't it?" Zacharias turned toward the jury, then back to Findley. "So then, you and Plez were both equally close to the place where Molly Capps was killed?"

A murmur swept through the crowd. Gabe leaned forward.

"Yes, but Plez was *coming* from the river, and I was *going* to the river."

"Ah, so he was, and so you were! Have you ever gone to the river before?"

"Now, Zach, you know doggone well I always raise a corn crop down there. Have for years."

"Just answer the question yes or no," Judge Theed said.

"Yes."

"Have you ever seen Plez down there before?"

"Yes."

"Coming from the river?"

"Yes."

"Carrying fish?"

"Well, yeh, I reckon so."

"Yes or no? Be definite about it."

"Yes." Gabe nodded.

"How were the other times different from this time?"

"Well, like I said, Plez was in a little hurry."

"Mr. Findley, would you say it appeared to you that Plez was drinking whiskey? Or anything like that, alcohol, that day in July?"

"Oh, no, Zach—er, sir. I never knowed Plez Shoe to take a drink in his life."

"The other times you've seen him near the river. Was he not ever in a hurry before?"

"Oh, Plez wasn't never one to lollygag along. He always wanted to get to wherever he was going, all right."

"*So?*" Renfrow eyed Harp, then the jury. He walked to his chair and sat. "No further questions, your honor."

The commonwealth attorney called Mae Dee Corlew.

"Plez was nervous, awful nervous that day," she told Harp. She held a palmleaf fan that she swished from time to time like the tail of a malevolent cat.

"Did you talk to the defendant, Plez Shoe, about the fish?"

"Oh, yes. I told him they was nice looking fiddlers. I asked him if he wanted to sell the fish, but he wouldn't let me have them. He just left. Nervous like." She sniffed.

"Nervous. In a hurry, and nervous," the prosecutor said. Nodding, Harp relinquished the witness to Zach.

"Mae Dee—er, Mrs. Corlew, was there any blood on the defendant?"

"No, not that I noticed—"

"Believe me, you would have noticed," Renfrow said in a low

voice. In the third row Naomi Ruth fixed her gaze on the witness.

"Now, Mrs. Corlew, tell the court about some of your *other* conversations you've had with the defendant in the past."

Mae Dee squirmed. One of the jurors fanned himself with an old straw hat. Time and motion languished. Zach stared at Mae Dee, his eyebrows knitted. The sun slanted across the floor in front of her.

Renfrow repeated his question.

"Well, I've never talked much with him. No reason to. I just help him with what he wants when he comes in the store."

"But this one time you just departed from your custom. You just started a conversation with him and he seemed nervous. Then you have had no occasion previously to notice whether he was nervous or not. Do you suppose that this out-of-the-ordinary conversation you started could have been what made him nervous?"

Harp jumped to his feet. "Objection, your honor, counsel is suggesting an opinion."

"Sustained."

Zach thrust his hands into his pockets. He remained silent for a moment.

"Mrs. Corlew, was Plez ever drunk, or drinking whiskey, any alcohol, when he came in your store? Ever smell it on him?"

"Not that I could tell."

"Now, Mae Dee—Mrs. Corlew," Zach said, a hint of reproach in his voice. "Surely you can recognize the stench of alcohol. Let me ask it this way. Did you smell whiskey on Plez that day last July, the Saturday after the Fourth, when he came into your store with those fish?"

"No, I did not."

"No further questions, your honor."

Zach slumped in his chair. He poured a glass of water, swallowing it in big gulps. Now and then a baby cried, causing its mother to look apologetically at her neighbors. The black coterie stood silent against the walls.

Harp called Gilly McCrae, the dead woman's sister, to the stand. Having forsaken her overalls, doubtless at Harp's suggestion, she wore black from head to toe, making her barely recognizable. Once seated on the stand she raised the veil that covered her face. The severe black created an ethereal contrast with her flowing white hair. Her fearful gaze swept the courtroom, the double doors, the tall windows.

"Now, Miss McCrae, would you tell the court what you remember of the morning when you found your sister's body?" Harp stood at a distance, not to obscure the tragic, grieving witness.

Gilly did not answer right away. One black-gloved hand tugged at the other.

"I had been at my camp in the woods up there. I was going down to Molly's." Her voice wavered. "I heared a noise like—like stepping on a stick. And I—I seen somebody going by at a—at a pretty good gait—" Her gaze fell on Plez. She stood and pointed. "It was him! Over there!"

The crowd broke into a frenzy. Plez twisted toward the door, panic in his eyes. Paul Luke half rose from his seat on the back row, as if fearing Plez might dash for freedom. Zach, sensing Plez's alarm, planted a steadying hand on his shoulder. Near the double doors the deputy sheriff took a few steps forward. Judge Theed pounded his gavel, causing the court reporter to jump. Bailiff Marbles Rickman ejected three people and the others quieted. Harp, appearing unaware of the outbreak, resumed his questioning.

"Were you concerned for your sister's safety at that time, when you saw—uh, this person, the defendant?" He pointed to Plez.

"No...."

"Did you then know that your sister lay murdered at her own door?"

"No." Gilly wiped her eyes on her sleeve.

"Your witness," Harp said, rising on his toes a bit.

Zach picked up his pencil and gave the woman time to compose herself.

"Now, Miss Gilly, when you saw the accused walking by—did you notice if he was carrying anything?"

"I don't know. I didn't see."

"What direction was he going?"

"Well, away from the river where my sister was at. That's all I know."

"And he was walking along the river road, I presume." Zach tapped the pencil against his chin. "That right?"

"Well I reckon." Gilly looked at him."There ain't but one road to the river, far as I know."

"In other words, the defendant was not skulking—hiding—in the woods?"

"Not when I seen him."

"Mrs. McCrae, a few minutes later, you, yourself, ran right down that very same road in the very same direction. Did you not fear for your own safety, following behind the man you have accused of murdering your sister?"

"No, uh, it was—I mean, I didn't—"

"Could it be, Miss Gilly, that it did not occur to you until days later, when suggestions had been made by others, that maybe you ought to implicate the defendant in this?" Zach wagged the pencil at her. "He had been to the river that morning; there was nobody else convenient to blame; in *your* mind did he become guilty? That guilt based solely on proximity to the crime scene?"

Gilly stared at him, confusion in her eyes. Harp half stood, but before she could answer, Zacharias spoke again.

"No further questions, your honor."

Harp studied the old lawyer. Plez was calm again. Nursie Baltz watched Harp, a remote expression in his eyes.

"The prosecution calls Sheriff Claude Meeks."

Every eye in the room was fixed on the sheriff as he strode between the double doors.

"Old Claude getting a little gut on him since he give up boxing," one observer said to his neighbor.

"Don't let that fool you none," the other replied. "Reckon you noticed how calm everything's been over to the jail. Wasn't nobody wanting that nigger bad enough to take Claude on. He may look kind of soft, but he's one mean son-a-bitch when he gets riled up."

Meeks leaned back in the witness chair and crossed his legs.

Harp rocked on his heels, hands clasped behind his back. "Sheriff, would you describe to the court how the defendant, Plez Shoe here, got to your jail? Be specific now."

The sheriff readjusted his large frame in the chair. "We went down to Memphis and brought him back. Deputy Virgil Bigler and myself."

Sharp stopped rocking. "*Memphis*? Why *Memphis*?"

"Beause that's where Plez went, after—"

"After the murder?" Harp interrupted with a shout. He whirled on one glossy shoe, his gaze glued on the jury.

"Objection, your honor!" Zach cried, leaping up. "Counsel is leading the witness."

"Sustained."

"Very well, your honor." The prosecutor walked to his table. He picked up an object, shielding it from the eyes of the spectators craning their necks to see. Harp approached the witness.

"Sheriff Meeks, have you ever seen this article before?"

Sharp's hand shot upward, stabbing the air with a long-bladed butcher knife. The sun's rays skipped across it, illuminating rust or dried blood. A commotion broke forth. Viewers bolted to their feet, pushing for a better view. Noise filled the room like a rushing wind. A few men gazed about. Were they supposed to protect wives and children against the gruesome weapon protruding from Harp's raised fist? Three young girls near the back began to wail.

"We got a knife like that!" one child squealed.

"Me see!" a toddler cried. He leaped from his mother's lap and bounded down the aisle toward the brass guardrails. Bailiff Rickman caught the youngster and handed him over to the woman with a reproving look.

Harp watched until Judge Theed's gavel restored order.

Sheriff Meeks took the knife. He examined it on both sides.

"Yes," he said, handing it back to Harp. "That's the knife that killed Molly Capps, all right. I scratched my initials on it, if you need proof. The day I took it off her boat, after the murder." The sheriff pointed. "Right there."

Harp eyed Renfrow.

"Your honor, the prosecution would like to enter this weapon into evidence as exhibit A for the commonwealth," Harp said.

Theed threw a quick glance toward Zach. "Granted," he said.

Harp's maneuver had not affected Renfrow, but Nursie Baltz, sitting beside him, detected a slight tremor of the hand gripping his notepad.

"No further questions, your honor." With a flourish Harp took his seat. Leotis Newton, Harp's assistant, leaned forward, whispering.

Zach laid his pencil beside his tablet, stood, and moved to Meeks. "Sheriff, about that knife. Do you by any chance happen to know who it belongs to?"

"Yes, it belonged to Molly Capps. It was her knife."

"The knife belonged to the dead woman. Are you absolutely sure about that?"

"Well, her sister identified it. Said it was Molly Capps' knife."

"The knife did not belong to the defendant, Plez Shoe?"

"No, Zach. It was Molly's knife," Meeks uncrossed his legs, turned, and crossed them again.

"Sheriff, what time of day was it when you first examined the body of the deceased?"

"It was mid-morning. I imagine it must of been between nine, ten o'clock."

"And when did the defendant go to Memphis?"

"Not till the next morning. Before daylight, so I was told when I went looking for him."

Harp sprang to his feet. "Objection, your honor! That's hearsay."

"Sustained," the judge said. "The reporter will strike that statement from the record." Decker Landiss blinked and his pen skittered up the page.

Renfrow ran a finger between the back of his neck and his shirt collar. "Sheriff, when you picked the defendant up in Memphis, how did he behave?"

"Good. Real good." Meeks squinted toward Plez sitting at Zach's table. "Made a tough job easier by a long shot."

"What did he say about running away? Did he offer you any reason?"

Meeks hesitated. "Yes, Plez said he ran off because he heard they would—" The sheriff surveyed the courtroom. "There was a cross burning like hell. Plez figured he'd be next. Said he was scared to death."

An uproar erupted from the crowd.

"This room will be cleared," the judge threatened. "But not before every one of you is fined twenty dollars for contempt of court!"

Harp hopped to his feet, standing until order was restored.

"Objection, your honor! That statement is self-serving. Of course the defendant would say he ran off because he was afraid."

"Your honor," Zach intervened. "The statement is not being offered as proof of fact. It is simply offered as evidence to the defendant's attitude. What he said. Surely the sheriff can testify as to what Plez Shoe actually said to him?"

"Objection overruled."

Zach turned back toward Meeks. "Did Plez have reason to be afraid?"

Harp objected again. "Calls for opinion, your honor."

"Sustained."

"Very well, your honor." Zach said, glancing at Judge Theed. "The defense will call another witness for that answer later on." He continued. "Sheriff, did *you* fear for Plez's life?" Meeks nodded. "Speak up, man. The reporter can't write sign language."

"Yes." Meeks squared his shoulders. "I saw that cross, burning down there. Spitting in the rain. Storm brewing. And I don't mean the weather. If Plez'd stuck around, we mightn't be having this trial."

Murmurs rippled through the throng. The judge pounded.

"Your honor," Zach said, "I'd like to reserve the right to question this witness further when the defense is presented."

"Counselor, if you have something more to ask this witness, ask him right now," Judge Theed said.

"Your honor, I need time to develop the line of questioning before I ask," Zach said.

"Very well," Judge Theed answered wearily. "Granted." The judge regarded Harp expectantly. He cleared his throat. "Mr. Prosecutor, do you have more?"

Harp stood, looking chagrined. "Uh—er—no, your honor. The prosecution rests."

"Your honor," Zach took a quick step toward the judge. "At this time the defense moves for an instructed verdict from the bench. Innocent on grounds of insufficient evidence. The defense believes the commonwealth simply does not have a case."

"I think you're going to have to let the jury make that decision on its own, counselor," the judge replied sharply.

"But, your honor—"

Theed paused. A pall of hostility engulfed the room. People nudged each other, their faces hard. Some of the jurors fidgeted. Lail Stratton regarded the judge from under half-closed eyes, his head tilted back. The cloth of Plez's shirt trembled.

"The court declares a ten minute recess. I will see counsel in my chambers."

Paul Luke walked into the hall, headed toward the wide stairs.

Mathelde, standing with Nora Ballard, called to him. "What's happening? We've been sitting with the children and haven't gotten the same viewpoint from any two people we've asked."

Paul Luke reviewed the proceedings, giving his own interpretation of the testimony.

"We're going in to watch now," Mathelde said. "The children are with Ruby Gem. They'll be all right in there with her."

Judge Theed closed the door to his anteroom.

"Now, counsel," he told Zacharias, "if the defendant walks out of this court an innocent man, he'll be a safer innocent man if he's pronounced so by this jury. I suggest that we simply move forward with this case."

"Judge Theed," Zach said, "the prosecution has precious little evidence. But emotions running as they do, my client could very well be convicted. He would suffer the consequences just as surely as if the commonwealth could prove its case."

The judge turned to Harp.

"Your honor, no, I don't have a lot of evidence," the prosecutor said. "The last thing a killer wants is to leave evidence. But the facts are these. The accused was at the crime scene. The dead woman's sister was certain enough of his guilt to bring a complaint. Furthermore, I believe the community in general considers this defendant guilty. I see no other way to resolve it, your honor."

The judge studied the two men. He turned to Renfrow.

"Counselor, you're just going to have to do the best job you can defending a man. This court's not going to tell that jury to find the defendant innocent without a trial." Theed glanced at the gold pocket watch on his desk. "This seems like as good a place as any to stop for the day. We might as well continue in the morning."

The men returned to the courtroom and the gathering hushed. Zach walked behind the others, his face grim.

"The request for an instructed innocent verdict from me to this jury is denied. The defense will call its first witness when this court reconvenes in the morning, nine a.m." Judge Theed banged his gavel.

Some nodded in accordance with the judge. Others gazed at the floor. Plez glanced at Nursie Baltz and slumped in his chair.

Chapter 13

The next morning Plez Shoe placed his hand on the Bible for swearing in to testify as Marbles Rickman recited the oath.

"Now, Plez," Zacharias Renfrow said, his voice sounding just as it had when he and Plez sat talking together in the jail. "Tell the court what happened the morning that Mrs. Capps' body was found. Where were you? What were you doing, exactly?"

"Well, sir, I went down to the river fishing early like I does. That's all."

"Did you see Miss Gilly McCrae, the dead woman's sister?"

"No, sir."

"You didn't see her see you?"

"No, sir, I never see her at all."

"Plez, you heard her say that she saw you on the river road. Were you on that road where she said you were?"

"Yes, sir, Mr. Zach, I be there all right."

Renfrow strolled toward the tall windows. He turned, halfway facing the jury. "Down there where she said she saw you, was that where you went fishing?"

"Oh, no, sir. You never leaves the river right where your fishing spot be. You do that, everybody know where it's at."

"I don't suppose you'd want to tell the court where that secret fishing hole is?"

Plez shook his head. "No, sir."

"Did you see Gabe Findley on the morning when the body was found?"

"Yes, sir, I did."

"He said you were in a kind of hurry that morning."

"Yes, sir, I were." Plez scooted in the witness chair. "When I goes fishing I tells Ruby Gem when to expect me home. But time pass so, I near always seem to be late. I have to hurry some, most usual."

"Plez, do you drink? Whiskey?"

"No, sir!"

"Did you ever buy whiskey from that lady, Mrs. Capps, who was killed down on the river?"

"No, sir. I tried to stay away from where that lady was at, best as I could."

"Did you ever know the procedure—the way—to go about buying whiskey down there?"

Plez looked puzzled. "What say, sir?"

"Did you ever 'put the money on the stump' to pay for a jug of moonshine at Mrs. Capps' shanty boat?"

"No, sir. I never do nothing like that."

Zach nodded toward Harp and sat.

"Plez," the prosecutor said. "You seem to want to be seen leaving that river at some spot other than where you actually were. Now, if you *did* kill Molly Capps, wouldn't you pull the same dodge, coming out of the river at some place other than where her boat was?"

"Objection, your honor!" Zach interrupted. "Counsel is leading the witness."

"Your honor, he's trying to save his own neck," Harp countered. "I'm *allowed* to lead a hostile witness."

"But, your honor," Zach argued, "If Plez answers yes to the question, it will sound like he's admitting he came from the murder scene; and if he answers *no*, he implies that he's 'pulled a dodge,' as counselor put it."

The judge peered at the two lawyers, then at the defendant.

"I can fix that. Now, Plez, if you answer yes, do you mean you came from the murder scene; or yes, you always go down river from your fishing hole?"

"I always go down the river from my fishing hole, sir, your honor."

Harp turned to Plez. "All right, Plez, tell us where this fishing hole is."

Plez glanced toward Renfrow, then at the judge, saying nothing.

"Now, Plez, you're going to have to tell him where your fishing hole is," Judge Theed said.

Plez tucked his head and mumbled so that none in the audience heard.

Harp's assistant, Leotis Newton, thrust a map toward Harp.

The prosecutor made a great show of consulting it.

"That's below the murder scene, I see. So you actually did walk right past Molly Capps' boat?"

"I walked right down that river road."

"No further questions, your honor."

Zacharias called Sheriff Meeks back to the stand.

"Sheriff, the court has just heard the defendant, Plez Shoe, testify that he doesn't use alcohol," Renfrow said. "Do you think he's lying?"

"Objection, your honor," Harp said. "The court is not interested in what the sheriff *thinks* about the veracity of the defendant."

"Sustained."

Zach began a circular stroll as if he had not heard. He stopped and turned back to the witness. "Tell the court, sheriff, to the best of your knowledge," he said. "You ever catch Plez Shoe lying?"

"No, never did."

"Sheriff, have you ever known Plez to drink whiskey? Would you be shocked if you saw him take a drink?"

"Yes, I would."

"Objection, your honor! We are here for *facts*, not the sheriff's moral judgments."

"Your honor," Zach said, "it *is* a fact that the sheriff would be shocked if he saw Plez take a drink. He just said so!"

"All right, go on, counselor," Theed said.

"Sheriff Meeks, do you know who drinks in this county, and who doesn't?" Renfrow stopped in front of the jury box.

Harp bounded to his feet.

"Objection, your honor! Counsel is *still* calling for expert testimony. Some people drink more discreetly than others. In private. The witness couldn't possibly answer correctly."

"Sustained." Judge Theed said. "Zach, if you're trying to go somewhere, then get there."

"All right, your honor, I'll rephrase the question. Sheriff, do you know who in this county gets drunk and causes trouble for you to see after?"

Meeks turned a sarcastic squint toward Renfrow. "Yeah, I know that all right."

"Sheriff, would you say that Bosh Tillson's boys, Daniel and Jack, would fall into that category?"

Harp bolted to his feet.

"Objection, your honor! No premise has been laid for that line of questioning. The Tillsons are not on trial here. Counsel is out of order!"

Zacharias raised his hands in a pleading gesture.

"Your honor, a man *is* on trial here for killing a known bootlegger. All this is relevant. I am *laying* the premise, which will become apparent. In the name of justice being done, your honor, I—"

Judge Theed interrupted. "Would counsel approach the bench? Counsel, where in the name of the Chief Justice are you going with this case?" Theed asked, looking at Zach with disbelief.

"In that back room a while ago, judge, you told me we're going to have to let the jury decide this. I respectfully beg that you allow me to show the jury what's been going on in this county, and *let* them decide. Otherwise, you might as well dismiss those twelve men and put a noose around my client's neck—your honor!"

Zacharias's words were harsh. Fatigue and frustration spawned recklessness; if the judge took offense, so be it.

"All right, counselor," Judge Theed said, after studying Zach a long moment. "I'm going to let you proceed."

The lawyers walked back to their tables, Harp clearly dejected, his jauntiness fading.

"The witness will answer," Theed said. "Clerk, read the question from your record." The judge assumed his praying mantis position. The clerk cleared his throat, and glanced about as if searching for a safe place to leap before reading the question.

"Yes, I've had trouble from the Tillson boys when they'd been drinking," Sheriff Meeks said.

The jurors leaned forward.

"What about their daddy?"

"Bosh? Oh, he don't drink. It's his boys."

"How does that set with Bosh?"

"Objection! Here we go again, your honor."

"Sustained."

Annoyed, Zach glanced at Harp.

"All right. Sheriff, are you aware of any indications as to how Bosh Tillson regards his sons' drinking habits?"

"Bosh is violent against those boys drinking. I've been called down there before, them fighting over it." The sheriff appeared ill at ease. He looked at the judge, then at the prosecutor.

"What about the Mabry boy?"

Harp objected.

"Overruled."

"Buck Junior? Yeah, he's been drunk a few times, too. Mainly when he's tagging along with Bosh's boys. You know he's not much responsible."

Zach leaned toward the witness. "Do you know who supplies the Tillson boys with their whiskey?"

The sheriff cleared his throat and brushed his trousers. Harp frowned.

"I expect most folks know that. Pert near all the bootleg consumed around here came from Molly Capps' shanty."

"Now, Sheriff Meeks," Zach continued, "your investigation apparently came to a halt with the arrest of `that nigger on the river road.' Would you confirm that Plez Shoe is the only suspect in this case? Nobody else is even under suspicion for the murder of Molly Capps?"

"That's right, Zach." Meeks squared his shoulders.

"Thank you. No further questions."

"Now, Sheriff Meeks, has anybody given reason—" Harp began, from his table.

"Objection, your honor," Renfrow said swiftly. "The sheriff is the prosecution's witness. Mr. Harp had direct questioning. He's already asked the sheriff his questions. I was just cross examining." Zach's glance traveled from Harp to the judge. "I'm through with the witness, your honor."

"But, your honor, counsel has opened a new area here that gives rise to some other questions." Harp rushed around his table, stopping halfway to Judge Theed's bench. "I need a chance to follow up."

"Aw, go ahead and follow up, prosecutor. Ask your question," Theed said, waving consent.

"Sheriff, has anybody else given reason to be under suspicion? Have you *arrested* anybody else?" Harp asked. "Plez Shoe *is* still the only one on trial here?"

Theed raised his hand to stop Harp.

"Is that the line of your questioning, counselor?"

"Yes, your honor."

"Then why don't we just allow the defense to go on with his next witness?" Theed looked at Meeks. "You're excused, sheriff." Harp threw his hands in the air.

"The defense calls Ruby Gem Shoe."

Ruby Gem passed through the double doors and hesitated. Zach Renfrow watched her, concern growing in his eyes. Nursie Baltz rose from the table. He approached the woman, took her arm, and led her down the aisle. At Marbles Rickman's direction she placed her hand on the Bible.

"Ruby Gem," Renfrow began, "the day everybody saw Plez with those fish, the day of the murder. Did Plez make it home with the fish?"

"Yes, sir, he did."

"Was Plez nervous or shaky?"

"No, sir." A wan smile crossed her face. "He a little late, but he weren't nervous."

"And you cooked up those fish and you ate them." Zach rubbed his chin. "Have you ever known Plez to drink?"

"No, sir, Mr. Zach. Plez a fine Christian man. He don't drink no whiskey since the day he born."

"And you washed his clothes, I presume. Did you notice any blood?"

"No, sir, no blood on them clothes. Just mud from out the river."

"Now, Ruby Gem, let's move back to the Sunday after the killing. Would you tell the court about an outing—a picnic?"

"Yes, sir," she said. "Mr. Paul Luke and Miss Mathelde say they has business to go over. They tell me, take Miss Mathelde children—Miss Rebecca and Miss Leighza and Mr. Will Roy. And they friend, the little Ballard child, to the park down there by Cartwright Lake. Right upside the river."

"Did anybody else show up at that park that day?"

"Yes, sir. Mr. Mabry what live in Mr. Tillson cow shed. He

come up from the river aggravating the children and all; he calling out about something. And he grab for Miss Rebecca arm."

"What did you do?"

Ruby Gem stared at her feet. Yellow and white cloth roses bobbled atop her straw hat. She looked up and her eyes met those of Naomi Ruth. Ruby Gem raised her head.

"I pushed him away from the children."

"No further questions, your honor," Renfrow said. Harp dismissed the witness with a wave of his hand.

Zach went to Marbles Rickman and whispered in his ear. A startled expression crossed the bailiff's face, and a frantic whispered exchange ensued between the two. Marbles gestured with both hands. Zach returned to his table. The bailiff shook his head as he approached Judge Theed.

"Judge, the defense calls Miss Leighza Phelps."

The onlookers began to babble.

"Put a child on the stand?"

"Never do it to my young 'un!"

"Surely they won't allow—"

Milton Harp, the prosecutor, jumped to his feet, objecting. The judge raised his gavel, but the crowd quieted on its own. Leighza Phelps stood just inside the double doors, clutching Mathelde's hand. The girl looked at her mother, then at the dozens of faces and eyes turned toward her. Her mother squeezed her hand and they began to walk.

"I object, your honor, on the grounds that counsel cannot qualify this witness. She's a young child, your honor!"

"Your honor," Zach said, rising from his chair. "A man's life is at stake here. I believe I can show that this child does know what the truth is. For God's sake, let me try."

"Let's give him a chance, counselor," Judge Theed said. "Objection overruled."

Zacharias took Leighza's hand. He led her to the witness stand and lifted her into the seat. Then he sat on the platform a step below Leighza's chair. The little girl peered into the crowd, looking straight into her grandmother's eyes.

"Now, Leighza, tell the—tell us how old you are."

She answered in a low voice, "Nine."

"Where is your home? Do you live here?"

"Cincinnati. But we're here now because my daddy's real sick."

"Your father's in Cincinnati?"

"No, sir. In Paducah. At the railroad hospital."

"What's wrong with him?"

"I—don't know for sure. Something awful."

"Leighza, what is a lie? Can you tell me?"

She cast her eyes toward the ceiling. One finger touched her front teeth.

"A lie is—a lie is—when you make something up and somebody gets in trouble, mainly you."

Zacharias nodded. A few smiles flitted about the audience.

"Leighza, which is right—to tell a lie or to tell the truth?"

"To tell the truth. You're supposed to tell the truth."

"Leighza, if I ask you some questions, will you promise to tell the truth?"

She nodded. "Yes, sir."

Through Zach's questioning Leighza confirmed Ruby Gem's testimony about the Sunday picnic.

"Leighza, did you notice anything about Mr. Mabry that day?"

"He's fat. And he smelled funny—bad."

"Smelled? Like what?"

"I don't know. Bad." She wrinkled her nose.

"If you smelled the `bad' odor again, would you recognize—know—it?"

Leighza ducked her head, swinging her feet from the tall chair.

"Would you, Leighza?"

"Yes, I think."

Renfrow walked to his table. Nursie Baltz handed him a small bottle.

"If the court please, I'd like for Mr. Harp and your honor to smell the contents."

The attorney for the commonwealth and the presiding judge jerked back, startled. "Outlandish Standish" Theed appeared ready to reject Renfrow's request. Zach, seizing the advantage of the moment, hurriedly passed the small bottle to Harp and the judge, then to Leighza.

"Is that the odor you smelled on Mr. Mabry that day, Leighza?"

"I don't think so. No."

"Let the record show that this bottle contains kerosene —plain, everyday coal oil."

Renfrow took an identical bottle and repeated his first action. Theed seemed dubious.

"Leighza, do you recognize this?"

Leighza shuddered and looked into the crowd. Her gaze traveled to Paul Luke; to her mother; and came to rest on Naomi Ruth. Twelve men she had never seen before sat together watching her. She stared into space. *That day in the park...the scent of grass...the sound of a twig snapping...the July heat...a hand closing around her wrist.*

"Yes! He smelled like that!"

"Let the record show," Zach told the court reporter, who was writing like a water spider skimming across a pond, "that this bottle contains a common form of alcohol known as moonshine, or bootleg whiskey. Let the record further state that the witness identified the odor as the one she smelled on Buck Junior Mabry after the murder of Molly Capps. Your honor, if the court please, I'd like to ask the bailiff to label these two bottles as exhibits for the defense. I can, of course, confirm that Sheriff Meeks himself prepared these same two bottles exactly as they are, at the defense's request. He has had sole custody of them since that time. I believe he will attest to the contents and that neither has been tampered with."

Theed looked at Harp, sitting next to his assistant like a morose peacock. "Any objection, counselor?"

"No, your honor. Not to the exhibits," Harp said, standing. "I smelled the contents, your honor. I believe counsel when he says one is kerosene and the other white lightning. I don't—er—partake myself, but I do recognize the—er—fragrance."

"Very well. The bailiff will do as requested."

Harp started to rise when Zach indicated that he had finished questioning the child. Noticing Judge Theed's expression Harp slumped back into his chair.

Zacharias called Rebecca Phelps, whose version of the picnic coincided with the statements of Ruby Gem and Leighza.

"Now, Rebecca, that Sunday at the park, was Mr. Mabry talking? Did he say anything? Do you recall?"

Rebecca looked at him with her grandmother's eyes. For a moment Zach was a youth again in the Presbyterian churchyard. Reaching to a tree above he plucked a cluster of the locust blossoms that drooped around him and the dark-eyed girl at his side. Naomi Ruth, eyes dancing, held his hands and buried her face in the fragrant mass. Time passed down the arches of the years. The white blossoms faded, to return anew. But the green of his youth had faded into the dust of age.

"Yes, sir. He was yelling at us." Rebecca was saying. She frowned. "He said she called—she called Junior a bad name. But Ruby Gem didn't say anything to him. None of us did."

The lawyer thanked Rebecca and she stepped down. Harp said nothing. Cross-examining the girl might produce little more than sympathy for the accused.

"Your honor," Zach said, turning to Judge Theed. "Earlier this morning I asked the deputy sheriff for another witness to be found and brought in. Can the court determine if he is here yet?"

"Deputy?" the judge looked toward the double doors.

"He is, your honor," Virgil Bigler, the deputy, said.

"Your honor, the defense calls Buck Junior Mabry."

"Objection! Objection! Objection!" Harp screamed, jumping to his feet. His arms sliced the air like windmill blades.

"Counselors, approach my bench," Judge Theed ordered. He pounded his gavel, glaring at the crowd.

"Your honor, counsel is calling a clinically-defined moron to the stand," Harp sputtered, his face flushed and contorted. "He cannot expect this court to consider the statement of a mental incompetent, your honor!" The judge turned a dubious gaze on Renfrow.

"Your honor," Zach said, "you know blamed well if Buck Junior Mabry said he saw Plez Shoe kill Molly Capps, everybody in this courtroom would accept it as the God's truth. Mabry is simple-minded, all right. But I believe I can establish that he knows right from wrong. Truth from fantasy. This jury is capable of judging. Indeed, it is *required* to judge—whether Mabry is babbling, or telling the truth from personal knowledge. This jury will have the final say, your honor."

Judge Theed made no response, other than to study Renfrow.

"You've made it rough on me, judge," Zach continued, desperation edging his voice. "Telling me I've got to have a trial here. I must call my witnesses—allow me that—if I'm to defend this man under the constitutional system. Even dogs let other dogs bark, your honor."

Theed leaned across his desk toward Zach. "Proceed with your witness. But carefully, counselor."

The bailiff opened the double doors to admit Buck Junior, accompanied by Deputy Bigler.

Buck Junior's hair lay flat against his head, matted with dirt. His overalls were held with knotted ropes tied across his shoulders. He yawned and rubbed his eyes and, looking like a sleepy goat, followed the deputy to the witness stand. His bare feet slapped the wooden boards. Several spectators studied their fingernails. Buck Junior Mabry laid his hand on the Bible, regarding Bailiff Marbles Rickman with suspicion while he administered the oath.

Mabry responded, after a simple explanation. He pulled at a hangnail on his thumb, casting oblique glances at Zacharias.

Renfrow seated himself on the step below the witness chair as he had when questioning the children. "Buck Junior, do you know what a promise is?"

"Uh-huh. Mr. Findley promise Buck Junior come in wagon. He run off. Fast. Leave Buck Junior at the store."

"Tell me this," Zach said, looking keenly at the witness."Who *is* Buck Junior?"

"Me!" he crowed. Grinning, he pointed to himself with both hands. "I!" After a moment the grin faded. He looked around, as though expecting to be refuted.

Zach smiled and nodded. Buck Junior appeared pleased.

"Buck Junior, you made a promise just now to all these folks." Zach took in the courtroom with a sweep of his arm. "...to tell the truth here. Do you understand?"

Buck looked around at the crowd, the jury, at Plez, and Nursie Baltz.

"Tell the truth," he echoed, nodding.

"Where do you live? Do you stay with your family?"

"No. Mr. Bosh. Family all die."

"That's the truth, Buck Junior."

The lawyer rose from his seat on the step, walked toward the jury box, then turned back to the witness.

"Ever go to the park down at the lake, Buck Junior?"

"Yep, to the park." Mabry grinned.

"Sometimes children play there. Ever see any children at the park, Buck Junior? Do you remember?"

Buck Junior's eyes took on a wary expression. He wriggled one bare foot, fingering the rope that fastened his overalls. The judge glanced at the commonwealth attorney.

"Don't 'member."

"Do you remember the Fourth Fest? At the park. Last summer. It was hot."

A wide grin spread across Mabry's face. He nodded. "Yep."

"Do you remember seeing some children at the park one day, after the Fourth Fest?" Renfrow persisted. "Do you remember?"

The witness scratched his ear and stared at the lawyer. "Yep. Buck Junior see children."

"Do you remember a colored woman at the park? With the children?"

Mabry changed in an inkling. He raised up in the witness chair, glowering.

"She a bad woman. Push *me*."

"Had you been drinking whiskey?"

Mabry leaned back into the chair. Then, leaning down, he examined the toes of one bare foot.

"Do you know the Tillson boys? Daniel and Jack?" Renfrow asked, taking another course.

Buck Junior lowered his foot and looked up, appearing puzzled. Zach repeated the question.

"Yep. Friends. My friends," he said.

"Did you ever go to Mad Molly's boat with them?"

"She call Junior bad. Bad name!"

"Why did you go there with them?"

"They get whiskey."

"Did you drink any whiskey?"

"Yep. They give me whiskey. Like this." He cupped his hands

and raised them to his mouth.

"Did you buy whiskey from Molly?"

"Naw. They buy. She bad. She bad woman."

"Did you ever see Bosh Tillson drink whiskey?"

"Objection!" Harp roared. "Mr. Tillson is not on trial here!"

Mabry's eyes rolled and his teeth started to chatter. Renfrow rushed to his side and put his hands on the man's shoulders. Deputy Bigler and Marbles Rickman ran to Buck Junior. Even Dexter Landiss, the court reporter, came forward with a tin cup full of water.

"I will see counsel in my chambers," Judge Theed directed. "Court will resume in ten minutes, the witness being recovered sufficiently."

"Judge Theed," Prosecutor Harp began, before the judge had time to close his door. "Your honor, I am disturbed at the turn this trial is taking. Never before in all my experience, have I been forced to object with every breath. The antics of opposing counsel—"

"Now, your honor," Zach interrupted, "I believe that we know the defendant did not kill Molly Capps. But you ruled to let the jury decide. And, of course, we agreed to that, Mr. Harp and myself."

"But we didn't agree," Harp snapped, "to come in here and make a fool out of me! I can't just stand by and allow you to create your own carnival! I won't!"

"Counselor," Zach said, "I am making no attempt to create anything here but a defense. A strong doubt as to the guilt of my client."

"Yes, but you—"

"Now wait a minute! Wait a minute!" Judge Theed said. "We agreed to go forward with this trial! Mr. Harp, I'm going to let you prosecute. Mr. Renfrow, I'm going to let you defend. I think we all know, deep down, that that jury's going to convict Plez Shoe anyway. No matter what we do. We'll give him every chance we can."

"But, Judge Theed," Harp wailed. "This case grows more bizarre by the minute. Bordering on outrage, your honor! First, you qualify children as witnesses. Then, the feeble-minded. Counsel has meandered all around the edge of justice. Hinting that first one and then another killed that woman. Anybody is guilty but his client.

Surely you don't intend to allow the testimony of a simpleton to implicate still another man, your honor!"

Your honor," Renfrow said, "this case *is* highly unusual in a number of ways not mentioned by Mr. Harp. For one, lay it to progress, or luck, if you will. This is the first actual trial I recall in this county involving a colored person, with any kind of effort made toward real justice. For another, I personally have never defended a man whose innocence I felt more certain of. The business of Bosh Tillson's guilt or not is for another day. This is Plez Shoe's day in court. And for hundreds like him. Let us keep to the task. Let's find out if that jury is, as you say, going to convict this man.

"There are a lot of things going on in this county. Drinking, fighting, bootlegging. Yes, even murder. But the only thing Plez Shoe has done is to go down to that river and catch him a mess of fiddler cats. If this jury can convict the man for that, then he stands guilty. But not to the charge of murder! I beg your honor—"

"We'll hear what Mabry has to say," Judge Theed told Harp.

The three returned to the courtroom. Mabry appeared calm.

"Now, Buck Junior, there's nothing to fear," Renfrow said, once more fastening his attention on his witness. "The people are out there because they want to hear you tell the truth. Remember? Nobody is going to hurt you."

Zacharias repeated his question. "Did you ever see Bosh Tillson drink whiskey?"

"Mr. Bosh drink no-o-o whiskey. He get mad. Get mad. Mean."

"Did you ever see Bosh Tillson buy whiskey from Mad Molly—er, Mrs. Capps?"

"No, siree! She bad woman. Mr. Bosh say. He want she—want she go dead."

Voices burst forth. The judge pounded for order. Zach walked toward the defense table. Buck Junior began to whimper. The noise abated when the throng realized it was unable to hear. The quiet restored Mabry's composure.

"Buck Junior, you ever have a dream when you sleep?" Zach questioned. "Do you know what a dream is?"

"Buck Junior know," he said, nodding. "Wake up. P-h-h- h-t. All gone. Lot of dream. P-h-h-h-t. Like that." He clutched at the air with his fingers.

"Where is Molly—Molly Capps—now, Buck Junior?"

"She go dead."

"Do you know who killed her?"

"She talk bad. Say bad name to Buck Junior."

"Did *you* go down there to that river? Did *you* steal her whiskey?"

"No-o-o. Put the money on the stump."

Milton Harp jumped to his feet. "Objection, your honor! This whole episode is a travesty!"

"No further questions, your honor. The defense rests."

"P-h-h-h-t. Like that." Buck Junior said from the witness stand.

Chapter 14

A rain had blown from up-river during the night but it did not diminish the number gathered to watch the final hours of Plez Shoe's murder trial.

Judge Theed had recessed after Buck Junior Mabry's testimony the previous day. Nothing remained now except the lawyers' final arguments to the jury. The lawyers sat at their respective tables inside the enclosure. Milton Harp wore a recently pressed pinstriped suit, and his old confidence. Zacharias Renfrow wore the same red bow tie—and more than likely the same shirt—he had worn the two previous days. Nora Ballard and Mathelde Phelps hurried into the courtroom and located vacant seats in the back next to Paul Luke.

The double doors swung open revealing Plez. He walked before Deputy Bigler to the assigned table next to Zach.

"Plez look bad," Ruby Gem cried, clutching Rejoice Tolliver's shoulder. "Like he ain't been eating!"

"Papa!" Willie Shoe shouted, hearing his mother's words. "Papa, wait! I got it!"

The boy broke from his mother's grip. As he ran he pulled a bundle wrapped in newspaper from inside his shirt. "Papa! Papa!" Willie Shoe yelled, worming his way through the spectators.

"Stop there! You, boy!" Marbles Rickman, the bailiff, shouted. "Catch him!"

Plez, about to sit beside Zach, heard his son's voice. He tried to turn, lost his balance and fell against the table. He looked down at his handcuffed wrists.

"Let him see his daddy," someone in the crowd called. "It won't hurt anything."

"Yeah," another agreed, "the boy ain't done nothing."

As he reached the enclosed area Willie Shoe grabbed for the wooden gate.

A firm arm grasped him around the middle. "Whoa there!" Paul Luke said.

"I got to see my papa," Willie said, squirming. "Got to give him—" He held the newspaper bundle aloft.

"Here! That ain't allowed. Give that here," Marbles Rickman said, pushing through the confusion.

With a lunge Willie Shoe freed himself and scrambled through the bannister gate.

"Papa! Here!" Willie tried to hand him the package, but Plez sat without moving. The boy gave him a strange look, then for the first time, he got a view of the shackles on his father's hands. Willie Shoe pulled back.

"I'll take that," Rickman said. He grabbed the little newspaper packet. "What's in there, boy?"

"Hold on, Marbles," Paul Luke said, reaching his side. "No need to get worked up." He put his hand on Willie Shoe's shoulder."What do we have here?"

"Biscuits and fried side meat's all it is," Willie said. "My dinner. But it be for papa, now."

"Your papa will be well fed," Paul Luke said. "I'll see to it."

He stooped and looked into the boy's eyes. "Now you run hug his neck and we'll go find your mother. She's worried, you know."

"Get him out," Marbles Rickman barked to Paul Luke. "Now. I'm in charge here. This is a court of law. Where's your respect?"

Paul Luke looked at Rickman. After a moment he said pleasantly, "Come, Willie," and took the child's hand. Rickman turned on his heel and resumed his post at the door.

After the commotion Judge Theed and the jury entered. Judge Theed called for the prosecutor's summation.

Laying his papers aside, Milton Harp rose and strode toward the jury box, buttoning his coat as he walked.

"Gentlemen," he began, "you have already used two days listening to the testimony in this case. You've heard the facts as presented. Molly Capps, a defenseless white woman was murdered, brutally and in cold blood. The defendant, Plez Shoe, was undeniably placed at the crime scene. The commonwealth submits that there were two people at that crime scene. Plez Shoe...and...the dead woman, Molly Capps.

"The defense has tried to show that there is a lack of evidence. Gentlemen, murderers never intend to leave *any* evidence! The

dead woman's *sister*, Mrs. Gilly McCrae, was certain enough to bring a *complaint* against him. A grand jury was certain enough to bring an *indictment* against him. Many in this community are convinced that Plez Shoe is guilty. Based, mind you, gentlemen, on their own conclusions, not on hearsay."

"Your honor, can we stick to the facts as laid out earlier in this room?" Zach said wearily.

"An appropriate suggestion. Do that, counselor."

Harp glanced toward Renfrow.

"The defense, in this room, has even tried to besmirch the name of the murdered woman. Members of the jury, it is easy—and weak—and, I think, lily-livered—to accuse the dead!" Harp bowed in silence for a moment.

"The defendant ran off to another *state* and had to be *dragged* back here to face justice. Gentlemen, what does this tell us? Does an innocent man run?"

Some members of the jury stirred angrily. Plez whispered to Zacharias, who shook his head without answering.

"Gentlemen of the jury, when you go into that room to decide your verdict, there is a scene I want you to examine over and over in your minds." Harp lowered his voice.

"A boat rocking on soft little waves. A devoted lady goes to that raft house expecting to visit her beloved sister. Instead, she makes a grisly discovery. The dead body of her dear one, throat slashed, blood colder than the flowing Mississippi."

Noise poured forth. The judge pounded.

Harp strode to the jury box and put his hands on the railing.

"Imagine further, gentlemen; the murderer—the killer of that poor, unfortunate woman—dabbling his bloody hands in this same river. Making good his escape to another state, to what he supposed would be freedom!"

The prosecutor looked toward some women and children sitting in the front.

"But, gentlemen of the jury, there is a way to defend your families. To release yourselves. To be forever freed from this scene. The very river cries for revenge! It's your duty! Find the defendant, Plez Shoe, guilty of killing Molly Capps!"

Milton Harp sat down, his triumphant gaze fixed on Zacharias.

The old lawyer rose, nodding toward the jury.

"Gentlemen, most of you, all of you, I dare say, know Plez Shoe, the defendant here; a member of this community—for how long now? Forty years?

"For the past two days, you have been subjected in this courtroom, not to evidence, but to the lack of it. This case should never have come to trial. The most significant fact here is this: Plez Shoe, the defendant, a Negro—a colored man—*was* brought to trial in a court of law."

"Objection! The court is not on trial here. Counsel is trying to appoint himself a judge." Harp said. "That approaches contempt, your honor!"

"Sustained. Watch your words, counselor."

"The defense has shown that Plez Shoe went fishing down at that river, God only knows how many times," Renfrow continued. "Plez hooked a mess of fish. He went home, and nobody died.

"That lady, the deceased, was down there at the river wheeling and dealing with moonshine whiskey. Plez was down there fishing. The prosecution has not even attempted to show that Plez Shoe was ever a part of any kind of lawlessness."

Zach walked to the jury box. "The very nature of Molly Capps' kind of business has built-in risks. When you operate outside the law, your associates are, of necessity, outlaws. Are common criminals worthy of trust? Can they trust one another?"

"Objection!" Harp cried. "Counsel does not appear to understand what your honor established early in this proceeding. The victim is not on trial here."

"Sum it up, counsel!" Theed said.

Zach threw a stony look at Harp.

"Plez Shoe goes out and catches fish. He brings them home to his dear wife. She fries them up and they eat. That's a part of his life, of their life. Left alone, that's what he would have done yesterday. Or the day before. Or today. And again nobody would have died.

"The only difference between what happened last July and what happened all the times before, is that Molly Capps was killed. Now, another thing *wasn't* different. Another thing that happened that day which had happened before, was that someone saw Plez Shoe on the river road. And—and, oddly enough, that sighting of Plez Shoe coming back from the river is the prosecution's whole case. Gabe Findley, among others, has seen Plez Shoe on that road many times. And there was no killing.

"Nobody cares that Gabe Findley was on that same road that same morning. Going, so he said, to tend his cornfields in the river bottoms. He could have been accused of this murder with as much reason as Plez Shoe. Ah, but Gabe Findley is a *white* man."

"Objection, your honor, "Harp said. "Counsel is waltzing with racism. This trial has been fair and unbiased, your honor. I would hate to see it cheapened at its conclusion."

"Objection sustained. Mr. Renfrow, this court will not tolerate prejudicial statements. You sweeten your words, now."

Zach, with a curt nod toward the bench, resumed his discourse. "We have shown proof that other people went down there to that shanty boat.That a retarded man, pitiably afflicted though he is, had a reason, distorted though it is. A motive. A propensity. Yea, you have heard even a *confession*, as it were. A confession absolving Plez Shoe of that bloody and brutal crime."

"Objection!" Harp shouted. "Only one man is on trial here, your honor."

"Sustained. Mr. Renfrow, you seem to be neglecting your client. Talking a lot about other folks. Careful!"

"Yes, your honor," Zach replied.

"But this court is to concern itself only with Plez Shoe. If Plez ever had a motive to harm *anybody* it would be those who masquerade around here in sheets. Those that burn crosses. Disrupt worship of the almighty God. Plez Shoe has a pretty good idea who these white-sheeted folks are. We all do. Yet Plez has not brought harm to any one of them."

"Objection! Your honor, the defendant never mentioned identifying any sheets. The commonwealth challenges the defense counsel's statement."

"Sustained. You know what he's talking about, Zach."

Renfrow walked to his table and stood beside Plez. "Plez Shoe does not use alcohol. The person who murdered this woman is involved with the only thing Molly Capps had to do with this community. Bootleg whiskey. Or the consumption thereof." Zach looked from the jury into the crowd. "Mad Molly didn't run around here wrapped up in sheets."

Hissing and murmurs rippled through the courtroom. The judge's thumping restored silence.

Harp rushed toward the bench. "Objection, your honor! He's conjecturing about sheets again."

"Sustained. Now, Zach, I don't have to tell you we can't honor any second-guessing in this court. Stay in your own pasture."

Zach walked close to the jury. "Members of the jury, many intelligent men, men learned in the law, have stood on this very spot. They have put forth their best persuasive arguments before a jury like yourselves. And having so done they sent that jury back there to deliberate its verdict. Who can tell when such an effort will or will not be for naught?

"I *do* know, *can* tell you one fact from experience. When that verdict comes back `guilty,' the defense counsel does some soul searching. A man may consider for a lifetime, some other words he could have used. Words that might have saved an innocent client."

Zach stopped. Lail Stratton shifted his weight. After a time, in a voice inaudible beyond the front row of the courtroom, Zach continued. "I could not live with myself thinking of words I could have said but did not say, should you, God forbid, find Plez Shoe guilty. You must be persuaded by now, gentlemen of the jury, not by words only, but by evidence. Plez Shoe is an innocent man.

"You may also suspect that one who took this very witness stand, one not legally competent, is the actual killer. If so, then there is a *perilous* danger. The danger that you might think, `The man who possibly killed Molly Capps is one I have scoffed at as one without value. A nothing in the affairs of this community.

"`Now he has taken a life. My God! What have I done to this man? Do I share in this man's guilt?'"

"Objection, your honor," Harp said with exaggerated boredom from his chair. "Does counsel have a late afternoon train to catch? He seems to be in no hurry to finish this rambling of his."

"Mr. Harp," Theed said, looking the prosecutor in the eye. "Justice tempered with mercy approaches divine law. It's too wet to plow. Let him continue."

"Thank your honor for your indulgence," Zach said.

"That man, dull-witted though he be, waged a war within himself. Finally, he killed. Pushed until the weakened vessel flew apart. The pieces lie at our own feet."

The rain stopped. Nothing moved in the courtroom. Harp half stood but said nothing.

"All this could go through your minds, members of the jury. Just as it could the mind of any other accountable soul." Zach said. The old lawyer was a battle-scarred gladiator, all right. "Accountable soul." When did he decide to loose that term on the jury? Was it spontaneous? Now he had them heading for glory or perdition on this verdict. Harp sagged deeper into his chair.

"Each of you could think if I let Plez Shoe go, then what? I am indicting myself to some degree, in the crime of this man that I scorned. This very reckoning is something we may all, each and every one, have to face in our own mirrors."

Zach fastened his eyes on the jury. "Now another thought might occur to you, gentlemen, while you are sitting back in that little room. You could think there is a way out. Hang the nigger! After all, this one got a trial. Nobody really proved he wasn't guilty!"

"Yeah, hang him!" one spectator whooped.

"Hang that church-going family man? That man kicked by the boots of some of the most respected men in this county when he was at worship? Hang him? Would this bring escape from that other guilt?"

"Objection! Now counsel wants to try the jury," Harp said.

"Sustained. Make your argument relevant, counselor."

Renfrow moved to the center of the courtroom. "These people in this audience will not be in that jury room with you. Yet, they have heard the same witnesses, the same words. You are not alone. But the chance to make this community bigger than it could ever imagine itself to be is on *your* shoulders, and yours alone. The chance to stand erect, to do the thing that's right *is* yours. This awful trespass we've uncovered we can overcome together, with God's help. But today let us undo today's wrongs. Plez Shoe is an innocent man.

"Whatever your decision is, you're going to have to live with it till the day you die. After that, it's what history will say when you're gone. How just or how unjust you were.

"The heavy business of conscience is on your shoulders. The weight of injustice multiplies. Time soothes many pains, but error compounded is not one of them.

"Gentlemen, you heard the charge the day this trial began. You don't have to say who killed Molly Capps. Your burden is to decide if the commonwealth showed enough evidence to prove Plez Shoe guilty. Do not fail this innocent man.

"Go on back there, members of the jury. Create greatness for yourselves. And may the Lord God walk with you into that room!"

From somewhere below came the faint strains of a harmonica, as the legless Simon Jarrett began another day.

Zacharias Renfrow walked to his table and leaned into his chair.

Naomi Ruth Lanier entered the courthouse a few minutes before ten the next morning. She spotted Zacharias and went to his side.

"No news?" she asked.

"None," Renfrow answered. "They requested that some of the testimony be read over, though. Some parts more than once."

"Morning, Miss Naomi. Morning, Zach." Whitsworth Moseby approached them.

"Good morning, Whitsworth. Had a busy night, did you?"

"That's the stomp-down truth," Moseby said. "Hardly ever hear of a judge putting a jury into seclusion like that. Glad he done it though. Sure filled up my boarding house. Had all them rooms rented at the same time only once before, as I recollect. Fifteen, twenty years ago. Big boat burnt in the river. Them newspaper people come from all over."

Whitsworth walked away grinning.

"Zach, the evidence is overwhelming in Plez's favor. The jury should have been back in five minutes. That it wasn't may be a grim prophecy," Naomi Ruth said.

"If they were of a mind to hang a rope and a guilty verdict around his neck they could have been back in five minutes, too," Zach reminded her. "In my thinking the delay isn't bad. At least they're arguing. Good may come of that."

Nodding, Naomi Ruth changed the subject. "You were powerful, Zach. All through this trial. I kept thinking of the `Bucket of Blood' murder, years ago."

"That does go a ways back." He looked pleased.

"Nobody gave you any odds on winning then, either. But you kept right on. Digging, arguing. You were young. People said you were wet behind the ears, and worse. But in the end you won." Her voice softened. "Afterward the newspaper called you a bright young attorney for the commonwealth, or something like that. People still remember, Zach."

"But there's never been a case like this one."

"Jury's coming in! Hey, Zach!"

"Where's Harp?" Zach shouted.

"Library in the basement. Somebody went to fetch him."

Zach managed to get ahead of the throng, but Naomi Ruth found herself almost trampled. Judge Theed was speaking when she reached the second floor.

"After a dozen or so communications with this jury I am convinced that these men deliberated as hard as humanly possible. They dedicated themselves to fairness.

"However, I am now persuaded that they will not be able to reach a unanimous determination. This jury is, in my considered opinion, deadlocked beyond any hope of a decision. Therefore, these jurymen are hereby dismissed of their obligation in the case of the Commonwealth of Kentucky versus Plez Shoe for the murder of Molly Capps."

In one motion all eyes swung toward the jury, each spectator attempting to decide who among the twelve held out for acquittal, and who for hanging.

The jurors' eyes were on Plez. Some flitting expression, a perceptible movement might establish guilt or innocence once and for all. But Plez's face revealed nothing but bewilderment.

A glimmer of satisfaction lit Nursie Baltz's eyes. Quickly he turned a piercing gaze toward Theed as though assessing the judge's own reaction.

At the same instant Plez twisted around, his eyes scanning the crowd.

Zach put his hand on Plez's shoulder. "We haven't lost, Plez! We're still in there! We haven't lost!"

"Thank you, gentlemen," the judge said to the jury. "I commend you for your service. You are now free to go back to your crops.

Your personal pursuits. Your daily lives. Counsel, I will meet you in my chambers in five minutes."

Sheriff Claude Meeks approached to return Plez to jail.

"What this means, Plez," Zach explained hastily, "is that you're not free. You're not condemned, either. They'll probably try you again. I'll do whatever I can."

The onlookers poured onto the stairs, the black coterie last, according to custom; but this time, by choice. Some were crying for joy. Some bowed in prayer.

Ruby Gem, clutching Willie Shoe's hand, leaned against Rejoice Tolliver. Reverend Antioch Pike put his arm around the boy's shoulders.

"Everything going be all right," Rejoice chanted.

"What happen, Mama?" Willie Shoe tugged on Ruby Gem's sleeve. "They let my papa go?"

Ruby Gem appeared lost for an explanation.

"They didn't exactly let him go," Reverend Pike interceded. "But they didn't say guilty, either."

"He going home now?"

"We got to wait and see," Reverend Pike said. "Wait and see. And pray and pray, and wait and see."

"Ain't the praying that bother me," Willie Shoe said. "It's the waiting and seeing."

Paul Luke tried to reach Zach's side, but failed, propelled toward the double doors by the throng. Nursie Baltz waved one hand in a loose salute.

Paul Luke grabbed the back of a bench and sat, a lone watcher in the quickly emptied room. Voices surged from Front Street.

"I knowed Lanier would get him off."

"It ain't over yet!"

"Maybe the nigger ain't guilty. The half-wit might of did it!"

"Nah, it was the nigger."

"Lanier will pay for this, come next election. You mark my words."

"All I can say is I shore miss them corn squeezings."

"You'll go to the devil for that!"

A grim foreboding settled over Paul Luke. Plez's trial had ended for the present, but uncertainty shadowed the days ahead.

Chapter 15

Zach Renfrow entered Judge Theed's chambers and closed the door, muffling the noise from the street. Milton Harp, his face ashen, strode about the room in vague circles.

As Renfrow settled himself Harp paused and stared at the chaos below. His wife, Madolyn, waiting at their home in another county, surely did not yet know of his discountenance.

Harp had married Madolyn with her father's doubts pursuing him like a swarm of hornets. The man would not be above hiring some clandestine observer to telephone from Moseby's Boarding House the minute the jury's decision was known. The Louisville law firm that the old man headed might even now be dissecting Harp's failure.

Harp shook his head as though trying to disentangle his thoughts. He and Madolyn must have a child right away. It would give him an edge in the old man's game. Voters' memories are notoriously short. That, coupled with a small amount of good fortune, would secure his election, proving his worth to Madolyn's father. One day the old man would surely offer him the partnership he coveted.

Judge Standish Theed, one foot propped against his desk, watched the pandemonium in the streets."What are your plans, Mr. Harp?"

The question startled Harp. "Judge, I—I—fired every volley I had. There just isn't any more evidence to be uncovered."

"Well, are you going to try him again?" Zach asked.

"I—don't know. Even I must admit that what little evidence we have is pitifully weak."

"I believe, Mr. Harp, if you'd faced that fact sooner you'd never have brought this case to trial in the first place. Yet, Plez is back down there in that jail right now. Seems to me you'd be better advised considering what to do with the half-wit."

"I know, I know," Harp said.

"What are your plans, Mr. Harp?" the judge repeated.

"I don't—I'm thinking."

"A day or two back the three of us sat in this very room," Zach said. "And we said just about the same thing you just said a while ago. There really wasn't any evidence. You could have cut Plez Shoe loose right then. But we agreed it would be better to go on with this trial. Let the jury settle it.

"We've done that. We gave it to the jury. They heard that little mite of evidence you were looking at that day. And they heard other things that Nursie Baltz was able to uncover." Zach looked over his glasses at Harp.

"I don't think you should put Plez Shoe through that ordeal again. And I don't think, Mr. Harp, you should put yourself through that again, either."

Judge Theed turned from the window. "The jury voted ten to two in favor of acquitting Plez Shoe."

Harp turned on his heel to face Renfrow. "There's no way I could pick up ten guilty votes from a jury when there were only two the first time around. We don't have enough evidence to get a rightful conviction. I am not going to wa—spend any more time on this case."

"Are you releasing him?" Zacharias said.

"I'm not going to prosecute him further."

"Are you releasing him, then?" Theed asked sharply.

"Yes."

"When?" Zach said. "And what about Mabry?"

"Zach," Judge Theed said, "Sheriff Meeks wanted to keep Mabry for questioning yesterday, but I discouraged it while the jury was deliberating. So Meeks had Mabry watched. Picked up by now, I imagine."

The judge looked at Harp. "Mr. Harp, don't you think we might ought to hold Shoe until some folks can come down here to get him? Assure his safety? People around here aren't used to this kind of a situation."

"Three o'clock seems like a reasonable hour to me," Harp said. "Enough time to get his family down here. Agreed, Mr. Renfrow?"

Theed interrupted before Zach could answer.

"Now, counselor, we've made a little history here, you know. You're through with Plez Shoe. The jury is through with Plez Shoe.

But I'm not all that confident that Hunt County is through with him. Maybe we'll know more about that when word gets out that he's being released."

The judge examined his knuckles. "I've been thinking on this thing quite a bit. Trying to figure out a prudent solution for all concerned. I can come up with only one answer. That is to—uh—suggest to Plez Shoe that he'd probably be a lot happier—and safer—if—if he just found himself another community to live in."

"You mean tell him to leave, judge?"

"Well, damn! Damn, Zach! There are several political careers at stake here." Judge Theed pulled a cigar from a velvet humidor. "Ordinarily, a jury trial would have ended the whole question, but we just landed right back where we started. Now you know, Zach, Plez Shoe will never live this down in Hunt County." Theed tasted the cigar in choppy bites, smacking his lips. "It appears to me it'd be much better for him—and his family—if they just went on off."

"It would be better for m—for us all," Harp said.

Zach watched Theed put a match to his cigar. The judge, it seemed, was a man with honor shining from one eye and ambition from the other.

The clock in the courthouse tower clanged half past two just as Paul Luke reached the private staircase that spiraled through the heart of the courthouse. The town and all its establishments appeared deserted. A silence too large engulfed Front Street. It overshadowed the adjacent Court and Ohio Streets and seeped its way to the river. Paul Luke knocked on Judge Theed's door. When there was no answer, he knocked again.

Finally the door opened. The judge, himself, rumpled, with a cigar clenched between his teeth, stood before Paul Luke.

"Zacharias Renfrow said you wanted to see me before I take Plez out of jail."

"Yes. Yes, I do," Theed motioned him inside. "Glad you stopped by." The judge cleared his throat and studied the top of his desk.

"Paul Luke, old Plez is a free man. That means he's free to go anywhere he wants to go." Theed removed the cigar from his mouth and squinted at Paul Luke. "Now I've been wondering just how free *we* are. Folks, if they're honest with themselves, will have to

say Harp did everything he could to hang Plez. And again, Renfrow did everything he could to defend him.

"Paul Luke, *you* stuck by Plez all the way in his defense." Theed flipped ashes into a crystal vase and examined the smoldering end of his stogie. "And folks would have to admit I was fair. But considering how people are not always honest with themselves I have a feeling it would just be a little bit easier for us to go on with our business in this community, if folks didn't have Plez Shoe around here as a reminder. Might be best too, for him, and his wife, and that boy if they all just went on back down there to Memphis, where he hid out."

Paul Luke stared at the judge. "Judge, you just said Plez is a free man."

"Hell, Paul Luke, he is!" Theed chewed his cigar and moved toward Paul Luke."It's just this. Everybody's life would be better if he went on back down to Tennessee. Shoe's got to realize that we saved his life—after all, the rest of this county is *accusing* us of saving it.

"You've got your own political future to consider. And so have I. You'd best think on it, Lanier."

A few minutes later Paul Luke left Theed's office and headed toward the jail behind the courthouse. Several farmers stood near the door.

"Come to get your nigger?" Loo Garvey asked, glancing up. Some of the others laughed and winked.

Paul Luke gave Garvey a direct look. "Plez Shoe is being released by the sheriff of Hunt County. I noticed you there at most, if not all, of that trial. You heard the testimony offered against Plez, and you heard the testimony in his defense. Now, do you honestly think he is guilty? Or not guilty?"

Garvey looked away. "Well, I don't know," he pushed his straw hat to the back of his head. "There ain't ever been a nigger accused and took around here before what wasn't hung. Not any that I know of."

"By the neck till dead." Goose Wiley said. Goose was Mae Dee Corlew's son-in-law. He spent most of his time playing checkers in front of the courthouse, listening to public opinion.

The livelihood of Goose Wiley's five little children depended

on the demand for their mother's sorghum molasses. She squeezed the syrup from cane in early winter, her white jennet treading around and around a sorghum press in the east county woods. "Till dead," Goose repeated.

"But this one got a trial," Paul Luke said. "Do you think he's guilty or innocent?"

"I don't believe I could of convicted him," another farmer admitted.

"I hear he's going to have to leave here. That true, Lanier?"

Paul Luke stared straight into Loo Garvey's eyes. Garvey glanced at the others but they said nothing.

"No, Plez doesn't *have* to leave," Paul Luke said, his words deliberate. " What's important now is that he *can* leave if he wants to. But that's up to him. This morning some folks around here wanted to *hang* him, but like Judge Theed said, now Plez is a free man."

Paul Luke started walking away, then he turned to face the men. "We're all free to leave," he said, heading toward the jail.

Early the next morning, Paul Luke took his coffee cup and walked onto the veranda. He looked toward his tobacco fields. The yellowing stalks had been cut and hung on straight sticks then stacked into teepee-shaped cones. The crop waited to be loaded on wagons and hauled into barns to dry in the rafters. As the crop dried, its aroma would emerge; a fragrance pungent as the perfumes of India, saturating the air; bewitching, yet faintly unpleasant; to be remembered, to be longed for, season upon season.

Paul Luke turned to find Plez standing at the bottom of the steps.

"Good morning, Plez. Come on up. I was just about to go looking for you."

"I've done me some tall thinking, Mr. Paul Luke. I been trying to figure how folks feel, now I been let out of that killing. White folks, I mean. Reckon I set half the night pondering. Then all the sudden I say, `Plez, you ain't done no wrong. You going hold your head up, like always.'

"You know what else I reckon, Mr. Paul Luke? White folks don't think I kilt that lady either—they done let me go! Praise God

A'mighty! He done let Plez go!

"Mr. Paul Luke, I'm thanking you for what you done. Standing by me. I going repay you. I don't know how, but I'll find some way. The Lord going show me a way."

Paul Luke set his coffee cup down on a white wicker table. "Seeing you free like this is pay enough for me, Plez. If anything, more of a chance for me to repay you. In time, perhaps people won't think much about it any more. I'm happy that you won't have to go through that again. You know you've made some history here."

"No, sir. I didn't make nothing in that jail house down there. Wasn't nothing I could make. Just wait."

"I'm talking about the trial. That business with the court will be remembered for a long time, all around this state, I imagine. It's going to take most folks here some getting used to."

Paul Luke turned his coffee cup around in its saucer like a circle of quicksilver. After a time he spoke, choosing his words with care.

"You know, Plez, the judge, and Mr. Renfrow, and myself, all of us—and even Mr. Harp—we have your best interests at heart. We have done a lot of thinking, just as you have. Trying to work this thing out for the best. Well, Plez, we all, to the man, believe that life might be a great deal more pleasant for you, and Ruby Gem, and Willie, if you just decided to move away, go to your kin. On down to Memphis, say."

"Move? Move, Mr. Paul Luke?" Plez sank to the top step.

"Plez, the last thing I want is to see you leave. You know that. I spared nothing to get you that trial. The sheriff did a good job protecting you in the jail. Now it's over. Nobody knows what's to follow. A few hoodlums in the night could undo it all. I'm afraid, Plez." Paul Luke's voice became urgent. "You can't spend the rest of your life dreading darkness. Scared of the shadows." Paul Luke moved to the porch swing behind Plez.

"Think about it, Plez. You know this incident will be around a long time. Even though the court set you free, some people forget slowly. Maybe not in our lifetime. Or Willie Shoe's either, for that matter." Paul Luke leaned back in the swing. "Making a fresh start where you have kin. It's not a bad notion."

"But folks here mostly think—they believed Mr. Zach—"

"Yes, most people do believe that you're innocent." Paul Luke's voice sounded distant. "But it's the few—the cross burners, the hell hounds—that could make your life one of misery. Now, Plez, you're a free man. Do whatever you want. Take this advice or not. But we think, the four of us, that you'd be safer, and probably happier in the long run, if you took your family and left. Start fresh. There'd be no hooligans to torment you. In fact, I'm not so sure but that my mother agrees."

Plez turned toward Paul Luke. "Miss Naomi Ruth, she think that, too?"

"She hasn't actually said so—"

Plez rose to his feet.

"Now, Plez, give this some thought. It's *your* decision. Whatever you do, I'll stand by you. Give you every support I can." Their eyes met. "You know you have a place here as long as you want it. Although there is a good possibility you'll have to stay close, at least for a while. Whatever choice you make you can count on me. I believe you know that."

"I got to think me on this. Talk to Ruby Gem. Pray over it."

Plez started down the steps and stopped. He turned back to face Paul Luke. "Today? You don't mean leave today, does you?"

Paul Luke waved his hand. "Oh, no, not today. If you decide to leave, wait a few days. But not too long. In the meantime, just be careful, that's all. Don't take any chances."

Plez walked along the path that edged the tobacco field. When he neared the hog pen, Willie Shoe ran out and caught him in an embrace.

"I love you, Papa! It be dreadful lonesome around here while you gone. I powerful glad it be all over with now." The boy clung to his father. "Papa, I been doing me some thinking."

Willie Shoe took Plez's hand and they began to walk.

"Now you out jail and all, you reckon could I go on back down there where Miss Meriwether at tomorrow? Reckon can you fix it now, Papa? Miss Naomi Ruth and Miss Mathelde, they try learning me. But I be missing that school, Papa."

Plez bent down and picked the boy up in his arms.

"Let's talk to your ma, boy." Plez looked toward the horizon. "Let's go talk to your ma."

Paul Luke, besieged by guilt, sat on the veranda for a while. He longed for childhood's carefree indifference; for an old man's wisdom; for escape to some less complicated time.

Tension mounting, he sought the open fields, tramping in long strides. His thoughts whirled like frost bitten leaves in the bitter winds of winter.

Plez, freed from a hangman's noose, now faced a new danger, one not subject to protective walls, nor judicial limits. Free. But not from the prejudice that lay smoldering, ready to flame.

Paul Luke stopped to pull at a limb wedged against a fence post. It loosened readily. He staggered backward, cursing. This county had elected him to the Kentucky State Senate, his proudest moment. Had it now reduced him to his lowest?

Judge Theed's words hounded him. His thoughts dissolved into confusion. With faith in the masses why should he fear losing his own senatorial seat in the General Assembly of the Commonwealth?

"The people make mistakes," Lucas Lanier once told him, "but over the course of time, these mistakes are inevitably righted. Trouble is, history records events in hundreds of years, but a man's life is measured in scores."

A black object, a shoe heel, lay in his path. Probably one of Plez's. Paul Luke visualized Plez following a mule team across the field. Plez would keep right on plowing till sunset in a shoe with no heel. That was his way.

Paul Luke strode forward. A discarded tobacco stick lay across his path. Stooping, he seized it and gazed down its length, judging its strength, its sturdiness. Its worth. The stick neither curved nor warped. Surely another Lucas stick. Paul Luke turned it over. The underside crumbled into rot and splinters.

The wind stirred. A cacophony of voices swept across the empty field. *"Where is that fishing hole, Plez?...."* *"Harp did everything he could to hang him...."* *"There was a cross burning. He was afraid...."* *"People are not always honest...."* *"This county is accusing us...."* *"Come to get your nigger?"*

"Damn!" Paul Luke brought the stick down across his knee.

Breaking it easily, he flung the pieces from his sight. "Damn the bastards to hell!" He raised his head toward the sky. Instantly a blurred image—a face, a child—rushed into his mind. "My God," he said, bowing his head.

Paul Luke crossed the field with rapid strides. Fragments of dead grass crunched and clung to his shoes like straw fingers. Arriving at the point where his own land intersected the road to Wickliffe, he chose the road.

When he entered Zacharias Renfrow's law office the sun had traveled two hours past noon.

"Zach, did you start all this?" Paul Luke demanded. "Or am I just now uncoiling from around the fingers of the people in this county? Theed thinks Plez will cost me my senate seat. That is, unless he leaves Hunt County." Paul Luke sat on the edge of a cut-velvet chair. "There could be trouble. I think Plez's safety is threatened, even his family. And I might draw an opponent. Lose the election next time around. But—asking Plez to leave is hard."

Zach closed the law book he had been studying. He came around his desk and leaned against it, facing Paul Luke.

"I haven't started anything. Things were just fine when Molly was selling down on the river. Peddling that moonshine. It might not have been proper. But speaking generally, Paul Luke, things were fine, compared to where we find ourselves today. Things were fine for you, and me. Fine for Plez. Fine, maybe even for Prosecutor Harp." Zach seemed about to chuckle. "But events have overtaken us all. Events coupled with our own instinct to survive.

"Whether you know it or not, or he knows it, Plez's life has changed. Hell, Paul Luke, it can't be the same again, ever. The decent people will leave Plez alone." He drew on his pipe. "But they're not the ones we're concerned with. It's those few out there who will keep on kicking the dirt. Busting the clods, till they start a dust storm. You know the ones.

"And I'll tell you something else. They're not above hurting Plez. Burning him out. Or worse."

"You're right, of course," Paul Luke said. "I agree. But I'm not so sure sending him away isn't the worst hurt of all."

"Paul Luke, I'm not convinced that you aren't being a tad selfish, wanting to keep Plez around. Somebody for you to run out and pick up every time some riffraff trips him. Oh, I know you owe Plez. Saving your mother—and yourself, too—in that fire, the way he did. He's dependable. Works hard. But you've done well by him. Furnished him a place, good wages. Going against the law to get his boy in school. You must have known that wouldn't hold up. What's more, Plez would've hanged for that murder if you hadn't hired Baltz to investigate. Kept after it the way you did with the Mabry thing."

Zach put his hands on his knees and peered over his glasses. "No matter what you pick up, Paul Luke, at some point in time, you're going to have to put it down again."

As the sun was setting two evenings later Paul Luke sat on the veranda considering Zacharias Renfrow's words. A wagon pulled into view. Plez was driving, accompanied by two young tobacco workers. The two men remained seated when Plez stopped the mules at the edge of the field, and jumped to the ground. He walked toward the veranda, pausing at the bottom step.

"I've been expecting you, Plez." Paul Luke stood. "I suppose you had a chance to talk with Ruby Gem about—about the conversation we had?"

"Yes, sir, I did. We talked it all out that night."

"And—ah, did she agree that it might be—?"

Plez stood straight, his eyes unwavering. "Mr. Paul Luke, I have something to say. Now it ain't out of no misrespect, or anything like that. We talked about it a whole lot, me and Ruby Gem. What we decide is, we *want* to go. That's exactly what we want to do. Get out from this county.

"I didn't kill nobody, but I be locked up in that jail anyway. Mr. Harp, he be always looking at me and yelling that I kilt that woman. And all the time, he must know I didn't.

"We love you all, Mr. Paul Luke. You and Miss Naomi. You all saved my life. Mr. Zach and Mr. Nurse Boss helped me a whole lot, too. But, yes, sir, we want to go. We make up our mind. That's what we aim to do.

"I reckon you stood by me because I saved your mama's life. And now, you saved mine. You don't have to worry about looking after Plez no more." He glanced toward the waiting wagon.

"Yes, sir, we going plumb away. Not to Memphis, neither." Plez looked straight into Paul Luke's eyes. "We going North, to Illinois. Me and Ruby Gem going work. We going put our boy in school."

The sun sank toward the western horizon, making silhouettes of the wagon, and of the triangles of tobacco stacked farther away in the distance. Beneath the steps crickets chirped.

"Illinois," Paul Luke mused. "Then you made your own decision." He stared at a crack in the wooden plank floor. Plez shifted his weight.

"Your family and mine are twined together like the roots of wild roses, Plez. So far back.... God, I hate to see you go." Paul Luke walked to the edge of the steps. "Things change. I believe for the best, this time. Not easy, but best. When you cross that river, Plez, you will take a part, a big part, of myself with you. Do you know what I am saying, man?" Paul Luke's voice broke. He rushed down the steps, reaching for Plez's arm.

"Take one of my wagons and a team of mules." Paul Luke regained his composure after a moment. "Any one you want. It's a small token at best."

"Much obliged, Mr. Paul Luke," Plez said carefully. "We figure on to leave early morning. Tomorrow. Reckon I best get on, now. I got some friends going help me."

Nora Ballard rose and dressed early. She dabbed toilet water at the hollow of her throat and grabbed a pale pink sweater. Today was Saturday. She planned to take Saree into Wickliffe to choose fabric for a new coat. Amos McCann would be along later in his car, after his mother gave the financial report at today's meeting of the Presbyterian Ladies' Christian Aid Society.

"That can't be Amos," Nora murmured, hearing a soft knock. "It's much too early." On her way to open the door she glanced out the window. A horse and carriage waited in the dirt road.

"Why, Paul Luke! What's the matter?"

"Nothing—. Everything. Plez is leaving. The whole family. Moving."

"Oh. I'd heard they might. When? Surely not today?"

"I'm afraid so. In a few minutes. A flatboat to Illinois."

She stood looking at him.

"I came to—will you ride to the river with me?"

"Me? Why me?"

"I'm going to need somebody with me when that raft pulls away from Kentucky."

Baffled, Nora nodded and took his arm. Little Granny came from the kitchen just in time to hear his last remark.

What appeared to be a small army stood on the river bank. The flatboat waited, secured by a rope tied to a cypress trunk.

Mathelde's children arrived in a red carriage pulled by a black and white pony, purchased by their grandmother on a recent shopping trip. Saree had ridden from the wye with them, having slipped away while her mother dressed. She scrambled from the wagon as soon as it halted.

Most of Reverend Antioch Pike's congregation stood around crying and embracing each other. The whole assemblage wore hats and their Sunday meeting clothes.

Spotting Willie Shoe, Saree ran toward him. The boy watched, but his enormous eyes stared past her.

"Miss—Miss Meriwether—"

The teacher reached his side, her breath coming in quick spurts. "I just heard you were leaving this morning, Willie. I was afraid I'd be too late, but I hurried." She thrust a bundle wrapped in newspaper toward him. "This is for you. Some jasmine to plant at your new school. I'll—I'll think about you, Willie."

Turning, she rushed away, auburn hair sleek above the collar of her green jacket. The astonished children watched until she vanished behind a fringe of beech trees.

Saree stared at Willie Shoe. Tears filled her eyes and rolled down her nose. "Oh, Willie Shoe! I don't want you to go!" She threw her arms around the boy.

Ruby Gem quickly pulled her away.

Willie Shoe bent down and rubbed Old Puddin's nose with his forefinger. "I'm going get me a dog. My papa going get me a fine dog."

A commotion erupted at the river. Whips popped as men tried to force the reluctant team onto the flatboat. The mules balked, with nostrils distended, walling their eyes. Shouts mixed with the sound of jangling harness. The wagon creaked under its load. The whips snapped again and the mules lunged forward. The wagon rolled behind them onto the floating platform that soon would be bound for Illinois. Plez had chosen to take Gyp and Tag, an unmatched set of young mules that was his favorite.

"Those mules always looked their proudest when you held the reins," Paul Luke said. He grasped Plez's hand one last time and turned away.

Willie Shoe stood close to Ruby Gem staring at Saree, at the red wagon, at Mathelde's children—his dark eyes troubled. One by one the black congregation shook hands with the woman, or fell on her neck, sobbing. As the last one passed, Ruby Gem turned toward Willie Shoe.

"Tell your friends goodbye, and God's blessing." She took his hand and started toward the boat.

Saree figured she'd never see Willie Shoe again. Or maybe they would pass on the river when they were grown up and never even know it. People change when they get old. Sometimes they don't even like each other. But Willie Shoe was her friend, and that would never change.

He had taught her how to mock the red bird's cry. In spring they ran through fields together, gaping at baby rabbits hiding in the red clover. When blackberries ripened Willie Shoe went into the brambles first, beating the snakes away. Once when a skunk sprayed Old Puddin', Willie Shoe felt so sorry that he sneaked a whole slice of ham off the breakfast table. Saree laughed at Willie holding his nose, not breathing, while Old Puddin' swallowed the meat in two gulps.

Saree remembered playing on a forbidden raft one spring day. When she toppled into the swirling river, Willie Shoe pulled her out. He didn't tell, either, so that she escaped Little Granny's high words.

And Willie Shoe always knew when the mayhaws ripened. In August he could find trees laden with sweet, wild black cherries low enough for her to reach along the edge of the road. Saree wondered if he remembered to take his old straw hat with the holes in the brim that let the sun shine through.

"Are they still in Kentucky?" Will Roy asked, walking up beside Paul Luke with his sisters. "Or are they in Illinois now?"

"Oh, I think they're still in Kentucky," Rebecca answered.

Paul Luke gazed across the space. Reverend Wakerich's words flitted through his mind. *"We all find ourselves in this situation at one time or another. Not too exactly sure where we are."* With a boundary as indistinct as that line out there in the river, perhaps his father Lucas Lanier, too, would have wavered.

"Well," Paul Luke said, roughing Will Roy's hair, "I'd say Plez is in Illinois by now."

The flatboat reached the middle of the river and headed upstream toward Central Illinois. Plez watched a grove of cypress saplings, staring till it passed from sight, and with it, his secret fishing hole.

"Soon as I learn to write I'll send you a letter," Saree murmured. "except I don't know where you'll be." She turned back to Rebecca's new pony cart, her shoulders slumped, downcast eyes hiding tears. Paul Luke and Nora returned to his carriage and watched until the boat became small as a bird in the distance. He clucked to the black mare and they headed away from the river.

"Thanks for being there with me today when I needed you."

"Paul Luke, you've been there for me. Remember? You still are, I think at times."

"Ah, Nora, Nora, how much I could be, if only—"

"Paul Luke, don't!" She grabbed his arm. They rode in silence until, at length, he spoke.

"Nora, we've shared dark days before. Days when the world seemed like a jumping off place. Today is another." He held the reins taut. "Tell me. I have to know what you think. Did I do the wrong thing?"

She toyed with a pink button on her sweater. "I think this was the only way." She tossed the hair from her eyes, and looked at him. "He, the three of them, would have suffered more. Why prolong it? We both know some people won't let things die." She twisted the pearls at her throat. "If it hadn't been for Mama, I don't know where I'd be now. But for Plez—for him, life would have been near unbearable. Always waiting for something. Nothing. Who knows?"

The reins slackened and the black mare slowed her pace. The carriage rolled through threads of autumn sunshine. Paul Luke opened his mouth to answer Nora, but he reconsidered and remained silent until they reached the Ballard house.

"Nora," he turned to her, but she was standing, ready to depart the carriage. He jumped to the ground and she took his outstretched hand. "Nora, we have to finish this conversation." He put his hands on her shoulders, looking into her eyes.

"No!"

"Sooner or later, we have got to talk. My God, Nora, after all this time! Why you're—"

"No—please—" Panic filled her eyes and she wrenched loose from his grip.

"This can't go on," he said. "It's absurd!" Paul Luke leaped into the buggy and popped the black mare with the reins. Nora stared after him, then stumbled toward the house.

Paul Luke returned from Nora's and stepped onto the driveway. Tobe Bandy, his new caretaker, rushed forward. The black mare snorted and arched her neck. Paul Luke entered the quiet house and started down the hallway. Over and over in his mind he watched the flatboat pass out of view, followed each time by the image of Nora's face, her eyes.

Naomi Ruth called when Paul Luke approached her door. He entered her sitting room, the scene of countless conversations between them in the past. "How do you feel?" she asked in her direct way.

"Confused. Uncertain. Pretty wretched, actually."

"Guilty?" Naomi Ruth raised her eyebrows.

"That, too. Mother, I helped send Plez away. I could have discouraged it. Stopped it, perhaps. I had my own selfish reasons not to. I feel guilty as hell, to tell you the truth."

"What do you mean?" She picked up her shuttle and began tatting a strip of lace.

"My own career. My future in this state. I've had pretty good support up till now. I like serving the people. It's a way to help make things better. I imagine I've been called `a nigger lover' behind my back. Probably will be to my face before this dies down. That's all right. I owed Plez. But after the trial—"

"After the trial, Plez would be a constant reminder that you brought a Negro to trial. `Got him off,' some might say."

"Yes. Just about every person in this community liked Plez. But as a group, they couldn't admit it. You know how people are. They overlook facts. Distort them. The truth becomes lost. Whispers and.... Well, they've destroyed more than one career." He spread his hands. "I don't want that for myself."

"You did for Plez what no one else could, or was willing to do. You helped bring justice closer to us all. For the first time in this county, being accused and colored has not meant an automatic lynching." Naomi Ruth watched him, the lacemaking abandoned. "What you did, Paul Luke, won't stop with Plez. He is merely the first. In another generation, maybe, people won't see a man's color before they see the man."

Paul Luke paced across the floral carpet to the window. Wheeling, he faced Naomi Ruth. "But I sent Plez away, Mother! You can't deny that."

"Paul Luke, no human being is totally selfless! No matter what one gives away, there's always a little piece kept back. Plez and his family, they had a secure life here, and not much else. That would have been threatened, too, had they stayed." Her fingers rearranged the ivory pins holding the hair at the nape of her neck. "Slavery ended a long time ago. Negroes aren't stuck on farms anymore. Sometimes devotion to an idea, a promise, has to end, too. It hurts us all. You, me, Plez. But let them make a better life, Paul Luke. There are schools in Illinois. Willie Shoe won't have to sneak in, or carry wood, or be humiliated."

Naomi Ruth picked up her tatting again. "You're concerned about what others think. Don't deceive yourself. You'd have insisted that Plez stay here if you'd thought that best for him. There's no stain on your honor."

Paul Luke stared out the window a long time. "Sometimes this room is so full of thoughts. They come and perch on my shoulder like—remember that pet crow Mathelde had? It used to do that."

He turned to leave, brushing his lips across the top of her head.

He walked through the house. An end to devotion, death to a promise? He examined the idea, turning it over in his mind, studying it; light and dark.

At some point in his thinking devotion and honor had blended, become one, the way colors merge. Even his good intentions had begun to collide with each other. That wasn't the way he wanted it. *"We all find ourselves at times not exactly knowing where we are."*

Paul Luke eased into the wicker settee. A few weeks ago he had dallied there with Lockett Lakewood. Weeks or eons? Where did he go, that light-hearted rogue?

Zach Renfrow's words came to mind. *"No matter what you pick up, at some point, you have to put it down again."*

Well, he had kept those promises; stumbled under their weight, but he had not betrayed his word. Perhaps the time was come to lay it all aside.

Even Plez had released him. *"You don't have to worry about looking after Plez no more."* Plez himself recognized the fulfillment of that debt. *"You stood by me because I saved your mama's life. And now, you saved mine."*

He considered the promise he'd made to Nora, the loyalty he'd shouldered. He had waited, biding his time, for the impasse to dissolve. Surely he had earned the right to turn his back, to walk away if he chose. To pursue his own direction. To do what he believed to be best for himself; for others, as he had done for Plez.

Hearing footsteps Paul Luke looked up. Naomi Ruth was standing beside him. "Zacharias came by while you were at the river.They had a hearing yesterday for Buck Junior. Didn't waste any time. Zach said some were afraid after the children testified."

She touched his shoulder. "Buck Junior's to be committed. Claude Meeks is taking him to Hopkinsville." Naomi Ruth turned toward the house. "I thought you should know."

An hour later Paul Luke's carriage stopped before the Ballard house for the third time that day. He leaped to the ground, barely pausing to secure the black mare's reins. Nora appeared at the door after his second knock.

"Nora, get your sweater. We're going to finish that conversation right now."

Chapter 16

Mathelde Phelps stepped from a trolley at the corner of Broadway and Jefferson Street. The train steaming its way from Wickliffe seemed to have gobbled her own meager energy, rather than the coal chunks in its bins.

Pulling her brown bowler over her ears, Mathelde turned down Broadway toward Water Street. Three blocks away, the Illinois Central Railroad Hospital overlooked the Ohio River. She needed a few moments to plan today's visit with her husband. The October air might nip some sharpness into her thinking.

Fleming Phelps' progress during his three months of confinement had been erratic. "He looked like a hat rack holding up a sheet," she once told Naomi Ruth.

Dr. Rusk Trevathan, the specialist, was a recovered victim of the pandemic Spanish flu outbreak five years before. Perhaps because of his victory over a deadly disease, Trevathan lacked tolerance—or compassion, Mathelde thought—toward a patient whose progress stalled.

"Your husband is—weak," Trevathan told her. "Depressed. You cannot expect to heal a man who offers himself up to futility. When you come here, do you worry him with home matters?"

Mathelde bristled. "Of course not! If you think that—Dr. Trevathan, of course my husband worries. But not because of me. We have children. He's lonely. He—" Seeing the skepticism in Trevathan's eyes, she bit her lip. "I'll—I'll try to do better."

Finally she reached Water Street, paralleling the Ohio, sighing at the end of the walk she had chosen. *I am not ready for this*, she thought, staring at the building.

The rectangular-shaped hospital consisted of two complete floors, and part of another. A window faced the street from the partial third floor above the entrance. A grove of turkey foot oaks surrounded the building, creating a drape against the sunlight.

Her own father, Lucas Lanier, once camped on that site as a

young soldier under the command of Confederate General Nathan Bedford Forrest. The Union forces had over-run Paducah, making it a Northern stronghold.

"It was a bad time, daughter, I can tell you." Her father's voice had grown faint, moving away from her into the past. A little girl of six or seven, Mathelde had left her dolls and play dishes to stand beside his chair. She watched the gold chain bobbing on his vest as he spoke.

"The Yanks came at us, but we stood them off. Took turns firing what few arms we did have. Things getting worse all the time. Mounts starving. Men sick. Wounded. No food. Medical supplies used up. Gone. Everything gone." Lucas frowned, leaning forward on his Irish blackthorn cane. Without knowing why, she shivered, brown pigtails jiggling on her shoulders.

"It was that desperation drove General Forrest to attack Paducah. March twenty-first, '64. Like yesterday. Three hundred of the South's finest men, all dead!" He rose and paced across the parlor, his cane striking the floor with angry bumps.

"And Paducah burned! The blue devils set her afire. Sixty houses to ashes. People's homes. Up in smoke!" The cane struck again and her tin dishes rattled in the corner.

"Never, never consort with a Yankee, daughter!" After a while Mathelde stole back to her dolls, wondering exactly what it was she had been forbidden to do with the Yankees.

Mathelde hurried into the lobby, pulling her jacket closer. The atmosphere discouraged germs, but it stunted the growth of other things, too, including hope. The institution whirred like a well-tended motor.

Reaching Fleming's door, Mathelde knocked. A withered man she did not recognize opened it wider than necessary.

"I'm sorry, I thought—" Looking past him, Mathelde glimpsed her husband propped on his pillows. The little man chortled and left, waving like some gnome from a fairy tale.

"Let me guess." Mathelde took Fleming's hands. "He's a dwarf. His name is Rumpelstiltskin and he was teaching you to spin straw into gold. Right?"

"No, not a dwarf at all. That was Thomas Weil. Lived in

Paducah all his life. Worked at the round house before—" Fleming had not been so vibrant in weeks.

"Oh? And does he also sprinkle magic dust that dispels illness? You look improved."

"No. Actually, Thomas talks about history. This town's history. He knows a great deal. For instance, were you aware that Jews were ordered out of Paducah during the war? Thomas Weil's family was forced to leave. Something the Commandant of the army dreamed up. `Violating trade rules' I think he said. Can you imagine?"

"That *was* heartless."

"No doubt about that. I'm considered a carpetbagger, I guess."

"Oh, people aren't still thinking about that war, Fleming. It's been sixty years!"

"Anyway, some of the patients make jokes. But even that can be agitating. Yes, it *has* been sixty years, plus a couple of foreign wars in between. But then when the trial came up—"

"The trial? You mean Plez? The murder trial?"

"Well, it was just a word or two in passing. Nothing to be concerned about. A lot of people know your brother."

"You just tell that `lot of people' that they can mighty well take that up with him. Or with me!"

"Never mind! I shouldn't have mentioned it."

She sat beside his bed. "I brought penmanship samples from the children. Leighza smudged hers and refused to send it, so I had to sneak it out." Mathelde spread the papers across his sheets. "Aren't they nice?"

He leaned toward her on one elbow. "Mathelde, remember the picnics we used to have in Cincinnati? The games? The silly stories? I hate that the children—we—have to miss all that now. And so much more." He caught her hands in his. "A sorry father I turned out to be, deserting the children like this."

"Fleming Phelps, you have not deserted the children! I won't listen to this! Feeling sorry for yourself takes a skill you don't have. You're very poor at it."

"Not sorry for myself. Sorry for the children. You. No father. No husband."

"The children miss you, Fleming, and so do I." She gathered

the writing samples into a neat stack, aligning the edges with her fingers. "As for the other, well, Paul Luke is there. He can't take your place, of course. Heaven knows, he would never try. But—"

"Which brings up another point." He moved the papers to a table beside his bed. He lifted her chin. "I'm thankful Paul Luke is there. They need him. But they're not his children! And with all his own problems, here he's had to stand in for me."

Mathelde rose and moved across the room. "He isn't standing in for you. The children don't think that. You were always strong. There, when you could be. Oh, they know you, Fleming."

He was at her side, holding her in his arms. She clung to him. Allowing herself one luxurious moment of desire, Mathelde touched his tawny hair, his eyelids. She leaned into him, longing for his strength to support her once again, struggling to pull free of the eagerness between them.

"You are incredible, Mathelde. And the children—"

"Fleming, the children, they're soldiers on your side in this war. They pray for you every night. They'd be here right now if they were allowed. You know that."

"How can they regard me except as weak? Ill. Not there when they need me." He wandered to his bed, his voice hollow.

"No, when you were well and strong, all those years. That's the father they remember. And love. They believe you will return. Well, and strong."

"I love you. Mathelde, I love you, and I love them. I *will* be well. I know it. I believe it." They touched in a brief embrace, and she turned to leave.

"*Mathelde!*" Tears filled his eyes. "Mathelde, I must see them."

"Fleming! What can I do? You know they can't come here."

"I realize that. But you have to find a way! And for God's sake, they mustn't see me! Not now. Not like this. Mathelde—"

"I'll try. I promise. I will try." She darted into the hallway.

When Mathelde reached the lobby Dr. Trevathan stood half-hidden near the outer door. He beckoned her into his office.

"Mrs. Phelps, after the latest series of x-rays and tests, we believe we now have an accurate diagnosis. We're more than ninety-nine percent certain that your husband has tuberculosis, consumption, if you will. Something we've suspected all along."

She caugh her breath. "Does he know?"

"Not yet. This diagnosis is only an hour or so old. You wouldn't have been permitted here had we been certain before. The prognosis is good. Your husband physically was—is—a strong man."

"What—what will we do?" She meant herself and the children.

"Isolation, of course. Right away. Rest and fresh air. Fortunately, the disease appears to be confined to one lung. We can go in, collapse the lung, and cure it." Easy.

"What does that mean, collapsing the lung?"

"A surgical process using a needle. The air is removed. The lung draws itself together. The disease—shrivels away." Trevathan toyed with the pencils on his desk.

"No! The lung dies, doesn't it, Dr. Trevathan? I know about that. The lung dies, along with the disease, and the person's *body* shrivels. And his strength. Fleming would be—changed, different. Wouldn't he, doctor?"

"Well, possibly—er—to some extent. A possibility. But it is a cure. Your husband could be home in a short time." His voice flowed like a stream over smooth stones.

"And weak, a shadow for the rest of his life? Your perspective is wrong, Dr. Trevathan." She stood.

"One other thing. This means that you, yourself, have been exposed. In all likelihood you won't become ill, but take care. We recommend an examination in a few weeks. A precaution."

She watched him, her turquoise-blue eyes steady. "What more can you offer for Fleming?"

"There is one other avenue we might consider." Trevathan fingered a paperweight. "A colleague of mine, Dr. Trudeaux, built a sanitarium in New York. In the mountains there. Trudeaux died a few years back. But I believe the work he started is continuing—an exercise and diet regimen. Amazing results. Very expensive, though." He looked at her, a question in his colorless eyes.

"Money is—I mean, the railroad is paying for Fleming's treatment. And even if it weren't—the children and I have—help. Dr. Trevathan, we'll pay."

Mathelde walked a few blocks down the street to Miss Lurlie Downey's boarding house, a school chum of her mother's. Mathelde had become a regular guest during overnight trips to visit Fleming, grateful for the calm that flowed from the older woman like Moses' stream in the wilderness of Zen.

After dawdling over lunch, Mathelde telephoned for someone to meet her at Wickliffe.

So it happened that when Mathelde settled herself beside her mother in the carriage a few hours later, she brought the usual greetings from Miss Downey. Tobe Bandy, in Plez's place but lacking his patience, held the reins. He urged the black mare into a trot, racing with the sun against darkness.

"I have to get the children there, Mother. But Fleming doesn't want them to know. I feel like the man in that story with the sword hanging over his head. The thread may break at any moment."

"Take the children to Paducah, Mathelde. Stay at Lurlie Downey's. A weekend excursion. Any excuse will do."

Tobe Bandy pulled the black mare to a halt in the driveway.

"Oh, and take Saree," Naomi Ruth added, dismissing Bandy with a wave of her hand. "She's seemed a bit mopey since Willie Shoe left. But with her geared up the others won't have much chance to wonder what's going on."

"About Saree—" Mathelde clutched her mother's arm. "Something else has been nagging me almost since I came back from Cincinnati. I shouldn't let it bother me, I know. But—"

Mathelde's hand trembled on Naomi Ruth's arm. "At least three people have mentioned it. Even Miss Downey today, innocent as anything." Mathelde chose her words with care. "I've been gone all these years. There's talk about Paul Luke and Nora. I don't know how to answer. You must have heard it? That Saree—Mother, what am I to—?"

"Oh, I haven't been spared. Yes, I've heard what you've heard. But only hints. Nobody has enough backbone to come out and say it to my face." They walked toward the house. "But I have faith, I believe if Saree were Paul Luke's child he would not deprive me of having that little girl put her arms around my neck and call me grandmother. Paul Luke has never said a word about that story, and I won't accept any of it. But I do believe the truth will out, sooner or later."

"Have you ever asked him about it?"

"No."

"Why not?"

"You explain, Mathelde. Why did *you* come to me, instead of him?"

One Saturday a few weeks later Mathelde stepped off a streetcar near the Illinois Central Hospital, followed by Leighza, Rebecca, and Saree. Pulling an imaginary cord and clanging lustily, Will Roy clogged along behind them. For once Mathelde welcomed his exuberance. The children would surely hear her heart pounding without it.

"Look, children! That's the hospital where your father is. The nurses' shift is changing. See?"

Will Roy froze in mid-clang. The girls stopped in their tracks. They looked at Mathelde, then turned long, slow gazes on the building. Without intending to, Mathelde glanced upward toward the window in the third floor isolation unit. What if Fleming didn't get her letter? What if they didn't give it to him?

"Is that where he is?" Rebecca asked, observing her mother. "Is he at that window? Watching us?"

"Oh, I doubt it. I imagine he's in his bed, resting. Getting well for us."

"My daddy's in there, and I'm going to see him!" Will Roy cried, dashing toward the door.

Rebecca grabbed his loose overalls, almost losing her balance.

"Let me see my daddy!" Will Roy cried. He kicked his sister and flailed the air with his arms.

His mother reached his side and firmly gripped his shoulder. "We have to go. Miss Downey has made us lunch. We mustn't keep her waiting."

The tiny window on the third floor was half open. Mathelde fancied she saw a shadowy figure.

"Now, shall we wave a good-bye to Daddy's hospital? No, not over there. Over here." She positioned the children in a line directly opposite the window.

Saree waved half-heartedly. A sick daddy would be better than no daddy.

An air of peace settled over Mathelde like the autumn sunshine

on her back. Leaves crackled beneath her feet, and a gust of wind dropped more on her shoulders. She turned, leading the way toward Miss Downey's.

"That's Miss Downey's house. Third from the corner," Mathelde said as they turned onto Bridge Street.

Saree stopped.

The house had not two levels, but three. Pink marble columns supported the roof. A corner tower, complete with a lightning rod, reached above the porch past the third floor. It was like a fairy house, and when the door flew open Saree expected a princess to emerge.

Instead it was Miss Downey hustling them inside for lunch. "Do you like the fresh creamed peas?"

"Oh, yes," Leighza said like a misguided diplomat. "We like them, we just don't *prefer* them."

It seemed that the meal might end well when Miss Downey appeared with a tray of gingerbread. "Oh, gee," Will Roy breathed, licking his lips.

But before passing the first piece to his mother, Miss Downey doused it with a ladle of lemon sauce. Ruby Gem launched her gingerbread under mounds of whipped cream. Will Roy's expression became melancholy.

The meal ended with gingerbread to spare. The children escaped to the sunny front porch. Miss Downey, raising her eyebrows like the backs of two swans, promised that her grand nieces from next door would soon appear for an afternoon of "glorious fun."

As if on cue a small girl, flaunting an assortment of orange-colored curls, came skipping up the sidewalk. Another girl followed. Her hair was plaited in elaborate French braids doubled behind her neck, suggesting the insignia of an admiral's aide.

"I'm Frances Earline," the braided aide announced, "and this is my sister, Emma Lou. Auntie told us you're from the country. We're to show you around and be polite."

"We're from Cincinnati," Leighza said quickly. "My sister and brother and me."

"I'm not!" Saree said.

"Oh, then *you're* the little country girl," Frances Earline said.

Saree puffed herself up in her red sweater until she resembled a gamecock ready to lob a fatal spur into a foe.

At that moment Mathelde and Miss Downey emerged from the parlor balancing demitasse cups. The distraction presented an opportunity for retreat that Frances Earline seized. She moved toward Emma Lou and edged behind her back.

Mathelde related to Miss Downey how she fulfilled her promise to Fleming. The shadow of the rose trellis crisscrossed Mathelde's face as she talked. Miss Downey nodded.

Saree and the children played on the steps all afternoon.

Near nightfall they walked down to the river. Saree hardly could comprehend that it was the same Ohio River they had at home; the one that met the Mississippi at Wickliffe, rolling to God knew where.

"It looks different because at home there are trees all around," Rebecca said. "Here there are no trees. Just some buildings. If you got on a boat, you could get off right at Wickliffe."

Saree knelt and put her hand into the cold water, listening to it slap the shore. She thought of Willie Shoe, then she pulled her red sweater close and buttoned it.

After supper—cold beef sandwiches and milk—the children sat on the steps eating Miss Downey's homemade shortbread.

"Want to play `Who's Got the Thimble?'" Frances Earline called. In the circle of light a silver thimble glinted on her index finger.

Saree thought the game the most amusing ever devised. When it was her turn to hide the thimble in somebody's cupped hands, Saree would cry, "Who's got the thimble?" signaling the others to guess which secret one she had chosen.

The next morning, following services at the Presbyterian Church, Mathelde herded the children toward the trolley.

"Look!" Will Roy cried, pointing toward the third floor of the hospital. "That window up there is still open."

"Yes. Why don't we all rest a minute on that bench right there?"

Leighza chased her brother until the streetcar screeched to a halt. They scurried toward it, Mathelde following behind. The window on the third floor closed with a gentle thud.

The train, its brakes catching in spasms, pulled into the

Wickliffe depot and stopped. The children yawned, except for Saree.

A bit of light seeped through the dingy office window onto the platform, and Saree spotted her mother. At Paul Luke's insistence Nora had accompanied him to meet the train.

"We saw big houses with lots and lots of steps. And street lamps. And the river same as ours," Saree blurted, running into Nora's arms. "Oh, Mother, why don't we live in Paducah? Granny could rake leaves and I—"

"S-h-h-h. I want to hear it all. Everything. But you must think about it until we get home, so you can remember every little bit. For Granny, too. Come, it's late."

"Thimble, thimble, who's got the thimble?" Saree sang, as Paul Luke lifted her into the carriage. The words echoed in the rhythm of the wheels as they pulled away from the station.

They rode in silence. All the children fell asleep except Saree. When they neared Corlew's Store Mathelde suggested that Paul Luke take her and her children home then double back to Nora's.

"I hope you don't mind," Mathelde told Nora. "But my three are sleeping and Saree is still wide awake. By the time you get home she might be sleepy, too."

When they stopped in the driveway Paul Luke lifted the sleeping Will Roy into Mathelde's arms. He carried Leighza, while Rebecca, blinking, followed. Nora and Saree waited in the carriage.

"Who's got the thimble?" Saree sang out.

"Dark tonight," Paul Luke observed, returning. He flicked the reins over the black mare's flank. "It's after nine o'clock. I wonder where the moon is?"

"Oh, it's the dark of the moon," Nora said. "Mama mentioned it. She always plants according to the moon. Her fall garden, you know."

"I have a lantern here somewhere, if you're afraid."

"What's there to be afraid of in the middle of nowhere? The horse knows the road. I do wish Cutter's Bridge had side rails, though. That's the only place. Horses can see in the dark, can't they?"

"She's not likely to run off Cutter's Bridge."

"What's that? Over there?"

Paul Luke looked. A light flashed in the woods beyond the

road. "Must be a hunter with a lantern. He's not up to any evil, though, carrying a light like that."

"I suppose not. Whoever it is, is in a big hurry. Must be chasing a fox."

They reached the corner again where Corlew's store stood unseen in the darkness. Saree, still awake, bolted upright and began to chatter. Her mother, sighing, allowed her to continue. "Will she ever go to sleep?" Nora wondered aloud. She turned to face her daughter. "There's school tomorrow, young lady."

"S-h-h-h!" They were nearing Cutter's Bridge. A sleepy bird shook itself and fluttered to a higher limb. Saree paused to listen, then continued jabbering.

"Quiet!" Paul Luke pulled the black mare to a halt. The buggy stopped. Nora and Saree looked toward Paul Luke. An owl hooted.

"What—" Nora began, and froze.

From somewhere a voice sounded, its ghostly echo rising and falling in the blackness. Now and then a light glimmered and disappeared.

"It's coming from the bridge.Something's wrong. I'm going down there." Paul Luke handed the reins to Nora. "You stay here. If there's trouble, don't wait. Slap the mare with the reins and hold on tight. Get home!"

His footsteps faded. Nora clutched the reins. Saree scooted close. Darkness engulfed them. In the distance a voice rose, muffled and wild.

"Nora! Nora!" Paul Luke said at her shoulder. "There's been an accident! Someone's hurt."

"Who is it?"

"I'm not exactly sure. Find the lantern, quick!"

Nora fumbled. Her hand touched glass. "Here!" she reached toward the direction of his voice. "I'm coming, too! Saree, you wait here. I'll be right back."

They were off. The phantom chant went on and on, then ceased. After a few minutes Saree crawled from the carriage and headed through the inky dark toward Cutter's Bridge.

Nora reached the creek on the heels of Paul Luke. He held the lantern aloft and she peered toward the water.

"But what's—?" Nora's hand flew to her mouth. She gasped.

A Model T lay on its side in the shallow water. The top caved inward as though battered by a giant fist. Pieces of tin lay about, forming waterfalls in the rippling stream. A few bits of paper floated across the water. The lantern in Paul Luke's hand smoked, expelling kerosene fumes into the air.

"But what—?" Nora began again. She stopped. From beneath the overturned vehicle the lower part of a body could be seen. Its legs looked like sticks that had been wrapped in cloth and pushed into shoes. The water tugged gently and the legs appeared to float. Paul Luke took Nora's elbow. Others stood just outside the lantern's glow. He raised it, revealing Reverend Antioch Pike and Tar Jack.

"We was huntin' possums," Tar Jack said, "when we come on it. Me and the reverend here, and my boy."

"The boy takened one of our lanterns. He went through the woods to fetch help." Reverend Pike said. "We try to pull him out the water, but they be snakes. One lantern wasn't near enough to see by. Water snakes all around. Lord have mercy! We be praying when Mr. Paul Luke come up."

"Mama!" Saree slid down the muddy bank behind them.

Paul Luke thrust the lantern toward Nora. He turned and picked Saree up in his arms. "It's all right."

"What happened?"

Nora came forward with the lantern, looking toward Saree. Saree's gaze fell on the feet protruding from the stream. She wriggled from Paul Luke's grip. She remembered those shoes, the odd metal buckles on the toes. The lantern light glowed in a crooked circle. *The flame blazed, became a torch, flared, crackled. A rock. A dull plop. Blood. She ducked under a bench, her eyes wide. She gasped. The shoes at the camp meeting, the shoes the Klansman wore.*

"It's Amos McCann. I was afraid it was his car." Paul Luke held some water-soaked papers toward the light. "Order forms from the canning factory."

"He's dead, isn't he?" The sound of Nora's voice seemed to float out of the night.

"I'm afraid—"

"Take Saree away!"

Wrapping his arms about Nora and Saree, Paul Luke herded them up the bank. "I'll be back in a minute!" he called to the men at the creek.

"Oh, Paul Luke!" Nora sobbed, leaning against his shoulder. "How can we tell Miss Nellie?"

The morning following Amos' death all the mirrors in Miss Nellie's house were turned to the wall. A cold spell blew in, bringing clouds that tarried just above the rooftops. Frost crackled. Neighbors stole into Miss Nellie's kitchen bearing enormous platters of food; church members sat day and night beside the casket in the cold parlor.

At the church Reverend Wakerich spoke in a somber voice. The choir sang, muffled by Georgie Rae Gardner's organ. Nora supported Miss Nellie, their faces white as the satin where Amos lay.

At the cemetery the wind stung Saree's face, burning her cheeks. Earth fell over the casket, swelling into a mound of wet clods. Saree never liked Amos much, but he had been kind letting her ride in his car. For a long time she thought about his shoes and the brush arbor flaming that night in Illinois.

Chapter 17

"**A** white Christmas makes a light graveyard," Little Granny said, peering at snow flurries through the kitchen window. "Or a green Easter," she added, seeing Nora's look. The most recent grave at the Presbyterian cemetery was that of Amos McCann.

"Ah, well," the old lady turned from the window, "Saree and I must deliver a dozen geese this morning. We'll take her little wagon."

Saree stirred her oatmeal. Her plans for this, the day before Christmas Eve, did not allow for going house to house with a wagon full of goose carcasses.

Raising and selling the fat fowls was Little Granny's way of earning money to insure a joyous Christmas for Saree. Long before December she "took engagements" from families whose Christmas dinner traditionally included one of Laura Ballard's succulent birds. From Thanksgiving until near Christmas the geese seemed to absorb every minute of the woman's time. They gobbled down an incessant river of milk and cornmeal mush, ground corn, and pork fat. A kerosene lantern burned in the hen house, and clean straw was strewn daily on the floor; all done for the morning when the geese would be brought forth one by one, hissing and flapping, for slaughter at the butcher block. Little Granny's merciless axe chop-chopped the outstretched necks, dispensing the whole gaggle in one bloody hour of carnage. After dipping the headless remains into her kettle of scalding water Little Granny plucked the feathers and eviscerated each fowl before hanging it in the smokehouse.

That afternoon, their deliveries finished for another year, the two trudged homeward through snow.

They passed Nellie McCann's house, abandoned a week after Amos' death. Snow blanketed the roof, and drifted against the sagging fence which enclosed the yard. Dried weeds leaned along the fencerow. A lone wagon wheel rested against a post, its missing spokes leaving gaps for filtering snow.

They rounded a curve in the road. Blue smoke from their own

chimney became visible. Nora would have hot soup and cornbread waiting in the kitchen.

Paul Luke's carriage stood in front of the gate, a plaid blanket covering the black mare. Holding cups of steaming cider Paul Luke and Nora met them at the door.

"I was just ready to leave," Paul Luke said, turning toward Little Granny, "but I was here to inform you that you're coming to our party tonight as a guest. And no, your offer to help is not accepted. Mother's arranged for all the help she needs." He drew on his leather gloves.

"Now if you find yourself able to fend off all the beaux coming to escort you." He started out the door. "And if you're so inclined, I'll be honored to have you on my *other* arm."

"Wait!" Nora cried, snatching her mother's shawl from a chair. Throwing the wrap about her shoulders, she closed the door behind her, bowing her head against the wind.

"Paul Luke, I want to ask you this now. I didn't want to bring it up tonight, with the party and all. Would—would you take me to the cemetery tomorrow, after church? With Miss Nellie away, there's no one else—"

"Nora, you know I'll be pleased to take you out there—or anywhere. All you have to do is say when."

The snow stopped falling at twilight, giving place to early darkness as Paul Luke's carriage pulled up before the Lanier mansion. He jumped down to assist Nora and Little Granny. Saree, wearing a red velvet coat trimmed with white fur at the collar and cuffs, bounced from the buggy. Quelling her excitement for a moment she paused, hands clasped, and drew in her breath.

Great swatches of cedar boughs festooned the veranda, meeting above the French doors. At each corner golden cherubs halted in mid-flight with trumpets raised, forever poised to sound a joyful blast. On both sides of the entry white tables held dozens of flickering red candles in hurricane lamps. The doors stood open. Inside, the air throbbed with warmth. Faces were illumined by a blaze of lights from the hall.

Leighza and Will Roy drew Saree into the vestibule. Nora, at Paul Luke's side, smiled while he and Naomi Ruth welcomed each

guest with handshakes and embraces. In the hall a stack of jellies, pickles, and homemade confections—Christmas offerings from their guests—grew enormous.

"The whole place smells so—so *Christmassy!*" Margaret Theed said, entering on the arm of her husband, Judge "Outlandish Standish" Theed. Their daughter, Pansy, followed.

"Just exactly like a Christmas painting!" Judge Theed pulled Paul Luke aside. "Now, Paul Luke, I—uh—I like my punch a little bit— um—sour." He winked, holding two fingers apart. "If you get my drift."

"Yes, indeed, Judge, I know exactly what you mean. I think you can be accommodated in the kitchen. Discreetly, of course."

Judge Theed made a beeline toward the kitchen. "The judge does enjoy his coffee on a cold night," Margaret Theed said.

A horse's hoofs clattered like a fanfare on the driveway. Lockett Lakewood alighted from her carriage in a flurry of emerald velvet. Beech Marcom and his wife, Letitia, Lockett's mother, followed. Nora stopped smiling and stood as though the merriment had ceased. In an instant she recovered.

"If I'd never seen Christmas before, I'd certainly have seen it tonight!" Beech Marcom said, taking Naomi Ruth's hands, and kissing her cheeks.

Lockett, seeing Nora, paused before rushing to her. "Dear, you are absolutely radiant!" Lockett said, hugging Nora.

Lockett turned to Paul Luke. After gazing at him for a moment as though they were alone, she kissed him full on the lips. "Merry Christmas, love," she whispered against his ear before leaning away to greet Naomi Ruth.

"Which punch is the safest?" Letitia asked.

"All these punches are safe," Naomi Ruth said, her hand sweeping the air above several ornate bowls. "The kitchen is the dangerous place—so I've been warned. You'll want to stay out of there."

The stream of arrivals trickled to an end and Naomi Ruth headed toward the pantry to bring in more trays of food. As she passed Zacharias Renfrow he caught her hand.

"Ah, Naomi, you are lovelier now than you were at sixteen."

"Pshaw, Zach! You're an old fool to talk like that."

"Yes, I *am* an old fool. But you—you are as lovely as ever I remember."

Naomi Ruth made no attempt to free her hand, and they stood silent.

"And Mathelde—will she be along directly?" Zach asked after an interval. "I've missed her lately."

"Oh, I thought everyone knew. Mathelde is in New York, with Fleming. He's being treated. Some specialist in the Catskills, I believe. We debated canceling this party, that no one would feel festive, but—"

"Nonsense! That's all the more reason for a party. Get your mind off of it. Everyone seems to be happy." Zach turned away. "Yes. Happy. Perhaps I should go back to the kitchen again. Check the mousetraps, so to speak." He saluted with his empty glass.

Saree, standing behind a corn husk angel as tall as she, overheard Zach's remark.

"*Mice!*" she chortled, the dimple appearing in her left cheek. "I didn't know about the *mice!*"

Saree headed toward the kitchen to see for herself, but Paul Luke met her at the door, marching her back to the sitting room.

"We'll look for mice tomorrow. They usually come out on Christmas Eve."

Judge Theed and Beech Marcom stood blocking the kitchen door so that Zacharias Renfrow was forced to stop but managed to pass his glass into the kitchen.

"Beech," Zach said, "I hear Gattis Todd may be defeated up in your neck of the woods. That the truth, or what?"

"Yes, he's about to get what he deserves, to my way of thinking." Marcom drained his glass. "You know he apologized for his outbreak at the Jockey Club Ball." He looked around, lowering his voice. "Near started a fight with his talk of bastards and all. Besides that, he's been plucking the voters clean as a chicken, collecting contributions. They're tired of him."

"Now if they'd just get rid of A. Dixon Murphy, the General Assembly might start shaping up pretty good."

Beech chuckled. "Who knows? Old Humpty Dumpty might fall off the wall yet."

"Now, now, now," Letitia Marcom scolded, passing the three on her way to the dining room. "That's not Christmas talk I hear!"

Zach twirled his glass. "A memorial for Cleveland Corlew's finally been approved. The army's sending a colonel or somebody. In March, I think."

"Thank the good Lord!" Judge Theed said. "If Mae Dee had been on their back like she has everybody else's, they'd done it a damn sight sooner."

"It's a fitting thing to be done, Judge," Zach said. "Honoring Cleve. Not just for Mae Dee, for the whole county."

"Yes," Judge Theed said. "Cleve was a hero, all right."

In the next room Margaret Theed and the Reverend Wakerich finished their repast of roast goose with orange chestnut dressing. Reverend Wakerich wiped the corners of his mouth, watching Nora and Paul Luke.

"You know, I wouldn't be a bit surprised to see a spring wedding between those two."

Lockett Lakewood sat alone in the corner. She yawned, appearing disinterested.

"Wouldn't that beat all?" Margaret Theed said, scraping a fork across her plate. "Oh, surely not!"

"Mark my words. They've been together an awful lot lately, especially since Amos—er—died."

Lockett hurried from the room. She looked around for Paul Luke, spotting him and Nora in the hall. Nora, her face turned up to his, was laughing at something he said. The moment appeared intimate, as if the two were sealed inside a private mantle. Lockett whirled and bumped into Saree, just as Beech Marcom caught her arm.

"I want you to meet the defense lawyer in that celebrated murder case." He pointed her in the direction of Zacharias Renfrow.

"But—" Lockett protested, looking back over her shoulder. Paul Luke was handing Nora a cup, their hands touching. They started toward Naomi Ruth, who was introducing Shard Mc Fadden, the legislator from Louisville, to Laura Ballard.

"I understand that's your daughter he's been monopolizing all evening," Mc Fadden said. The rest of his words were lost amid the voices and laughter.

Lockett looked at the smiling Zach and backed away, her hand covering her mouth, eyes large. She mumbled and wheeled toward the hall, where the guests' wraps hung on a rack. Marcom started to follow, but her expression warned him away.

Managing to reach her coat, Lockett flung it over her shoulders, and darted out. She gulped the cold air. Without a sound Paul Luke appeared at her side.

"What's the matter, Lockett?"

"Nothing. I have to leave."

"Why?"

"You know why."

He stared into her eyes. She turned and hurried toward her carriage. Unwinding the horse's reins she stepped up onto the driver's side. Paul Luke rushed after her.

"I can't let you leave alone like this. What will people think? Your parents won't have a way home—"

"Somebody will take them."

"No. I'll take you, if you must, and bring the buggy back."

"Well, if you're going to insist, at least get your coat. I don't want to be the cause if you die of pneumonia. I'll wait. Promise."

He returned shortly wearing his wool greatcoat. He climbed up and took the reins with a firm hand. Lockett scooted across the seat.

"Well," he looked down at her. "Here I am again. Seems I always find myself gazing at that little left ear of yours." He pulled the lap robe across their legs and clucked to the horse.

They rode in silence. Lockett breathed in quick shallow bursts, like a winded pony. An occasional yellow square glowed on the snow as they passed houses with lamps shining through the windows. Corlew's store stood dark against a lighter dark, silhouetted by the moon at its back. The snow-covered benches and nail kegs stood forlorn under the persimmon tree. The hoofs of My Kate, Lockett's horse, made crunching sounds in the snow.

"Do you know how long we've been seeing each other? Six years, Paul Luke. More than six years!" Lockett said, her voice dismal. She leaned forward and looked into his face. "All that time

I thought that eventually.... But I see now. Nora's hold on you is, well, like a steel cord. Even stronger than I suspected."

"I do care for you, Lockett, and I always will." The scent of roses, Lockett's perfume, hung in the cold air. Roses and snow.

"But not like you care for her. Not like that. When I saw you together, all I wanted was to be back in Louisville. You're in love with Nora! How long?"

"Nora and I are old friends—"

"Hah! More than friends. Longer than six years, Paul Luke?"

"Not what you think, Lockett. Not that."

"I did manage to get you away from her once. At the lake. We were all together. The night Cleve left," she mused, her voice low. "And even then, even though Nora was with Cleve, I thought you preferred her. When I saw the two of you tonight—" She looked down at her gloved hands and bit her lip. "But now I'm through dilly-dallying while you make up your mind. I will not be humiliated. Life is too full of a number of things. I haven't exactly been sitting in Louisville pining. After all, when you're not there, someone else is." Her breath spurted in ragged clouds as she spoke.

Paul Luke cast an oblique glance toward Lockett. Shadows hid her face but he was accustomed to her flushed cheeks and the stormy eyes that accompanied that tone of voice.

"I can't imagine you sitting and pining for anyone."

She jerked about on the seat in a gesture resembling a flounce.

"I am not a good loser, Paul Luke. I don't stay around to lose. We have a lot of years between us. Too many. I'm leaving Hunt County. For good. Escaping, you might say, to Louisville. In every sense of the word."

"But Beech and I are friends—"

"Oh, you're welcome to visit my stepfather. Any time, of course. Alone or with others. That's of no concern to me." She stared at him in the moonlight. "But you and I are through, Senator."

"Lockett—" He turned toward her while My Kate chose her own path. "Let's discuss this later. You're angry."

"No, I am not angry, Senator, I am *through*."

My Kate stopped in front of Beech Marcom's farmhouse. Lockett started to leap down from the carriage, but Paul Luke caught her arm and lifted her to the ground.

The unlocked door swung open at his touch. Laughter and voices burst from the kitchen.

"The help is celebrating the season." Lockett shrugged. "Would you tell my mother I'm home safely?"

"See what you've done? You've spoiled their party."

"No, I'll be joining them. And I hope to God they've got lots of `dew' from Golden Pond. I feel like helping them dispose of some. Thank you, Senator Lanier, for the favor of seeing me home. Good night." She started in the house but he caught her shoulder.

"Not good night, Lockett. Not like this."

"Excuse me, Senator. I meant *good-bye*."

"Lockett, how can we say good-bye, after what we've—what you've meant to me?" He took her face in his hands. An unexpected wetness covered her checks.

"After *is* the correct word, Senator." She removed his hands. "It's *after*, and it's also *good-bye*. Please go." She closed the door. The bolt clicked.

He left, longing for the light and warmth of home. He popped the reins. My Kate clipped through the snow at the fastest gait she could deliver, snorting hotly when they pulled into the driveway.

"Where've you been?" Naomi Ruth asked, seeing him enter the hall. "People are looking for you."

"I'm sorry, Mother. Lockett was not feeling well. I took her home. She asked me to give you her regrets. Would you let Letitia know?"

Shard Mc Fadden's wife, Ella, approached him. "Senator Lanier, you've got us all in the dark," she said, her drawl soft as Georgia cotton. "Are you still going to run for governor? We're all *dying* to know."

Obviously they had been discussing the trial. What they really wanted to know was how he assessed his damages. Paul Luke picked up a glass. Spending his life running the farm with his mother, for whatever years were left to her, seemed not unappealing. Then there might be love. Not bad for a fallback position. Not many men had, or wanted, more.

But he refused to concede his political fortunes to anybody. He could take defeat, if it was inevitable, but they would have to hand it to him standing on his chest, with him flat on his back. And, by God, they would know they'd had a fight! Paul Luke's gaze swept slowly over Ella Mc Fadden, and he smiled.

"Being governor does appeal to many men in public service. However, I have yet another term to finish in the Senate. After which, you might just pose that question again."

Ella Mc Fadden blushed and retreated a few steps before his amused gaze. "Yes, Senator, I'll certainly do that," she stammered, turning in the direction of her husband.

Nora appeared at Paul Luke's side. "Your mother wants you. Some of the guests are leaving."

He took a sip from his cup. "Let's go."

"Were you with Lockett?"

"I took her home. She's gone."

"Mama had to leave, too."

"Oh?"

"Yes, Tobe Bandy's wife is having her baby. Dr. Haas didn't think he could get there in time. Mama's delivered so many. Tobe came by to see if she could attend till Dr. Haas comes. The baby wasn't due till next month."

"It'll be all right." He squeezed her arm. "Let's get you and Saree home."

The next morning Saree seemed to be coming down with a cold and Nora insisted that she stay in her warm bed.

"But I'll miss the Christmas pageant." Saree had a one-word part. An older child was to read the Scripture depicting the birth of Christ. When she read the words, "And the angel said—" Saree was to step forward and say, "Lo!"

"Maybe someone else can say it. Oh, not like you, but they can make do."

Little Granny returned home at daybreak too tired to attend the Christmas Eve services. Soon as Reverend Wakerich finished his sermon on the greatest gift of all, Paul Luke and Nora left for the cemetery.

Nora shuddered as they neared Cutter's Bridge where Amos died. The boards of the bridge vibrated one by one, hollow sounds. The black mare hastened, appearing anxious to be done and back again in her warm stall.

"It's so awful. I don't understand why he was out after dark like that, with no lights on his car and all."

"Yes, well, he stayed at the canning factory too long. The darkness overtook him. I guess he thought he could get home, but there wasn't even a moon. Pity."

Nora knelt to pray at the snow-covered mound. She laid an evergreen wreath she had made against the headstone, and they left. Snow began to fall. Gusts of wind swirled it against their faces.

"I'll come by tonight," Paul Luke said when they reached her door. "But it may be late. I have a lot of calls, political obligations. Parties, gatherings, like that."

She nodded and hurried inside.

Saree stayed in her nightgown the whole day, busily creating Christmas drawings for every acquaintance she had.

"And this one is for Willie Shoe," she said, pasting a lop-sided star on the peak of a waxy paper tree. "Merry Christmas."

"Is all that for Santa Claus?" Saree asked, observing from the kitchen door. She pointed toward three strands of wire suspended from wall to wall across a corner. They held plates of Christmas sweets.

"I doubt he'll take the time," Little Granny said. "And the mice can't get across the wires to it, either. So, there'll be plenty left for us tomorrow, even if Santa's hungry."

After her bath Saree sat with Nora on the side of her feather bed while Little Granny read from Luke, Chapter Two, the Christmas story. The oil lamp cast comforting shadows. Warmth radiated from the chimney that rose through the attic from the room below.

After a time Nora stood and lifted Saree, whose lashes lay against her cheeks, into the middle of the billowy mattress.

The two women kissed the child and made their way down the narrow stairway. Little Granny went first, bearing the lamp above her head, like a beacon for Nora. Although flames already danced in the fireplace, Nora added another log. Little Granny fetched a box from her bedroom and they set about arranging fruit and toys under the Christmas tree. After a while Little Granny went off to bed, leaving Nora sitting beside the fire.

Nora awoke startled and chilled. The fire had burned to embers. A persistent knock on the door summoned her.

"It's me. Am I too late?"

Nora cracked the door. Paul Luke stood in the dimness looking apologetic.

"I—I don't think so—no—what time is it? Oh, of course not! I—dozed off. Come in."

"I am sorry. I wouldn't have come, but I had to get this doll here for Saree." He handed Nora a cardboard box. "Go ahead. Look at it."

Nora flipped the top off and folded back layers of tissue paper. She moved into the circle of lamplight to examine the doll. Its face, hands, and legs were of hand-painted bisque porcelain. Luxurious brown curls, adorned with pink ribbons, tumbled to its waist. A red gingham pinafore and polka dot blouse covered the body.

"Oh, no. You must give this to her yourself. Mama made her a Christmas doll. This one must be from you."

"Then save it for later, and tell her—whatever you wish." Paul Luke placed the doll back in its box and set it on the floor. From his coat pocket he fished two boxes.

"This is for your mother, and you must promise that she gets it—this morning. It's a silver thimble, very practical, and a millefiori paperweight that caught my fancy."

Nora hesitated, at a loss.

"What's this?" he produced yet another box and frowned in mock surprise. "Ah, yes, my memory returns. I believe—yes. Yes— it is for you. Merry Christmas, Nora!"

The gold foil box was tied with a scarlet velvet bow. She sat down, her eyes traveling first to the gift then to him.

"Open it."

Her hands trembled. She tore the foil away revealing a cherrywood box with inlaid gold designs. He knelt beside her and raised the top. A melody chimed from the box lingering on the air like exquisite perfume.

"The Emperor Waltz," he said, "in honor of our dance at the

Fourth Fest. But there's more." He picked up another small object. "Your comb was broken that night, too. How could I forget?"

In the attic above, Saree stirred, her slumber disturbed. She turned on her side, dreaming.

She sat with her mother and Little Granny in a room filled with Christmas, a fire warming her face. Evergreen and spices mixed in a bewitching scent. Dolls and fruit and candy spilled across the floor and onto stacks and stacks of presents piled at Little Granny's feet. Next to her mother, beside an immense Christmas tree, a man sat laughing, his back toward Saree. Snow gleamed outside the window, its luster dispelling the darkness of the night. Inside, the house glittered, even the corners, and there were no shadows. Somewhere across the snowy fields bells pealed joyous sounds.

A silvery dawn lit the eastern sky. Saree's eyes fluttered open. She ran to her window and scraped away the frost. Snow had not conquered the night as it had done in her dream. Darkness gave way to daybreak above the white earth. Each remained still, the sky and the earth, where it had always been, in its own place. Beneath her window, down where the snow and first light met, Paul Luke walked toward his carriage.

On the Wednesday following Christmas the Magistrates' Court convened for its final session of the year. Paul Luke was present, along with Zach Renfrow and a committee appointed to plan Cleve Corlew's memorial.

Miss Maude Jett, last surviving relative of the Boatwright family, sent her permission for the park to be renamed. Her letter was read into the official minutes while Mae Dee Corlew sniffled on the front row.

"I have a telegram from the War Department," Zach said, standing."It says they're sorry no one was able to attend the planning sessions. But they do promise to send an official speaker for the dedication in March."

"Can we count on that?" Paul Luke asked.

"I think so. That date has been on their agenda for a good while."

Zach looked speculative for a moment before turning his attention to the magistrates. "Now there was some talk of building a new wall around the park. Gentlemen?"

One of the magistrates leaned forward. "That's out of the question," he said. "This county is near out of money. We're hard put to meet payroll as it is."

"Would it be possible, then," Paul Luke said, "to rebuild the archway at the entrance? I favor leaving the Silas Boatwright plaque where it is. We could put a new sign at the front."

After a lengthy discussion the magistrates agreed to Paul Luke's idea. Following promises of donations and volunteer labor the meeting was adjourned.

"That was a fine Christmas party you all had," Zach Renfrow said as they left. "Mighty fine. Naomi Ruth knows how to put one on. Give her my regards, will you?"

Paul Luke nodded as he climbed into his buggy and headed out of Wickliffe. He went to Nora's. She and Saree were making snow ice cream in the kitchen.

"We finished plans for the war memorial today. The ceremony will mostly honor Cleve."

Nora turned pale.

"I think you should plan to be there. You and Saree and your mother."

Nora's eyes searched his face. She walked to the window and stared at the falling snow.

"Yes," she whispered, twisting the pearls at her throat. "We'll go. I want Saree to—to be there."

Chapter 18

Mae Dee Corlew stopped opposite the entrance to Boatwright Park, staring at the space her son's nameplate would fill after today's ceremony. A sign announcing the name change from Boatwright to War Memorial Park dangled from the arch.

"There's Mae Dee!" Whitsworth Moseby yelled.

"That the mother?" a photographer from the *Paducah Democrat Express* inquired. He readied his camera without listening for an answer.

Whitsworth appeared glum. The train conveying the War Department dignitaries was two hours late and a noon dinner at Moseby's boarding house had been cancelled. A formal briefing to acquaint the speakers with Cleve Corlew's "little corner of Kentucky" as he once called it, also had to be omitted. Now the government officials might find themselves with not much more than Cleve's name to honor at today's ceremony. But Whitsworth's concern centered on his own lost revenue. He had anticipated that windfall ever since Judge Theed and the Hunt County Magistrates approached him with the plan in late December.

Dabbing her eyes with a handkerchief edged in black lace, Mae Dee looked every inch the grieving mother. Even her hat bore a cluster of black velvet roses on its crown, from which cascaded a veil. She glanced around with satisfaction. Most of the county had turned out to pay its respects to her son.

"If only T. J. could have lived to see this day," Mae Dee sniffled.

Georgie Rae Gardner patted Mae Dee's shoulder. T. J. Corlew had dropped dead one morning five winters earlier while carrying a chamber pot to the privy behind Corlew's Store.

"He would have been proud."

Many spoke to Mae Dee as they arrived; others hastened to find seats on benches borrowed from the Presbyterian Church.

Reverend Wakerich seated himself among the empty chairs on a platform at the front.

Sheriff Claude Meeks arrived, his Model T emitting black odorous smoke. "They'll be here in five minutes!" he shouted.

Paul Luke stopped his buggy next to Sheriff Meeks' car and jumped down to help his mother.

"You go ahead. I'll wait for the others." His eyes darted over the crowd.

"Are you all right?" He nodded and squeezed her arm.

Eli Mayes pulled up in the late Amos McCann's refurbished Model T. With Eli were a Lieutenant Colonel Jacob Cross and a former soldier named Abner Cooksey. The two had been present when Cleveland Corlew died, so the War Department had designated them to lead the dedication. Also riding with Eli was Miss Maude Jett who gave Hunt County permission for the name change to War Memorial Park.

Eli Mayes looked around, cleared his throat, nodded and began walking toward the platform. The others followed, Paul Luke last; his eyes, with that same odd expression, searched the crowd. When Nora, Little Granny, and Saree slipped into the back row his tension eased but he remained watchful.

"It was that awful battle of the Somme seven years ago that claimed our hero and Hunt County son, Corporal Cleveland Corlew," Eli Mayes said, following Reverend Wakerich's invocation. "We have in our midst Lieutenant Colonel Jacob Cross. He was at that time Captain Cross, commander of Cleveland Corlew's volunteer regiment. Lieutenant Colonel Cross is with us today to dedicate this final and lasting tribute to Corporal Corlew."

Solemn applause acknowledged the Lieutenant Colonel. He strode straight as a wooden yardstick across the platform to the podium. His brass buttons appeared to juggle the sun's rays from one to another and back again.

Paul Luke watched Nora. She caressed Saree's golden hair, never lifting her eyes.

"Several years ago few people knew of Corporal Corlew's death," Cross began. "He was one of over four million Doughboys, soldiers who stood with our allies for freedom, and received little recognition. More than one hundred and twenty-five thousand of those Americans never laid eyes on this country again. Many of them lie under unmarked soil. Others were lost and buried at sea.

They are that great brotherhood, these near-forgotten casualties, who preserved for us, and our allies, the freedom to choose our own ways.

"Corporal Cleveland Corlew was among those fallen heroes. Another brave, loyal American, he gave that last, and greatest, measure of devotion for liberty. He died that men might be free, that women and little children might be safe.

"Ladies and gentlemen, when I was first approached about today's ceremony, I naturally conducted a little review of that fateful battle which claimed Corporal Corlew's life. In doing so I was fortunate to come upon one who knew Corporal Corlew much better than I. Indeed, one who was with him in his final moments of life. It is also fortunate that that one is able to be here with us on this stage. I present to you, Sergeant Abner Cooksey, Corporal Corlew's sergeant, now a civilian of Knox County!"

Restrained applause filled the air. A man wearing snug blue serge took the speaker's place. His face showed a hint of perspiration in the chill afternoon. Since leaving the army three years earlier Abner Cooksey had worked in a feed store at Stinking Creek. Never before had he faced an audience this enormous. Pulling a handkerchief from his back pocket he dabbed his face.

Nora looked up at the podium then lowered her eyes. Cooksey gripped the edge of his rostrum and stared into the crowd.

"Corporal Cleve Corlew was a lover of his home," Cooksey said. "His happiest minutes was when he thought about his family. When his country, and his friends, needed him, he went, with that same love and loyalty he showed to them at home.

"Cleve Corlew died that November day in '16 standing in the trenches. Yes, *standing*, I say. Standing and firing! Defending our position against them—those—German artillery shellings that was loud enough to deafen a stone." Cooksey paused.

"When Corporal Corlew was hit and down—dying, I say—his last words was about his loved ones at home. 'Lord,' he said—his very last words—'Lord, take care of the folks.'" Cooksey bowed his head. "'Take care of the baby, Lord.' That's what he said."

Gasps from the listeners followed Cooksey's statement. A sad reminiscent smile hovered about his mouth.

"I remember the night before that battle. We all sat around

talking. But Cleve, he didn't say much. He was scratching on his helmet, on the inside, like it was kind of private. When he died we found it there beside him. `Nora.' That was the things he did, his very last night on this earth."

Abner Cooksey paused again. If he noticed the stricken faces of the audience, he attributed it to his own eloquence. His voice rose to greater heights.

"And I want to say, to tell you folks, how proud I am to be here, and to have a part in these doings to honor my brave soldier buddy."

Cooksey sat down. Silence enveloped the onlookers. Lieutenant Colonel Jacob Cross glanced about. No mention had been made to him of a child. None occupied the platform; nor was anyone present who resembled a grieving widow. Cross had seen it often, this tragedy of a soldier's death, reaching backward, obliterating not only a life, but all that had gone before as well. Lieutenant Cross scanned the front row. Still no sign. Heads began to pivot. Necks twisted and eyes turned.

Nora half rose to leave, but Little Granny pulled her back onto the bench. Saree scooted closer to her mother. Lieutenant Colonel Cross once more took the speaker's stand.

"I don't see those folks here," he turned questioning eyes toward Eli Mayes. "I assume they have—eh? Lost contact? Moved? Seven years is—er—" Cross'uncertain glance swept the crowd. He hesitated; perhaps he should relinquish this entire business to one of the civilian officials. But after an awkward silence Lieutenant Colonel Cross salvaged his poise and walked to an easel draped in blue velvet. "Let us—er—continue in our duty to honor this brave, fallen hero."

"You're drunk, Cleve," Nora said.

"Yes, drunk, maybe. Drunk with love. That possible, Paul Luke, to be drunk with love?"

"Let up, Cleve. You've had too much."

"But not enough of Nora." Cleve reached for her. Nora slid away, disentangling herself from his arms.

"Well, I want to go for a boat ride on the lake," Lockett Lakewood said. The moonlight through the trees cast leafy shadows

on her face. "Come on, Paul Luke, you promised." Lockett grabbed his hand, pulling him to his feet.

"That was earlier. I don't think Cleve has any business out in a boat."

"Well, then, Cleve and Nora can wait here. Just a short ride, Paul Luke?"

Paul Luke looked at Nora but she waved them away with a lightness she did not feel.

"Come on, Nora. You know I love you," Cleve said. The sound of oars dipping in the water faded as the canoe glided across Boatwright Lake.

"Just a kiss for a soldier boy off to war." Cleve seized Nora's arms.

"This is Europe's war, not ours," she said, trying to sound calm. "And you're not a soldier boy. Not yet."

"But tomorrow I will be. Or is it today? What time is it anyway?" He tightened his grip.

"It's late, Cleve. I have to go." The stench of whiskey on his breath revulsed her. She tried not to struggle.

"But I love you!"

Suddenly he threw her against the grass, falling across her, holding her face in his hands, kissing her. She struggled, but it was too late. Vomit rose in her throat. Burning like acid it spilled into her nostrils. Cleve pinned her to the ground with his knees, his hands clawing, ripping into her. He stifled her screams with his mouth. She bit his lip, tasted blood, salt, felt his hands on her flesh. Pain careened through her body, flooding her soul. After a briefness Cleve sank into a stupor. Nora crawled from beneath him. She started running, the pain subjugated only to her overwhelming abhorrence.

"Where's Nora, Cleve? Cleve!" Paul Luke bent down, shaking him. Cleve raised his head.

"Uh—Nora? Nora? Uh—Nora got mad. She ran off." He dropped back into the grass.

"She ran off? Where, Cleve?"

"Her house? J'ya see her?"

"No, I didn't see her. I went to take Lockett home. Is Nora all right, Cleve?"

"*Yeah. She got mad and ran off. 'Cause she's mad. I'm running off, too. In a minute.*"

"*You have a train to catch, Cleve.*"

"I don't—I don't—" Mae Dee murmured. She lifted her veil and her face appeared grotesque beneath its cover of flesh-tinted powder. Paul Luke moved next to her.

"What's going on, Paul Luke? What is this—Nora, a child? Somebody tell me! Why? My boy's dead, and I—why didn't somebody—"

"That was up to Nora," he said. "Always."

Nora fell onto the steps of Corlew's General Store, a pathetic bundle of rags. The rattle of a carriage sounded in the distance. In a moment Paul Luke stood over her.

"*Nora! What happened to you?*"

"*Cleve—he—he—*" *She held her hands out, beseeching him, unaware of her bare breasts, the shreds of cloth hanging about her shoulders.*

"*My God! You've been—! Cleve? Not Cleve.*" *Stunned, Paul Luke threw his jacket around her.* "*Oh God, not Cleve!*"

"*He broke my necklace!*" *Nora screamed, holding up a thread of shattered glass beads.* "*The son of a bitch broke my necklace!*"

She screamed and screamed, sobbing, beating her fists against Paul Luke's chest while he held her. Finally she lost consciousness. He put her gently into his carriage and drove her home.

"*No, we won't tell her,*" *Little Granny said later, blowing out the kerosene lamp as dawn broke through the windows.* "*You'll stay right here and hold your head up.*" *The gaze she turned on Paul Luke carried a warning.* "*Nobody need ever know. You won't give her the satisfaction of saying you lied on that `soldier boy' son of hers.*"

"I'm shaking so. I don't know if I'm going to be able to—to do this," Mae Dee said, clutching Paul Luke's arm. "I wish—"

Lieutenant Colonel Cross stood by an easel, waiting for Mae Dee to pull away the blue velvet that covered Cleve Corlew's brass plaque.

"I think I can help," Paul Luke said. He walked slowly from the platform, down the aisle between the rows of spectators. Jacob Cross waited in the immense quiet, but every eye followed Paul Luke.

A few weeks later Paul Luke appeared at Nora's door bearing a pink beribboned box. "I'm going to have a child," Nora told him.

"Why then you must tell—"

"No. No one would believe me now. They wouldn't have believed me then, either, Mama said. She forbade it."

"They would believe me. Don't you know I feel responsible, leaving you alone that night, with him drunk out of his mind?"

"Do you really and truly think they'd believe you, Paul Luke? No. People believe what they want." Nora began to pace, her face agitated, tears spilling down her cheeks. "Besides, Mama wouldn't allow it. After all that trouble with the tobacco planters—that court case—Mama thinks it would be like surrendering. Giving them something. Revenge, maybe. She's stubborn. She has—pride. She would rather die than go to Mae Dee. You must give me your word."

"That's foolishness, Nora. Not pride; foolishness. My father aligned himself against the Planters' Association, too, you know, and it didn't keep me from being elected."

"Yes, but it was my mother who sued them. And won. That was a long time ago, but some grudges last a lifetime. Oh, they won't provoke Mama outright, but something like this?" Her eyes pleaded.

"Please, Paul Luke, don't say anything. To anybody."

"All right. But only till Cleve gets home. In the meantime, I'll write. He must know about this right away. What will you do with the child?"

Nora looked blank. "The child isn't to blame. Maybe I'll love it all the more because of that—its innocence."

"Nora, I have—feelings for you. We could—"

"You? Feelings for me? After I was raped and cast away like trash by your friend? Like dirt? You left me with him that night. Don't try to make it up to me. Ease your own conscience. I don't need you!"

He left. Months later Nora opened the box. Inside was the most exquisitely matched string of luminescent pearls to be found in the state of Kentucky. She put them away in a drawer beside the glass beads Cleve had broken.

Halfway down the aisle, Paul Luke realized that Nora and Little Granny, along with Saree, were coming to meet him. Nora's cheeks were flushed and her eyelashes shimmered with tears. Saree appeared confused. Walking a little behind her mother she clutched Little Granny's hand. They paused and Paul Luke stooped beside her.

"Saree, you're going to learn a lot of things today. Things you've wondered about. Important things. Things you may not understand till you're older." Paul Luke put his arm about her waist as he had so often done before.

"Paul Luke, is *he* my daddy?"

"Your daddy was a hero."

"Then, why—?"

Taking Saree in his arms Paul Luke stood. Lieutenant Colonel Jacob Cross waited, looking more bewildered than anybody.

"Do you remember when I told you that flowers grow in some folks' gardens, and weeds in others?" Saree nodded. "Well, today all the flowers in your garden burst into bloom, and I'd like for these people to see. Will you come with me?"

Saree glanced toward her mother and Little Granny. "Well, all right. I'll go with you." She turned perplexed eyes toward Jacob Cross. "He's my daddy?" Paul Luke carried Saree to the platform and sat her beside Mae Dee.

"Not here! Not by her."

"I received this letter from Cleve," Paul Luke said, stepping in front of Nora as she walked in the road beside his tobacco fields. He had not succeeded in his attempts to see either Nora or her mother since the day she announced her pregnancy. The window shades remained drawn and there was little sign of life at the house. Even Little Granny's beloved garden had gone unplanted, overrun with wild hemp and mustard plants.

Nora tried to sidestep, but Paul Luke prevented her. She looked ill, her face pale.

"Paul Luke, please! Can't you leave me alone?"

"This letter concerns you. Cleve must have written it on the train the day after he left. I think you should hear it." Walking slowly by Nora's side, he began to read.

"'I don't know what I did. I was stinking drunk. I've always loved her. You know me better than anybody in the world. My God, Paul Luke, it must be a nightmare. Whatever I did, I will beg Nora to forgive. You must help me with this. I love her.'"

Other letters followed. The ones to Nora were returned unopened.

The crowd dispersed, moving in hushed groups, their eyes downcast. Naomi Ruth made her way to Little Granny and touched her shoulder.

"My whole family has walked on coals more than seven years. I believe I deserve some kind of explanation for what's happening."

Little Granny squeezed Naomi Ruth's hand. "I'm sure Paul Luke will explain it all to you."

Whitsworth Moseby stood near the road watching cars and wagons loading up to leave.

"We got a special on pork chop dinners over to the boarding house," he called, gripping his short-brimmed hat. "We got a special—"

Nora rushed toward the platform where Saree waited with Paul Luke. He stepped into her path. "Nora!" She tried to go around him but he blocked her way.

"You have to listen! I've tried to tell you but you stopped me. God, I wanted to!" Nora stared at him.

"There was always that blotch over us. Over Saree. Then, after Cleve died, it was yours to decide. I could only wait. But now—"

He raised his hands, palms up. "I've been on a fool's errand. I'm tired to death of deceit."

"It isn't over, Paul Luke. There's still so much. I'm not sure if I can ever—" Her shoulders sagged. "I'm tired, too."

"I can take you home."

"No. I just want to be with Saree. I think we'll take a shortcut through the field."

"It'll be cold on Sandy Ridge. The wind's up."

"I know." She pushed the hair off her cheek. "I need the chill to cut through this numbness inside." Tears filled her eyes. "I've made a terrible mistake. What do I do now?"

"Now, Nora? The end is in sight. We'll go on till we get there." He handed her his handkerchief. "Right now somebody must talk to Mae Dee."

"I'll ask Mama to do that. But who's going to talk to the rest of Hunt County?" She reached down and took Saree's hand.

"Mae Dee can. She's good at that." Paul Luke headed toward his carriage. Lail Stratton sat in his wheel chair a few feet away.

" Guess you know *you're* no hero, Lanier. You worked your backside off all these years. Everything you've done has been devoted to the good of these people. Your constituents!" Stratton laughed, a mirthless sound. "They think a lot of you, I reckon. You enjoy some degree of status around here. Yeah, you've got your comforts all right, Lanier. But a hero you're not." Stratton rocked back and forth.

"If a man just set out to make himself a hero," he continued, "you'd be one. Don't guess I know anybody who's put as much effort into it. But you're no hero, you see, because heroes just *happen.*" Stratton spat on the ground.

"Take your buddy Cleve, for example. What'd he do? Got drunk, most likely. Took a gal here. Give her a baby. Went off to war like a lot did that wasn't heroes. But you know what? Your buddy Cleve probably did something dumb over there. Got himself killed. Got himself a big to-do at this park that was renamed on account of him. Now *there's* a hero for you." Stratton laughed again. "And it just *happened* to him. But you'll die, Lanier, and somebody else'll come along and pick up your load. Lighten it a bit probably. And they'll fall into that little band of poor devils just like you that keeps things going and clicking." Stratton twisted his hands like a knife.

"That don't make you a hero, Lanier. Nobody's going to name a park for you. Or even give you any credit for all your pains." Stratton, warming to his tirade, grinned. "But human nature being what it is, folks don't make heroes out of people based on the effort they put out. That would put the screws on. Folks think `I'd have

to go through all that crap myself to be a hero. It's not worth it.'
Most folks don't cotton to that much, putting out effort. But you?
Naw, Paul Luke, you'll just have to get used to living with it. You've
busted your ass, all right, but you're nobody's hero."

"You've done a lot of that busting for these people, too, Lail,"
Paul Luke said as he climbed into his carriage. "I guess it's a good
thing neither of us ever set out to be a hero, isn't it?" He flicked the
reins and the buggy rolled away.

Paul Luke stopped for Mae Dee trudging toward her store.

"Was they married, Paul Luke?" She twisted her handkerchief.
"Secretly? I can't make any sense out of it all. Did Cleve marry
that—Nora—before he left?"

"No, Mae Dee. Nothing so kind as that."

"So kind? What're you saying? You mean this is all just a passel
of claims she's making against my boy?"

"No, Mae Dee. Cleve was drunk the night he left. Don't you
understand?"

"Are you telling me he took advantage? That's a lie! This whole
business is one of her lies! Stop! Turn this buggy around! Take me
back! I've got to get the truth out!"

"Mae Dee, I have letters. From Cleve. My God! He was my
best friend, and he's dead! I've protected him all these years. Would
I lie?"

Mae Dee leaned back into a shriveled, trembling heap. "There's
so much I don't understand. Why did you keep it from me all this
time?"

"That was Nora's say. She wanted to find the right time. For
herself. For Saree. But it never came. Besides, you wouldn't have
believed her."

"I don't know what to say. If I'd a-known that little girl was—
I would have—I never would have—"

"Now wait a minute, Mae Dee! Nobody tricked you into being
uncharitable to Saree." He gave her a piercing look. "You'll have
to wrestle with that matter on your own."

At the store a crowd waited beneath the persimmon tree. Paul
Luke held the screen door open while Mae Dee fumbled with her
key.

He followed her inside. "Might as well get my mail."

A Model T screeched to a halt near the persimmon tree. Several men jumped to the ground shouting.

"Lail Stratton just dropped dead!"

"Old Doc Haas was still at the park when Lail collapsed. Fell right out of his wheel chair, he did!"

"Doc said he's dead a-fore he hit the ground. Done already carried Lail to Crice's Funeral Home. Right straight!"

"Well, old Lail ain't been hisself since that horse kicked him," Guy Childers said, buttoning his tight brown coat against the chill.

"Pretty sour individual," Goose Wiley said. "Pretty soured on life."

"The man isn't even cold yet! We owe him his due," Paul Luke said from the doorway. "Lail Stratton represented Hunt County in the state legislature for eighteen years. He cast a tall shadow over this entire county. Everything he did benefitted us all."

Paul Luke raised his hand and pointed. "Lail Stratton got that bridge built over Cutter's Creek. The levee on Boatwright Lake. He expanded the railroad. I'd say Lail Stratton was a kind of hero."

Paul Luke closed the sagging door behind him and took a step toward the persimmon tree. "I don't recall any scandal in public office during his terms, either. Seems to me people forget a man's accomplishments pretty fast, but his shortcomings go on forever."

He looked at the crowd. A shaggy form brushed against his legs, and he glanced down. "Puddin'?" Paul Luke said. "You're not supposed to be here!" Stooping, he patted the dog. At length he spoke again.

"Lail got older as we all will, please God. He had his faults like the rest of us. Now, he's gone. Some seem obliged to wave those faults like a banner. Forget the good he did." The silent cluster stared at him, not moving.

"And, yes." Paul Luke nodded toward Goose Wiley and Guy Childers. "Lail Stratton was a mite dour, bitter even, after that accident. But all he craved was a bit of praise. Maybe he felt worn out, discarded. A jot of thanks, my friends, for all he did in this county, could have made the difference. Given the opportunity now, I would say this to that man lying over there in Crice's back room.

"When I gasp my last breath, if you people are kind enough to wait till then, why you'll stack all *my* shortcomings up in one big pile, too. And you'll dance around them. But I can take that. And so can Lail! Seems to me that's better, all things considered, than for you to flounder around, trying to figure out something good to say about somebody that never did any." He glanced about. "You'd be better served by all your effort right now if you spent it finding yourselves another Lail Stratton."

Little Granny had been standing near the edge of the gathering. She went forward and gripped his arm.

"You can count on it, Paul Luke. Only them that do, get criticized." She embraced him. "But I owe you some thanks, and I'm not going to put off saying so."

He put his arm about her shoulders. "For that, I'm offering you a ride home."

"No, I have come to see Mae Dee." Little Granny started in the door and turned back toward him. "I expect I'll be here till way after dark."

Old Puddin,' his ears perked, sat at Paul Luke's feet staring up at him.

"Rejected twice in one day," Paul Luke said, shaking his head. "Let's go, Puddin.'"

Gathering Old Puddin' into his arms he walked toward his buggy. He sat the custard-colored dog on the seat and climbed in beside him.

In the mountains of New York, Mathelde Phelps gazed from her hotel room, which faced a fresh air sanatorium. Light from the setting sun poured through oblong windows forming patches on the leaf-patterned carpet. Below nestled a courtyard veined with sidewalks that led to a cloistered bench. Mathelde, looking down into the enclosure, thought of her children playing at the Illinois Central Hospital in Paducah. She smiled, remembering the joy of their father watching through a window from the third floor.

On a back street in Decatur, Illinois, Willie Shoe sat in a warm kitchen. Bending over a book his teacher had sent home, he read aloud. Lamplight flickered across a picture showing a little girl who looked like Saree. An aroma of baking cornbread reminded Willie of the Lanier kitchen. Inhaling deeply, he glanced at Ruby

Gem and grinned.

Little Granny stood beside a potato bin waiting for the last customer to leave Corlew's. In the corner past the pot-bellied stove stood two empty chairs. Picturing Georgie Rae Gardner and Mae Dee cradling their iced tea jars, she wondered who they would shell along with their beans in the summer to come.

Paul Luke flicked the reins across the black mare's flanks and the carriage began to move. Without deliberation he chose one of two dirt roads that converged and formed a wye creating the space occupied by Corlew's General Store.